# THE BLOODLAND CHRONICLES

## THE CRUSADE BEGINS

# J. KRUZA

Book design and layout by Presentation Graphics Studio

ISBN: 979-8-9877523-0-2 Paperback
ISBN: 979-8-9877523-1-9 EBook

Published by Presentation Graphics Press
Printed in the United States of America

# THE BLOODLAND CHRONICLES

THE CRUSADE BEGINS

J. KRUZA

# Dedication

To the University of Michigan Writers Community, who gave me the critique I needed. To Lucas Renno who inspired me to pursue making my childhood dream come true.

And to everyone who bought this book: thanks for making me feel good about myself. May you find joy in a book about vampires in a region of the world no one cares about.

# Table of Contents


Dedication .............................................................. v

Map of the Prussian Coast ........................................ viii

Historical Background ............................................. ix

CHAPTER 1: Hellfire ...............................................11

CHAPTER 2: Savages ...............................................19

CHAPTER 3: Swintamistan ........................................29

CHAPTER 4: Idol ...................................................47

CHAPTER 5: Angel .................................................65

CHAPTER 6: Nightmare ...........................................81

CHAPTER 7: Bloodletting ........................................ 101

CHAPTER 8: Afterlife ............................................ 111

CHAPTER 9: Anew ................................................ 125

CHAPTER 10: Bonds .............................................. 151

CHAPTER 11: Revenge ........................................... 171

CHAPTER 12: Revenant .......................................... 183

CHAPTER 13: Loss ............................................... 201

CHAPTER 14: Fox ................................................ 215

CHAPTER 15: Capture ........................................... 225

CHAPTER 16: Flogging .......................................... 243

CHAPTER 17: Bloodbath ......................................... 263

EPILOGUE ....................................................... 269

Endnotes ........................................................ 281

About the Author ............................................... 283

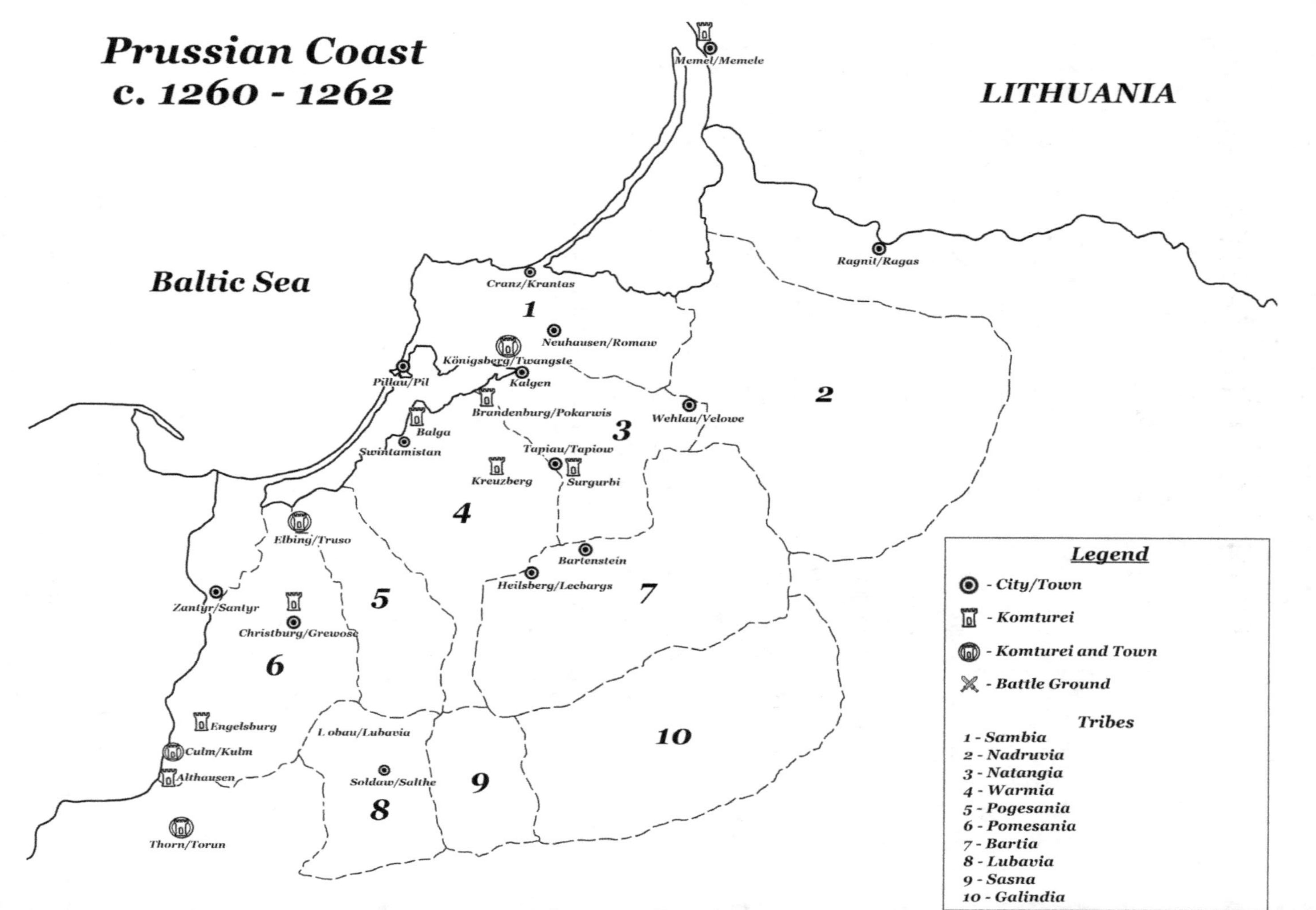

Prussian Coast
c. 1260 - 1262
Memel/Memele
LITHUANIA
Baltic Sea
Ragnit/Ragas
Cranz/Krantas
1
Neuhausen/Romaw
Königsberg/Twangste
Pillau/Pil
Kalgen
Brandenburg/Pokarwis
Balga
3
Wehlau/Velowe
2
Swintamistan
Tapiau/Tapiow
Kreuzberg
Surgurbi
4
Elbing/Truso
Bartenstein
Heilsberg/Leebargs
7
Zantyr/Santyr
5
Christburg/Grewose
6
Engelsburg
L obau/Lubavia
10
Culm/Kulm
Althausen
Soldaw/Salthe
9
8
Thorn/Torun
Legend
- City/Town
- Komturei
- Komturei and Town
- Battle Ground
Tribes
1 - Sambia
2 - Nadruvia
3 - Natangia
4 - Warmia
5 - Pogesania
6 - Pomesania
7 - Bartia
8 - Lubavia
9 - Sasna
10 - Galindia

# Historical Background

In the first millennium A.D., new kingdoms were emerging all over Europe. Slowly and surely, the whole continent of Europe became Christianized. However, there was one area on the continent that remained uncharted, unmapped, and avoided by the Christians: the area by the Baltic Sea. This area was inhabited by pagan tribes. These people were known as the Balts, but they were often just labeled as barbarians or heathens. There were several Baltic peoples in this area, all of which were pagan: Galindians, Prussians, Yotvingans, Selonians, Semigallians, Curonians, Skalvians, Latgallians, and Lithuanians. The most notorious of these peoples, the Prussians, inhabited the Prussian coast, later known as the Frisches Haff, an area that would be fought over for centuries. The Prussians were made up of several different clans: Nadruvia, Sambia (or Samland), Natangia, Bartia, Warmia, Pomesania, and Pogesania. This area is now part of modern-day Poland, Lithuania, Latvia, and Russia. Eventually, the land of the Balts became the only non-Christian part of Europe, and many kingdoms sought to convert these pagans. However, every attempt to do so ended in failure. These tribes resisted significantly, violently rejecting peaceful missionaries and fending off crusades that were launched against them.

The Baltic pagans also had a fearsome reputation outside of their wartime affairs. According to sources, they would loot and raid other villages, murder their inhabitants, enslave the women and children, and make human sacrifices from the men. As Germans (or rather, those from the Holy Roman Empire, as Germany was not yet a concept) from the West began to expand Eastwards, they were met with brutal attacks from the Prussians, who were also known for murdering any priest or missionary that would attempt to convert them. These pagans committed many acts that were considered un-Christian. Some tribes practiced polygamy. Most worshiped idols of their many gods. Some, such as the Lithuanians, saw suicide as an honorable alternative to surrendering on the battlefield, a taboo in Christianity. Many tribes practiced strange rituals and witchcraft that were seen as Satanic by Christians. These rituals often involved human or animal sacrifices to the gods.

The Catholic Church decided that they could not let these pagans continue their sinful ways. In 1217, Pope Honorius III called for a crusade on the Prussian lands. The Prussians responded by invading Christian lands outside of their region. In 1226, after numerous attacks, Christians called upon the Teutonic Order, a German Christian military order, to take care of the Prussians in aims to keep the Christians safe. The Pope promised the Teutonic Order any land they conquered if they could drive out these pagans. Thus, the Teutonic Order began their crusade against the Prussians.

The Teutonic Knights had a theocratic elective monarchy. The Generalkapital, all the priests, knights, and half brothers, were divided into Kommenden and Balleien and spread across the land that was conquered. The members had an organized hierarchy. The Hochmeister was the highest officer that was elected by the Generalkapital and was considered as the prince of Prussia, but this was mostly a formal position. Großgebietiger were five high officers appointed by the Hochmeister, in charge of a specific role for the whole order. This include the Hochmeister's deputy (the Großkomtur), the treasurer (the Treßler), one responsible for hospital affairs (the Spitler), the dressing and armament manager (the Trapier), and the chief of military affairs (the Marschall). There were three national chapters in Prussia, Livland, and within the Holy Roman Empire. The Landmeister, or country master, ran each chapter and were elected by regional chapters.

Since the Teutonic Order's territory was spread out, a local regional structure was established in the form of Kommendes. Ruled by a Komtur, in charge of administration, district reeves, and tax collectors. In his Kommende, also called a Komturei, three different kinds of brothers lived a monastic life. The knight brothers, also known as Ritterbrüdern, were the elite soldiers of the Order and some of the most feared warriors in history. These were highly experienced noble knights that took monastic vows, devoting their lives to the Order. Their uniforms were pure white and their helmets were often decorated to resemble archangels. In order to become a Ritterbruder, a man had to have 50 kills on the battlefield, 5 years of service, and be of noble birth. These knights were trained in a way that made them skilled and efficient killers with monastic vows. The Diendebrüdern, or servant brothers, were non-noble volunteers. Also known as sariant brothers, these were the first non-noble European knights who would later become a lesser nobility. They helped lead the volunteering commoners and made up the bulk of the Teutonic Order's army. These brothers wore light gray and were often referred to as gray cloaks or Graumäntler. Lastly were the half brothers or Halbbrüdern. These were volunteers that did not take monastic vows, and therefore could be married. They also wore gray and were not obligated to perform any military role outside of emergencies. These knights mostly were involved in economic activity and trading. There were other members of the order as well. The Priesterbrüdern, or the priest brothers, were primarily clergy. The novices working to be knights, volunteer adventurers and crusaders of both noble and non-noble birth, lay knights, and mercenaries all had their own role in the Teutonic Order.

One by one, the Teutonic Knights, along with a few other religious orders like the Livonian Order, began to drive out the pagans, giving them the choice of conversion or expulsion. These knights may have lived a religious life in their Komtureis, but on the battlefield, they were known to be ruthless.

At first, the crusade went smoothly with the Eastern clans suffering many defeats and Samland being conquered by the early 1250s. But when the Teutonic Knights started turning their efforts towards the Prussian tribes, they were met with a resistance they didn't expect. The Prussian clans banded together with the help of a Natangian leader known as Herkus Monte (or Erks Mānts, as the Prussians called him). Herkus was a Natangian Prussian who was captured by the Teutonic Order in his youth, learned of their tactics and returned to his homeland to fight for his people, using the Teutons' strategies against them. And so, with Herkus Monte's help, the two groups waged a decades-long war.

# Chapter 1: Hellfire

# 1258 AD

Rapid thumping sounds. A high, shrill shriek. Sharp crackling. Distant murmuring. Gailimantas shifted to his other side. As he stirred awake, he realized he was covered in sweat. The wooden house was unbelievably hot, hotter than it had ever been before. He threw off the blanket covering his body. His closed eyes were filled with an orange glow that could only come from a fire. Why would his brother be awake so late at night? And why would he light a torch in here of all places?

"Melstis, what are you doing?" the child groaned, opening an eye. Both of his eyes snapped open when he saw the blazing inferno in front of him. He instinctively scrambled to his feet, forgetting his shirt and nearly tripping over himself trying to get to the door. The entire front doorway of his home was engulfed in flames. Gailimantas screamed in terror. Panicked, he rushed to the door only to recoil at the intense heat. He frantically looked around the house for a place to flee. The crackling became louder as the inside of the cabin grew brighter and hotter. The fire spread, consuming more and more of the house. Gailimantas saw a beacon of hope out of the corner of his eye. *The window!* He rushed to it and tried to crawl out, but the strength of his nine-year-old body couldn't quite pull his weight. He wailed in frustrated panic.

"Māti! Eimants! Vudevutas… Please! Where are you? Help me! Help me please!"

From his tear-blotted vision he saw the fire begin to creep towards the table. A chair for each of the eight members of his family and the other four who shared the cabin encircled it.

As the growing flame ate one of the chairs, he had an idea. He quickly dashed over to the table, snatched one of the chairs, and dragged it over to the window. By the time he got there, the entire table was consumed by the hellfire. He hopped up on the chair and tumbled out of the cabin, landing on the ground with a hard thud.

He looked up to see his village ablaze, every single wooden structure now fuel for the fire. There were people from his village, neighbors and friends, sprawled out on the ground, unmoving. Strange men in stark white uniforms with shiny silver heads were scattered throughout the village, shouting and carrying torches. The screams of terror harmonized with the crackling fire that resounded inside the wooden walls surrounding his home:

"Run! Run!"

"Grab your sword!"

"Māti! Help! Don't go!"

"Komants! Please don't take him from me!"

"By the gods! Don't hurt me!"

"My son is in there! My only son!"

Gailimantas had heard something about a war. Something about strangers from the West attacking other tribes and villages, taking the people hostage, cutting down holy trees, hunting in sacred forests, and burning their towns to the ground. He couldn't remember their name. Some kind of Teutonic Order, though he wasn't sure what a Teuton was.

It was the reason that he and his family left their home in the countryside and moved within the walls of the wooden fortress on the hill. His mother told him that there, everyone would be safe if they were attacked. Her words of promise seemed to disintegrate like the burning buildings surrounding him. Foreign soldiers in strange helmets were fighting against everyday men, women and children were being tied up in ropes, and mass panic swarmed around him as those who weren't yet caught were trying to flee. The few Prussians that were running away had the men in white chasing after them. Their bodies were drenched in sweat, their desperate faces covered in ash as they painstakingly tried to avoid capture. Those that failed were lying motionless on the ground, most likely dead. Some of them had pools of blood under their bodies. Others were burned corpses; it was clear people tried to save them, but were too late. Gailimantas's heart jumped as he spotted a noticeable article of clothing on one of the women on the ground: a dark blue headscarf.

"Māti!" he cried, dashing to his mother. He knelt down by her body. "Māti?" She was completely still, eyes and mouth wide in terror. There wasn't a single sign of life from her. "Māti? Māti? Are you hurt? What happened? Māti!" He kept shaking her shoulders, tears spilling down his cheeks. He did not want to believe that the tragedy in front of him was real. "Māti! Please…"

"Gailimantas!"

The boy whipped his head around to see a tall, familiar figure.

"Tāws!" Gailimantas ran to his father, who had a relieved look on his face. "Tāws! What's going—"

"Gailimantas, you need to run."

"Huh?"

"Run! Go! Into the forest! Before they find you!"

"What's going—"

"There's no time to explain! Just go! Run until you reach Swintamīstan!"

"What about everyone else? We can't leave Māti—" His father cut him off by picking him up and throwing him over his shoulder. He started running away from the action, towards the entrance of the town. "Wait!" said Gailimantas. "What about Māti?"

"There's nothing we can do," said his father. "She's in Peckols's hands now." Gailimantas felt a pang of sorrow in his chest. But he was given no time to grieve. He heard a shout from behind them. He looked up to see a man cloaked in white about a meter away, charging after them, brandishing a sword. His father noticed this and slowly put Gailimantas down. He then whipped around and pulled his own blade out of its sheath.

"Gailimantas! Run!"

"Tāws!"

"I'll meet you in the forest! Just go!"

His father thrust his sword at the enemy, but it was parried with a sideways swipe. Metal clanged on metal. Another powerful swipe sent his father reeling backwards. A third blow almost met its mark. It was close. Too close. Gailimantas jumped to his feet, blitzing towards the opening in the wall. He was halfway to the entrance when he was suddenly pulled backwards, making him lose his balance and fall to the ground. He whipped his head around to see a very young man cloaked in a white uniform, holding the back of his clothes. The boy couldn't have been more than fifteen years old. He had short golden hair that looked red with the glow of the blaze surrounding him, and a cocky smirk as he held Gailimantas in a chokehold. His small, icy blue eyes were flecked with an amber so bright, it almost looked like splats of fire. They held so much passion and hunger. He yelled something in a language that Gailimantas didn't understand.

*"Oy! I caught a kid!"*

*"Put him with the rest!"* another warrior yelled back to him. Gaili-mantas couldn't understand what was being said, but he knew he had to run away. He thrashed with all his might, but the other boy kept a tight grip on him.

"Let me go! Please!"

"Stop fighting me or I will hurt you," the boy growled in Prussian. Gailimantas froze for a second, surprised that the enemy spoke to him in his native tongue. The other soldier said something in the unfamiliar language they were speaking earlier.

*"Don't worry, kid! You can still be saved if you come with us. Stop struggling and we won't hurt you!"* The other man attempted to talk to Gailimantas in his throaty language, but his words fell on deaf ears. Gailimantas contin-ued to resist as he was pushed towards where the other men in white were.

"Let me go!" he cried. "Tāws! Tāws!" He looked back with teary eyes to see his father with a sword in hand, bravely fighting against the heavily armored man. The blaze in the background illuminated his fa-ther and shined off his sword as if he were a holy spirit. A holy hero from the old sagas told to him as a kid, fighting for the glory of the gods. Gailimantas then gave the boy a sharp kick to the knee with all his might. The boy yelped in pain and fell on the ground. Gailimantas then noticed the boy had dropped something. He quickly snatched the small blade. He felt the boy grabbing him again, knocking him off his feet. Gailimantas then took the blade and stabbed it into the boy's thigh. As the boy howled in pain, Gailimantas bolted towards the entrance of the crumbling town walls. He looked back at his father who was still battling the menacing knight. Remembering his father's instructions, Gailimantas burst past the burning walls and ran down the hill, gaining momentum from the incline to the point where he couldn't stop his feet. He contin-ued running away from the fortress and fled into the forest. He didn't think. He kept running until he was in complete darkness and out of breath. Gailimantas looked around, realizing he couldn't even see light from his village anymore. He couldn't hear anything over the loud chirping of crickets.

"Tāws?" he called out. He was met with silence. "Tāws! Tāws!" Only the crickets responded. Gailimantas plopped onto the ground. "He'll come. He'll meet me here. That's what he promised." Gailimantas continued calling for his family. "Tāws! Kirsne! Eimants! Vudevutas!" He was screaming with all his strength, hoping anyone would hear him. Begging that someone would hear his cry, be it family, a stranger, or a god. Hoping anyone would find him in the woods and rescue him. Wishing that someone would embrace him and tell him everything would be okay. Gailimantas sat and waited for what felt like hours, but heard and saw no signs of life other than the insects and the owls. "Tāws! Melstis! Eimants! Please! Answer me!" Gailimantas felt cold, tired, and itchy from the grass. Giving up hope, he began to weep. "Somebody... Please..." He was startled when he heard a rustling in the leaves behind him, realizing that he was alone in the middle of the woods, at night. Without his shirt and shoes, the chilly summer breeze made his scrawny body shiver. The trees were so thick, blocking out the weak moonlight from the crescent moon, Gailimantas could hardly see anything. His young, boundless imagination started racing with stories of the evil creatures who lived in the woods that were sure to come for him now. He panicked, sobbing even harder.

"I'm going to die..." he choked. "I'm going to die. I don't want to die!" He collapsed on his hands and knees again, trying to breathe between cries. "Māti..." he cried. "Tāws..." He began to pray. "Deywis... Please! Help me! Help me please!" Gailimantas swallowed. "I don't—I don't want to be alone... Why? Why did this have to happen? Why? Deywis! Please! Help me…" Everything then faded to black as exhaustion took over his body, and Gailimantas's cries finally ceased.

# Chapter 2: Savages

"Ow!"

"Hold still!"

"Demons! All of them! I can't believe the little infidel got away!"

"I recommend resting for a few days," said the monk before leaving the boy's sickbed in the infirmary.

Friedrich von Rotenkreuz scowled. His first real mission could now possibly be his last thanks to that tiny pagan boy. All he had worked for, all his training, could be going down the sewage canal now. After years of training as a page under a family friend in the Order and doing things like cleaning up after the horses, retrieving arrows from corpses, and polishing armor, he was finally a novice of the Teutonic Order and a squire under Brother Heinrich von Andernach, attending to his every need on the battlefield. After a required year of probation, where he learned how to live in the convent, the hardships he would endure, and how to be a man of God, he finally professed his commitment to the Order. He had been working hard on his training, learning the prerequisites for knighthood like climbing, weaponry, and swimming, all while wearing armor. He was finally on the battlefield, taking part in the Prussian Crusade like he'd always wanted. He was ready to plunge into battle and take revenge on the people who ravaged his life. The Order also provided him food, a place to sleep, a great reward in Heaven, and amazing adventures to places no one else dared to go, things Friedrich saw as additional bonuses. But now all those thoughts were starting to melt with his current mood. Today was the first day he got to actually test his fighting skills against a pagan. He felt humiliated and weak after his performance today. The fact that his friend was in the infirmary with him made him feel all the more self-conscious.

"A kid did that to you?" snickered a slightly older boy with short, dark red hair. He, like Friedrich, was a new novice. Friedrich scowled.

"Don't remind me," Friedrich growled.

"I think that maybe you shouldn't have been so brash," said Simon. "You know their language, don't you? Why didn't you try speaking to the kid?"

"I tried!" Friedrich replied. "Well kind of. I don't like using that language. It makes me shudder. It reminds me of…things I don't want to remember."

"What are you two talking about?" asked their Ritterbruder, Heinrich, a pale, older knight with dark hair. He had a bandage around his face. Even though he was older, he still had a youthful appearance compared to the rest of those in his position, or at least, compared to those Friedrich had seen.

"Friedrich here knows the infidels' language," explained Simon.

"Kind of," interjected Friedrich.

"You never told me about this," said their knight, a hint of intrigue in his tone.

"I thought everyone knew. It was part of the reason I was accepted to take part in the fight in this area," Friedrich elaborated.

The Ritterbruder's eyes widened in shock. "Brother Friedrich! Your leg!" he said.

"He was stabbed by a child," Simon explained. "It's not as bad as it looks." Friedrich scowled again.

"I wouldn't be surprised," their knight said. "Forcing their children to fight on the front lines so young… It seems befitting of a heathen."

"Sir, if you don't mind me asking," Simon said, "what happened to your face?"

"One of them managed to knock off my helmet and scratch my face," the holy knight replied. "It looks far worse than it is. No worries. It is a small price to pay for what I did to him. God gave me the strength to finish him off."

"Well, I should check on Brother Franz," Simon said. "He was injured quite gruesomely. I shall keep you in my prayers, Brother Friedrich!" Friedrich cracked a smile as Simon left. Heinrich put a hand on Friedrich's shoulder.

"Do you mind if I talk to you, Brother Friedrich?" the knight asked. Friedrich's heart skipped, worried about what his knight might say to him in private.

"Of course," he nodded. Heinrich sat down next to Friedrich on the small bed in the infirmary.

"Is something troubling you, Friedrich?"

"Well, kind of," he replied.

"Does this pertain to your performance on the battlefield?"

"Yes," admitted Friedrich. "I just… I feel so weak. To think that could happen to me… It's embarrassing. As a member of the Teutonic Order I should carry around my title with the greatest honor, not allow it to be ruined so easily. I know that the mission was successful and that I shouldn't be thinking about my personal defeats, but Brother Georg had to save me from being decapitated by a pagan! I feel like maybe I just don't have the physical strength to fight. I worry that I may hold the Order back in the future."

"Brother Friedrich, failure is not permanent," reminded the knight. "Have you learned nothing from your studies? Did Joseph give up after being sold as a slave and locked in a cell?"

"But he didn't fail a mission given to him by God," retorted Friedrich.

"But we were successful in conquering the fortress. And it was a nightly ambush, something that is especially difficult even for the most skilled of soldiers," reminded the Ritterbruder. "In war, men have to fall in order to bring victory to their cause. You must also remember that you are still very young. You're not even a knight yet. This was your first time on the battlefield. You have many years to grow and improve yourself."

"But what if I don't improve?" asked Friedrich. "What if I keep failing time and time again and it ends up costing the Order a victory? What if I never become a Ritterbruder?" Friedrich looked into the knight's eyes. He couldn't help but notice the strange color. Amber eyes were not unusual, but Friedrich thought that he saw smaller flecks of red. He blinked, thinking it must be the dim candlelight.

"I remember when I heard of the incident with your father," he began. "Such a shame. Your father would have been a wonderful leader. But then when I heard that Laurentius von Rotenkreuz's son was still alive, I was astounded. And to think he was assigned as my squire."

"I'm surprised they didn't kill me either," Friedrich said. "I was just a kid after all. I guess I got lucky," Friedrich replied.

"There is no such thing as luck, Brother Friedrich," the Ritterbruder said. "For you to survive all those years under the rule of the infidels, clearly you are blessed. It is very unusual that you were sent to the place you desired to be. Being in this order means giving up your personal desires to fight for God. Do you know why you were sent here?"

"Well, I want to fight because my family couldn't. Maybe they saw how passionate I was?" Friedrich guessed. "Maybe they knew they could put me to good use here."

"It is because the Order heard your story and knew you were blessed by God," Heinrich answered. "God kept you alive for a reason. Your father and brother's death were not the devil's work, but God's. He put you on this path and led you to us. God gave you strife to fill you with faith to fight in His name. The Order knew that you had a holy destiny to fight in the North, so they sent you here because the Lord was clearly calling you." Friedrich listened intently. "Your first fight may not have been as fulfilling as you were hoping, but believe me when I say you are going to be a great knight, Brother Friedrich." Friedrich felt a warm feeling all over his body. Hearing those words from his knight made him feel strong and valuable.

"I owe my life to the Order," Friedrich stated. "And I will die fighting against these people if I must. Thank you, sir."

The knight gave a smile. "Don't delve too much into yourself," he reminded. "Vanity is still a sin."

Gailimantas awoke, shivering. He was cold and wet from the dew on the leaves and grass beneath him. He sat up, looking around at the forest surrounding him and the stream trickling beside him. The birds were loudly chirping, announcing the morning. He rubbed his eyes, which felt like they were burning. His throat was incredibly dry. He leaned down to the stream, cupping his hands and drinking from the shining creek. The cool water satisfied his thirst as he kept drinking more and more. He had been following the stream for weeks, ever since the raid, persevering on, determined to find his father. His father promised they would see one another again. And the way to do that was to find Swintamīstan. The holy place. He had no idea where to start nor a clear direction. In fact, he still wasn't sure if the direction he was going in was correct, but he had to be brave for his father. Once he found him, everything would be okay. After quenching his thirst, he looked at his reflection in the water. Mud and leaves caked his messy brown hair, which had grown past his chin. He washed his gaunt, place face, which was smeared with dirt, and began to walk again.

It had taken him a few days to get over the loss of his mother and siblings. It was hard to believe that they were really gone, but sitting in the forest crying only made him tired, thirsty, and hungry. He had been surviving off whatever nuts or berries he could find as he didn't have any tools or skills for hunting. He tried to chase after the game he found, but the animals were always faster. How he longed for a nice roasted pheasant. He would even settle for squirrel meat at this point. He desperately missed meat and the way his mother would cook a freshly caught deer before serving it with the soft fluffy bread she baked. He had run out of the pears he had swiped from a tree. Despite the hunger pangs and exhaustion, he continued on.

It was a particularly windy day. The forest talked to him throughout his journey. The trees swayed from side to side, their leaves rustling. Fallen leaves crunched at his feet. The creek next to him trickled along. The birds twittered away. But instead of pleasant sounds, their messages carried a tinge of despair. The trees whispered to him, telling him things he didn't want to hear. The leaves at his feet told him to turn back. The creek mocked his cries and complaints. The birds gossiped about how pathetic he was. He just walked along, ignoring them. Even if he didn't find Swintamīstan, he would find someone who could.

He walked for a few hours, only stopping when he found food in the form of a bilberry bush. The sun was setting now, and everything was becoming harder and harder to see. He knew he had to find a place to rest for the night. He kept his eyes and ears peeled for any kind of shelter. Whenever he found none, he just slept against a tree. Last time he encountered a snake, so he didn't want to do that again.

As Gailimantas traveled along, the stream seemed to grow louder and louder, growing from a trickle to a soft roar. *Is it raining?* he wondered. *The sky is clear. I don't see any rain clouds.* He then stared straight ahead, the sound of the water roaring in his ears, his eyes widening in awe at the magnificent sight before him. The stream that he had followed stemmed from a river that led high above a cliff, cascading into a magnificent waterfall as it hit the lower ground. It was only about twice Gailimantas's height, but the fresh, flowing water and the smooth, welcoming rocks were more than enough to make him feel relieved. The last rays of the setting sun seemed to make the cascades sparkle and the color of the mauve sky on the stream made the scene majestic.

Gailimantas began to explore the landmark. How could such an abundant, beautiful place not be sacred? The gods must have seen his suffering and provided him with this oasis. He felt something under his foot. Upon closer examination, he had stepped on what looked like a comb. *So there are people nearby!* He felt an immense sense of hope spread throughout his body. *Maybe they know where Swintamīstan is!* He looked behind one of the cascades to see a strange, large, dark patch on the light rocks. He reached out, but felt nothing. This was a cave. Gailimantas slipped inside and saw mostly darkness, but he figured the cave would be great at protecting him from the cold and the animals. It became quieter and darker in the cave the deeper he went inside.

Gailimantas then heard what sounded like a rat squeak, but it was much more high pitched. He turned his head towards the sound. The cave was dark, but he was able to make out what appeared to be a dark figure hunched over. It looked like a person, but it had something in its hands and was making a slurping sound. He backed further away. He didn't know this stranger. What if he was dangerous? But what if he could help him? Gailimantas would have asked him about his identity and for help, but something in his gut was screaming at him to get out of the cave as soon as possible. He slowly backed away, but knocked into something that made one of the rocks beneath his feet scatter across the cave.

*Clack, clack, clack...*

The figure turned its head and noticed him, its eyes glowing red. Gailimantas screamed and ran as it let out a menacing hiss. Gailimantas didn't look to see where he was going. He just ran as fast as he could to get away from what he could only assume was a monster. Half of his body was wet from getting splashed from the cascade, but he managed to run away from the waterfall and back towards the forest. Dusk had set in, and it was getting darker outside, but Gailimantas didn't care. He ran until his lungs begged for mercy, only collapsing when he couldn't take it anymore.

He gasped for air, the world around him spinning from shock and hunger. Why? Why couldn't the gods just give him a break? He had finally found someone else, and that person happened to be a demon. *What did I do wrong? Why are the gods of fate so cruel to me? What did I ever do to you?* Gailimantas began to sob again. *I'm all alone. This is my life now. Why did the gods damn me to a life so cold?*

Suddenly Gailimantas felt a cold grip around the back of his neck. As his body was lifted up, he gasped and struggled, but to no avail. He opened his eyes to face his opponent. The demon looked like a human, but had long, clumped, filthy, white hair that fell over its gaunt face and skin that was a grotesque purple-red, with a light green crusted around the lower half of its face. There were smears of blood around its drooping, bluish lips. Open sores festered on its bloated limbs, creating a foul odor. Blood stuck to its long, scraggly, silvery beard, and wrinkles lined its face. Gailimantas felt its untrimmed nails dig into his skin as he shivered in fear, staring into its hungry, red eyes. But the most distinguishable feature of the creature was its long, sharp, yellow fangs. The pungent smell of rotting flesh engulfed Gailimantas's senses, causing him to freeze in terror.

"P—Please… D—Don't kill me," he begged. "Tāws…is still waiting for me." Gailimantas may have imagined it, but the being seemed to hesitate, just staring at him for a moment. It closed its eyes very briefly, as if it was intensely pondering. Gailimantas then felt a sharp pain in his neck as the creature bit him. His body slowly began to feel numb, and he felt his eyes starting to close in exhaustion as his energy was drained from his small body. As he gave into the creature, everything faded to black.

# Chapter 3: Swintamīstan

# 1252

"That little German girl is pretty cute," he heard someone comment. "I think I'll have her as one of my wives in the future."

"No way! She seems pretty rebellious. Besides, the noble German women we capture hardly know anything about doing actual work. Prussian women at least know how to cook and clean."

"But the foreign women are the best," said the man. "Their bodies are different, they age very well, and they give you a better time. I have enough wives to help around the house. I need a new one to greet me when I come home from a hunt. Besides, she seems to know how to do basic things, unlike her mother."

Friedrich walked faster with the pail in his hands. *I've got to get out of here. I don't have much time before I start becoming a man. And then they'll burn me alive! Or I'll be sold to some heathen who will try to make me his wife, which will only expose me faster.*

Friedrich put the large pail down for a second, exhausted from smashing through the ice to get some water for the animals and dragging that water all the way back to town. All that work warmed him up a bit, making him forget just how numb his hands and feet were from the cold. Ever since Wilhelm disappeared, Friedrich had twice the work. This work was especially hard to do while wearing a dress. His mother told him and his brother to pretend to be girls or else they would disappear like his father. Seeing the terrible things these Prussians did to their male prisoners, Friedrich was constantly afraid of his masters finding out

who he really was. In the pagans' world, women were the ideal servants, while the male captives were to be sacrifices. It had been four years since he had a haircut, so he definitely looked like a girl. As long as he didn't have to strip, he would be safe. He didn't want to end up like Wilhelm, who was still missing. He had gotten an earful of it yesterday. He picked up the bucket again and continued towards the stables, the icy air gripping his body again.

*Women are so lucky. They aren't under the constant threat of death. These heathens don't butcher and sacrifice women. They get to stay in nice warm houses with their men without a care in the world. No battles to fight, no need to worry about who you're with. Just do as you're told and you'll have all the food, warmth, and men you want. Such a simple way to live that guarantees a long happy life of hardly doing anything.* Friedrich finally reached the stables, setting the bucket down to open the door. *I hope I live long enough to live in my own house.*

Friedrich had just opened the door when he felt his arm being forcefully grabbed and yanked to the side. His eyes darted up the arm that grabbed him to meet the face of Rudayko, his master.

"WHERE IS SHE?" Rudayko screamed.

"Who?" Friedrich asked after a bit of hesitation.

"You know who I'm talking about!" Rudayko snarled. "Where is your sister?"

"I told you, I don't know!" Friedrich said, losing his patience. "She's been gone for a few weeks. She probably was eaten by—" Rudayko cut Friedrich off with a slap to the face.

"Stop with the excuses! Where did your sister go?" Rudayko growled.

"I don't know!" Friedrich repeated. The Prussian grabbed Friedrich by his long hair and gave him another hard hit to the cheek before tossing him back into the snow.

"You little bitch! It's not worth lying to me. Where's your sister?" he yelled again.

"I told you, I don't know!" Friedrich said, tears streaming down his face. "She just never came home! I was told she went to get water and never came back!" The cold snow helped ease the pain in his face, at least. "I didn't want her to go either, sir. I want her to come back too." Rudayko let out an aggravated sigh.

"If you really don't know, then at least don't slack on the job!" Rudayko lectured.

"But it's really hard for me to take care of both the stables and—" He was cut off by another slap.

"You need to learn your place," Rudayko growled. "Don't slack off on your duties, or I'll sell you to Vidmants this Summer, and you'll never see your mother again." Friedrich took a deep breath. He wanted to strangle this man, but he knew his hands were too small to fit around his thick neck. He had to comply to survive for just a bit longer. Just hold out a bit longer.

"Apologies, master," Friedrich forced himself to say. "It won't happen again."

"Good."

Friedrich balled up some more snow and put it on his face to help ease the pain.

"By the way, you missed a few spots while cleaning the stalls today!"

Suddenly, Friedrich's vision was obscured by darkness and a pungent odor suffocated his senses. He felt himself covered in a squishy, foul substance. He grabbed the wooden bucket off of his head, dung dripping onto his clothes from his head as half of the bucket's contents were covering him. Hearing the pagans' laughter surrounding him as he tried to wipe the dung off of his face only made him feel more enraged and humiliated. He wanted to cry, scream, and punch something. But instead he just sat there, freezing, exhausted, aching, humiliated, and covered in dung. *I can't take much more of this. God, please, send someone!*

# 1258

Friedrich awoke. He looked around, noticing his brothers were fast asleep, confused as to why he had suddenly snapped awake. The candle in the corner of the room was still lit, now halfway melted. A light had to be kept on as they slept as part of the Order's rules. It had been a few weeks since his last raid, but even though Friedrich improved his skills, the pagans forced them to retreat. Friedrich didn't know what he dreamt about, but he remembered (detail). He wasn't sure why he was awake. He thought he heard a loud noise, but he wasn't sure, since no one else was awake. He wouldn't dare ask around, as speaking after evening prayer was forbidden unless commanded to or in the case of an emergency. Friedrich sat up. His mat was near the entrance of the tent, so he tiptoed around his brothers so he could slip outside. He wouldn't leave the tent. He just wanted to look outside to see if everything was alright. The moon was nowhere to be seen tonight. The camp was empty. Not a single soul around, not even the guards whose duty it was to stand and watch over the camp.

A feeling of dread and unease punched Friedrich in the gut. *Wait a second, this isn't right. Where are the guards? The entrance to the camp is right over there, and yet I can't see them.* Friedrich then heard sounds coming from a few tents away. He looked in the direction of the sounds, but he didn't dare move. Someone was definitely in the supply tent. He rushed back inside his tent when he saw the tent's sides begin to ripple. He watched silently from the slit in the tent to see who was there. Two men dressed in furs exited with quivers full of arrows, numerous bows, and a couple swords. Friedrich recognized them instantly. He turned around and looked at his sleeping comrades. Should he yell? Or would that alert the enemy? Should he just wake up one person?

"Oy! Oy!" Friedrich hissed. "Pagans are in the camp!" No one opened their eyes. Friedrich sighed. He then gave a half-shout, something that would at least wake up his nearest brothers. "Thieves! Thieves!" Instantly, a couple of rows of brothers opened their eyes. One or two shot to their feet. Commotion slowly began to rise as the brothers woke one another.

"Brother Friedrich, what is this about?" asked an older novice.

"Thieves! Heathens have raided our camp and are running away with our weapons!"

A few brothers charged outside.

"Brother Michael and Brother Jakob are on watch tonight," said another brother. "Surely they would have alerted us."

"I didn't see them outside, Brother Conrad," Friedrich said.

A few more brothers rushed out of the tent. There was some yelling and shouting outside. Friedrich and Brother Conrad hurried outside to see other brothers running around, checking on things. Even some of the priests awoke and came out of their tents.

"Brother Friedrich, are there really thieves in the camp?" asked Heinrich.

"I saw them with my own eyes!" Friedrich said.

"Because so far, no brother has spotted them."

"Huh?"

"Herr Heinrich! Herr Heinrich!" A page ran up to the knight with a grim expression on his face.

"Speak, my young page."

"Brother Michael and Brother Jakob are dead," the page reported. The camp became quieter.

"D—Dead?" repeated the knight.

"Someone attacked them," the page replied. "We found them slain by the entrance."

"So heathens really did raid the camp?" Simon questioned.

"Hey!" yelled another brother. "A large stock of our weapons is missing!" Heinrich and the Komtur reported over to the weapons tent, Friedrich following behind him. "The majority of our arrows and over half of our bows are gone," the brother reported, "as well as some of our swords."

"What is going on here? Why is there commotion after evening prayer?" the Komtur came out of his tent, a novice by his side.

"I woke up and I saw heathens in the weapons tent so I woke everyone else up," Friedrich informed him. "I think they raided the camp and killed our guards."

The Komtur looked crestfallen. "Brother Tomas?" he called.

"Yes?"

"Pick four Diendebrüdern and tell them that they are to be on guard the rest of the night," he ordered. "You will guard the weapons tent. Tomorrow we shall host a vigil for Brothers Michael and Jakob."

"Yes, Komtur," Tomas responded.

"And you," the Komtur said, turning to Friedrich. "Thank the Lord that you alerted us of this. They could have burnt down the whole camp if you hadn't."

"I just did what God wished me to do, sir," Friedrich said.

"Good. Tomorrow, we will have to make more weapons. We will get up early to collect the materials or find a nearby town. So get some sleep, brother."

"Yes sir."

Friedrich returned to his tent, but he couldn't go back to sleep after that. He decided to stroll around camp for a bit, as everyone else was in disarray. He went over to the group of brothers that were huddled near the entrance. He figured they were checking out Michael and Jakob's bodies. The moon was nowhere to be seen tonight, leaving only the stars to light the night. Friedrich looked up at the sky for a moment, admiring the stars. *God creates such wonderful things like the beautiful night sky. So why on Earth would he make heathens like this?*

"Didn't the Komtur tell us to return to bed?"

Friedrich was startled when he heard Simon behind him.

"Well, I can't sleep now," Friedrich whispered. "Not after all that drama. Also, it's against the rules to talk after curfew so shhh!"

"But we have broken that due to the emergency," Simon said. "Everyone else is out and talking so I think it's okay, right?"

Friedrich shrugged. He was still trying to figure out which rules were okay to break sometimes and which ones would get him in serious trouble.

"To think the creatures that killed Brothers Michael and Jakob were also created by God," Friedrich thought aloud.

"But they were corrupted by Satan," said Simon. "He introduced the dogma that they follow, right?"

"I know we're supposed to save them," said Friedrich, "but I don't think they deserve it at this point, after all they've done."

"You hate them so much, yet, you speak their language," Simon pointed out.

"That's because of their horrendous actions!" Friedrich snapped. He paused, suddenly realizing something. "Have I really never told you why I know their language?"

"You mentioned that they killed your father," Simon responded.

"I was forced to be a slave for them for five years. So naturally, I became familiar with their tongue," Friedrich tried to give a short explanation, hoping the conversation would drop.

"That was you?" Simon said, with a look of shock on his face.

"You've heard of my story?"

"It's been circulating around camp for months!" Simon replied. "The story of a new novice whose father was killed by the infidels and forced into servitude until he was freed and raised by the Order. I didn't know that was you. What were you doing there as a slave?"

The pride Friedrich originally had in this story had faded. The murder of two of his comrades tonight tainted the story in a different light. It became a tale that made his blood boil, giving him the desire to rant about every horrid detail, rather than the heroic origin story he used to see it as. The worst memories of his childhood of servitude to the heretics began to surface as he narrated his story.

"When I was very young, my family moved to the Prussian coast to establish an estate. My father was a volunteer knight and earned property here through his time on the battlefield. We were going to start a new life here, set up for a life of peace and prosperity. But the place was attacked by heathens, and we were captured. I don't remember it happening, I just woke up in a cage like a wild animal," he explained. "While my father was sacrificed, my mother, brother, and I were forced to be their slaves, doing a lot of dirty work like cleaning up after animals and building sinful shrines for them to worship their idols. We were like dogs to them. They fed us scraps only a pig would eat, would beat us if we stepped out of line, forced us to sleep on the ground… In the winter, I would just freeze in the dirt alone. It was a horrid environment to grow up in."

"Is it true you and your family were rescued by the Order?"

"My brother disappeared when he was there. Probably taken for one of their human sacrifices. My mother and I were liberated when the Order took the town. But my mother perished shortly after, so the Order took me in." Friedrich turned his gaze away from Simon, looking at the night sky, taking a moment to collect himself. "That's why I joined the Order. I owe my life to it, so I want to repay them by smiting the infidels that took away my family. No Christian should have to suffer what I did." he continued. "So I'm going to become a Ritterbruder and be the best knight out there."

"You want to become a knight brother?" Simon asked.

"Of course! They're the elite knights that are the best on the battlefield! And I'm going to be up there some day. And I'll lead my own novices into battle in about five years."

"You need to have around 50 kills on the battlefield though!"

"I'm already at seven, and I'm just a squire. I'm sure to get to 50 shortly after becoming a knight," Friedrich smirked confidently.

"Wow. You really are going to make it up there Fritz…" Simon let out a sigh. "I'm probably going to die on the battlefield before I get that far."

"What makes you say that?"

"I don't think I have the same skill or stride as you do," Simon replied. "Plus, the Lord has blessed you with this destiny."

"Why did you join the Order, Simon?"

"My family forced me into it," said Simon. "I'm the youngest of 14 sons. I don't receive much inheritance anyways."

"Well, you will in Heaven," said Friedrich.

Simon smiled. "Yep. If I have a selfless life here, Heaven is going to be paradise for me." He sighed, looking up at the stars. "But for now, we have to do God's work."

"Then we can finally rest together in paradise."

Gailimantas awoke to the smell of something delicious. It smelled like meat. Juicy, savory meat being cooked over a fire. *I must be so hungry, I'm imagining things*, he thought. He opened his eyes. Confusion set in as he realized that he was in a comfy straw bed inside a wooden house. Was he home? Had the past few miserable weeks in the forest all been a dream? He sat up to see that he was not in his house. The long hand-made table with the crafted chairs encircling it was replaced by a much smaller one. The house had a stone oven, one that was dark, as the summer had been a hot one. There was a small carving of one of the gods on top of the smaller table, bedecked with only four chairs. It was too far away for Gailimantas to identify who it was. Judging by the wavy hair that stuck out of the idol's head like the rays of the sun, it was probably Perkūnas, the god of the sky. This wasn't *his* home, but it was definitely *a* home. The question was, whose?

"I see you're finally awake."

Gailimantas looked around the room, startled. He saw an older woman, her gray hair braided and coiled around her head. Her wrinkled face was lined with a sympathetic smile. In her hands was a tray. A tray with what looked like golden-crusted bread with a fluffy white inside next to a bowl of pale brown stew. Gailimantas didn't recognize this woman, but his eyes grew larger when he saw the food. He felt his mouth watering and his stomach began to cramp up again. He had come to ignore this sensation, but now that he was in the presence of real food, he could feel the hunger pulling him in.

"You look so gaunt, dear boy. Why don't you eat?"

Gailimantas didn't need to be told twice. He ravenously bit into the bread, feeling its soft insides nourish his stomach. After he wolfed that down, he desperately slurped the warm, savory stew, only stopping to chew whatever vegetables were inside, but only for a few seconds. He sighed happily when he was finished, his body feeling warm and for the first time in weeks, satisfied. Gailimantas looked at the holy woman that had given him nourishment.

"Th—Thank you very much," he bowed his head. The old woman just smiled. "But do you know where I am?"

"This is my home," she replied. "I live here with my son, Trenis, and his family. A fine warrior, he is."

"D—Do you know how I got here?" Gailimantas asked.

"Last evening we heard some commotion," she explained. "My son went to see what happened, and they found you being attacked by some demon. We thought it had killed you, but you were breathing perfectly fine. You must have had quite a scare." Gailimantas closed his eyes, trying to recollect everything that happened the previous night. "I'll let Stantiko know that you are awake," she said.

"S—Stantiko?"

"He's the one who keeps us all safe," she answered. "He leads our fighters. He is a brave soul. Even took in a few poor souls from a nearby town about a moon ago."

She stood up from her chair. Before Gailimantas could even ask for her name, she slipped out the door. After a bit of pondering, he finally remembered the monster that had attacked him. He was sure that it was

Baubas or some kind of demon that Melstis used to tell him about. He shivered, surprised that he survived.

In stepped a tall man with wavy black hair tied back into a ponytail and a long beard covering his neck. His small, amber eyes seemed fixed in a serious, intimidating stare. He was wearing a long black tunic. Next to him was the old woman. Gailimantas's smile quickly faded when he saw the man approach him. He sat up straight, staring up at the man towering above him.

"Greetings stranger," the man greeted. "State your name."

"G—Gailimantas," he stammered.

"You speak our language," the man began. "And you use our vernacular… What are you doing so far away from your home?" Gailimantas then relayed everything that happened to him. From waking up to his house burning to him running into the forest and living there for the past few weeks. "I see," the man replied. "My condolences about your family." He balled his hand into a fist. "Damn those Teutonic Knights! They've been causing us trouble for years now."

"Teutonic Knights?"

"They've been attacking settlements around ours," he explained, "but whenever we have had enough people, we've been able to hold our own. Hence why this place has not been captured. So you survived one of their attacks, yes?" Gailimantas nodded, completely still in intimidation. "I suppose you want to know who I am. I am Stantiko, son of Arwist. I am in charge of the local army."

"The army…" Gailimantas wondered why such an important person was taking time to talk to him.

"As you know, we have been fighting against these invaders for years now. We need as many men as possible to fight these people, and we have already lost too many. You are a young and healthy boy. So I am going to offer you a deal." Gailimantas became invested in this man's words. "We will let you stay here and live with us. But in exchange, you must train with us and join the army when you are older. What do you say?" Gailimantas was very tempted to say yes. After all, he would have a new place to call home and never go hungry again. He would get to fight for his family and prevent these people from hurting anyone else. He would be a hero, like his father. But he still had his promise. He sighed and shook his head.

"I'm sorry sir," he began. "I would join you, but there is something I must do first. I made a promise to someone that I need to keep."

"A promise?"

"If—If you don't mind, I need your help," he requested. The man was quiet, his expression unchanged. "My father promised to meet me out here. During the attack, he told me to keep running until I reached Swintamīstan. I…I don't know where that is so… I—If it isn't too much trouble, could you please help me get there?" Stantiko slowly blinked, his expression slightly changing. Gailimantas thought that he heard a scoff from the man. He prepared for a negative answer.

"Swintamīstan?" he replied. "This is Swintamīstan."

Gailimantas's eyes widened. He stood up and slowly walked to the entrance of the house, opening the door. He couldn't believe his eyes. Surrounding him were dozens and dozens of houses, shops, and stables; there were more than twice as many as his village, and they were bigger than any man-made structures he had ever seen. Some of the buildings were colorful and had beautiful designs carved onto the doors. Each was made of wood with roofs of hay or sticks, just like his village, but something made these houses seem extraordinary. Some were still being built, stacks of logs piled outside incomplete structures, men stacking them on top of one another. Numerous shrines to the gods made out of pyramids of stones and animal bones dotted the clearing. All the huts were arranged in a circle around one of the biggest trees that Gailimantas had ever seen. It wasn't that much taller than the others he had seen, but its trunk was incredibly thick, and its branches expanded across the clearing, stopping just before the ring of houses. Most peculiar were the busts of the gods Perkūnas, Peckols, and Potrimpo nestled in the tree's branches near the center. Peckols, the god of death, had a long beard and twisted crown of vines around his head. The statue of Potrimpo, the god of the earth and sea, had such precision that Gailimantas could even see the veins on his crown of leaves. The smooth carvings were so detailed, it was as if he was staring at actual human faces painted like stone. Surrounding everything were wooden walls higher than any walls Gailimantas had ever seen. It was as if the town was encircled in one big building without a roof. This town was one big home, and the heavens were the roof.

"Swintamīstan..." he breathed. He could understand why this was named the holy place. He felt a hand on his shoulder.

"Swintamīstan is a sacred place, built for the gods," said Stantiko, "centered around a holy tree." Gailimantas looked up at the older man. "So, now that you're here..."

Gailimantas nodded enthusiastically. "I want to become a warrior," he answered.

Stantiko gave a soft smile. "Welcome to your new home," he replied. "I'm glad you like it."

"Stantiko!" called a blonde man with a full beard, body clad in armor, who was walking quickly towards the two. Behind him, near the front of the camp, a group of armored men were heading towards a tent, carrying a bunch of weapons and a couple of large deer.

"Yes, Eydraus?"

"I just wanted to inform you that our raid was a success," Edraus replied.

"Excellent."

"We obtained about thirty quivers of arrows, eight swords, three shields, twenty and a half bows—"

"A half?"

"It's a long story," Eydraus replied, his eyes finding Gailimantas. "Who's the kid? Is he yours?"

"No. He recently fled from his village," Stantiko explained. "Teutonic Knights…"

Eydraus sighed. "We had a few refugees come here a month ago," he said. "It seems those Teutons are after all of us. Deywis knows where they'll strike next…" He smiled at Gailimantas. "Well, welcome to Swintamīstan. Maybe you can be my apprentice."

"This is Eydraus, son of Dywans," Stantiko said. Gailimantas didn't know what to do, so he bowed his head very formally to the elder man, in a way a slave would to his master.

"I am Gailimantas, son of—"

"Gailimantas?"

Gailimantas turned around to see a tall man with dark red hair and a thick mustache. His gray tunic was still covered in sturdy, dull armor. His green eyes were wide in disbelief, as if he were staring at an illusion that he couldn't rid escape from. The man began to approach him. Gailimantas couldn't believe the sight in front of him. He stared in awe at the man whose eyes were identical to his, tears beginning to form. It was as if he had been locked in a dark box for weeks, and he was finally being released, light shining on his skin and fresh air circulating through his lungs.

"...T—Tāws?" Gailimantas suddenly bolted, dashing to the man at full speed. Finally reunited, the two embraced in a large hug. "Tāws!"

"Gailimantas, I—I can't believe… How did you…"

"I knew I would meet you here! I knew I would!"

Gailimantas clung to his father with an iron grip. His father in turn did the same.

"I thought you were gone…" his father gasped. "I thought I was…"

"I thought I wouldn't see you again," Gailimantas sniffled. "But you promised to meet me here and… I just knew you'd come…"

"Sarginus, this is your son?" Stantiko asked.

"My son…" Sarginus sighted, reluctantly breaking free from the embrace, still holding his son's hand. "This is my fourth and youngest son, Gailimantas."

"I thought all your children were captured by the Teutons a moon ago," said one of the warriors.

"The gods have granted me grace," Sarginus said with a large smile on his face. "The gods have given me my son back!"

At that moment in time, Gailimantas had never felt greater joy. He had lost his mother and siblings and spent the longest time hungry, cold, and alone. But being held by his father once again made all his terrible experiences vanish, replacing them with gratitude. *The gods have not forsaken us,* he thought. *Evil may have had its way, but in the end, good still prevailed.* Gailimantas looked up at his father. *And I'm going to fight to keep it that way.*

# 1261

Friedrich huffed as he struck down another pagan, blood staining the snow beneath his feet. He was starting to get tired, regretting that they had split the troops in two, as they were severely outnumbered. But this did not kill Friedrich's will to fight. On the contrary, it fed it. It was up to him now to lead his squad to victory, despite the unfavorable circumstances. He didn't know where Heinrich was. He would get a lecture about going off and fighting on his own again, but given the dire situation, who could blame him? *Damn it! When we first got here, there wasn't a heathen in sight. Now the place is swarming with them! Those sneaky bastards. It's like they knew our tactics all along! But I don't care what it takes. I'm going to end our losing streak here! We have to take back Pokarwis! It's the least we can do! And I'll slaughter each and every one of these infidels if I have to do so myself.*

He scrambled to his feet, hopping up just in time to block the incoming swing. But the enemy struck him across the head with his shield, causing his helmet to twist, obscuring his vision. He felt a kick to his stomach as he struggled to take off his helmet. When he was finally free, he used the helmet to block an incoming sword attack. The blade went through the eye slit, causing the helmet to be stuck on the sword. Friedrich used this diversion to get back on his feet, dash behind the enemy, and swing at him. But the pagan was too clever and moved at the last second, causing the sword to strike the base of his helmet, knocking it off. Friedrich now had the advantage. He had an intact sword and the enemy was impaired.

As the enemy turned around, Friedrich couldn't help but stare. He felt like he knew this boy, but Friedrich couldn't think of where he knew him. It couldn't be that he had fought him before. He had killed every soldier he battled against so far. At least, every soldier with a face. The enemy's brown hair was down to his chin, wet, and clinging to his face from the snow. His face was pink from the cold and seemed rather youthful, as he lacked any kind of facial hair. He looked to be about twelve or thirteen. When he noticed Friedrich, his forest green eyes locked on him.

Gailimantas scanned his opponent. Something about those unusual eyes seemed so familiar. The orange-amber flecks brought up some sort of nostalgia. But right now he could hardly think, as he was clearly at a disadvantage. He knew he had to search for a way out, but he couldn't figure out why this man seemed so familiar, and why this man was staring at him instead of attacking him.

The two stood there, gazing at each other, a sword's length away; finally reunited on the battlefield.

# Chapter 4: Idol

To commemorate our victory in battle today, we offer a sacrifice to the gods as a token of gratitude," proclaimed the commander. "Before me, three prisoners stand. The priests have drawn lots, once again. Now they will tell us which prisoner has been chosen."

The priests came up to where the noble leader and the prisoners stood, dice made of bones still in hand. Three prisoners had been captured from the last raid, all of which were Teutons, shackled by tight rope and guarded by Prussian warriors. The prisoners quaked in fear as the priests approached. The priests picked up the one on the left, indicating the choice in sacrifice.

"Please don't do this to me!" the sacrifice begged. "Herkus, please! In memory of all I did for you back in Magdeburg, please free me from this!"

"Hirtzhals, I have shown you sympathy and redrawn the lots thrice already," the commander said, switching to the noble's language. "But the gods have chosen you three times. While I am not the most devout believer, I will not defy the divine will of the gods. It is the gods' will that you are to be sacrificed."

The men led him to a tree in the forest, where a horse was tied up, legs bound, eyes covered by cloth, and mouth gagged, still adorned in its armor. The man's arms and legs were tied to four birch trees and he was straddled on his horse. Around him were piles of wood. The Kriwe, the pagan priests, then began to chant a prayer. Another man then came over and lit the pile beneath him, the crowd staring in awe as the fire began to engulf the wood, and with it, the holy knight and his horse. The elected leader and his men watched as the flames suffocated their sacrifice, sending him and his steed to the gods above, singing their praises to their deities.

# 1262

"And so I told him, may the Lord have mercy on your poor soul. And may your wife have mercy on your ears!"

The brothers laughed as they whittled away. After a silent dinner, as per the rules of the Order, the men had some free time and decided to whittle. After all, it was the only form of entertainment allowed for members of the Order. It had been a year. Exactly one year since the Prussians had taken their enemy off guard, killed and captured all but a few of their men, and left the rest to flee in terror. It was the first time Friedrich failed to finish off his enemy since he received his new sword. Today, exactly one year later, was their revenge. Revenge that was extra savory. With the help of some reinforcements from the Rhineland, troops had driven out the Prussians from Königsberg, a very important city.

"Praise the Lord, that food was wonderful!" Simon sighed.

"We finally were allowed to have meat and vegetables!"

"It feels so good to eat a full meal again," Friedrich added. "I thanked the Lord with every bite I took. I never want to starve like that again. I'm so happy we have access to food again."

"It was a great idea for the Rhinelanders to suggest a celebration, " commented a brother. "We had missed many feast days while trapped in that bloody castle…"

"Making up feast days was just an excuse from the Rhinelanders to have a party," Brother Tomas said. "Typical of those from the heart of the Reich, who know no struggles with heathens and supply."

"Oh come on, Brother Tomas, we deserved that feast," Brother David said.

"I don't think we deserved a whole fresh calf…" Tomas commented. "That should have been saved for a holy day."

"It is a holy day!" Brother Franz said. "We finally took revenge on those infidels for all the castles they've taken from us! The tides have finally turned, and it is a step in the right direction."

"The Rhinelanders go home tomorrow, right?" Simon asked.

"Yes," said Friedrich. "I quite like them. I hope we get to work with them again someday."

"Apologies for going off topic. Brother Friedrich, what are your thoughts on the new pope?" asked Brother Kennet.

"I have not heard much about him," Friedrich replied. "He was just appointed last August, after all."

"I'm still surprised we allow popes that have not been cardinals before," Brother Tomas commented.

"Not all holy men are necessarily cardinals first," argued Brother David. "Many saints were ordinary people."

"I suppose…" admitted Brother Tomas. "Still, I can't believe some of the people we let into the Order these days. Even as volunteers. Take a look at Brother Jockel, for example. He was born out of wedlock!

What a world we live in where bastards can become holy knights!" It was quiet for a while. Simon noticed the tension and decided to speak up.

"I miss going into the city," Simon admitted. "I know we are supposed to set an example, but I miss seeing the springtime festivals."

"I do too, but you know that we must abstain from those sinful events," reminded Brother Tomas. "Those are frivolous events, emanating with pride by which the devil is served. Besides, numerous women are there, especially young maidens. And temptation is abundant."

"I go to those events all the time," Brother Kennet said. "They are a good place to talk to potential converts."

"I agree," David said. "It is a good way to increase the reputation of our order. Not that many people can relate to us."

"What do you mean by that, Brother David?" Tomas asked.

"I grew up in a sinful family who rarely attended Sunday mass," confessed David. "My father was a drunkard and a belligerent barbarian. Profanities were part of their vernacular, they took the Lord's name in vain, and had many shameful indulgences." Everyone surrounding him looked shocked. "I grew up always believing that the church hated people like me. That I was forever to be shunned for my family's actions. But then, I met a member of the Order and I learned about Christ."

"But you are a nobleman, Brother David," said Kennet. "You have to be of noble blood to be in your rank. Unless, of course, you lied to achieve your rank." David shook his head.

"Even though I am of noble blood, my father was the youngest in his family, inherited next to nothing, and married a peasant woman, becoming estranged from his family," David elaborated. "I was later adopted and mentored by my uncle. I may be a nobleman, but my upbringings were far from pure. When I met a brother of the convent, he told me that Jesus Christ surrounded himself with sinners. When I learned to read, I learned that Jesus Christ befriended the tax collector and the prostitute and the beggar. People like me and my family could still be saved." He turned to Tomas. "So I do go out to the city. And I go to what you call sinful events. But I talk to the sinner instead of shunning them." It was quiet for a while. Tomas's face was as white as a ghost's. Simon suddenly stood up.

"Oh. I am feeling a bit of a chill," Simon said, excusing himself. "Excuse me, brothers, I am going to the chapel to pray." Friedrich wasn't the best at sensing the atmosphere, but he felt that something was off about his friend. Besides, he wanted to get away from this conversation as soon as he could.

"I am feeling cold as well," Friedrich said. "I will join you." He hurried after Simon, putting his work in his pocket. He quickened his pace to catch up to his friend.

"What the matter?" he asked, jogging next to his friend. "You look a bit pale." Simon looked worried, biting his lip and avoiding eye contact. "Have you something to confess?"

"No," Simon replied, a hint of his friendly smile stretching across his face. "Don't worry about me, Fritz. It's just me worrying about something that does not matter."

"It troubles you enough to the point of worry," Friedrich insisted. "We have to check up on our brothers' well being. It is our responsibility as brothers." Simon chuckled slightly.

"It's just me worrying…" Simon started. "If I hadn't joined the Order, would I have become like Brother David's father? Can nobles like us really turn to that kind of lifestyle?"

"I don't think you would have become that," answered Friedrich. "I believe you are not the kind of person to become a sinful drunkard. Besides, you made the right choice by joining the Order. Your faith alone separates you from those people, doesn't it?" Simon smiled. The two had been friends ever since they were admitted into the Order together and after all these years later, they still had a strong brotherly bond. Friedrich had expected to be primarily focused on the war and training, but Simon made being in the Teutonic Order a lot more enjoyable.

"Let's prepare for evening prayer," said Simon. "The Grand Master said that we have to be on our guard. We may have defeated them for now, but they could easily come back."

"Agreed," Friedrich said, smiling. "There's a lot I need to pray about."

"Tonight we celebrate our victory!" Stantiko proclaimed. The rest of the men cheered in agreement. They all raised their glasses full of alcohol. "A healthy one after a healthy one, one after another!"

"To Natangia!"

"Natangia!"

"To Prussia!"

"Prussia!"

"To Herkus Monte!"

"Herkus!"

With a clunk of the cups and the blowing of the horns, the drinking and festivities had begun. Earlier they had sacrificed one of their prisoners along with a horse to the gods and the priest had sprinkled them with blood for protection and blessing. Many large fires had been kindled across the settlement, people dancing around them. Gailimantas smiled. Sieging Kreuzberg Castle had been a long, arduous process, but it was worth it. It had taken about two years. Two long years of being on the battlefront and starving out the garrison. Finally, the garrison gave up. Now they could relax for at least a little while.

"Thank you for your aid today, Gailimantas."

Gailimantas turned to see his father behind him. "No problem," he said. "I saw you were in trouble and I went to help. I took care of him, don't worry."

"He took me off guard," Sarginus said. "I'm fine now, but he really knocked the wind out of me. Maybe I'm getting too old for the battlefield."

"You still have a few summers left," assured Gailimantas. His father chuckled.

"So, what do you think of Herkus?" his father asked.

"Herkus? He's brilliant!" Gailimantas praised. "He sees through their every move! It's amazing! When the Germans tried to sneak away, he had us charge after them. I can't believe how scrawny they were!"

"They were starving up there for months. I can imagine they'd look quite shabby."

"And then we slaughtered all of them except for two, which we left alive to tell the rest of their kind of our victory!" Gailimantas continued. "Oh wait, they probably told you that already."

"I would have only left one…" his father said, taking a sip of his drink.

"Well, one is probably food for the other," Gailimantas joked. His father laughed in response.

"You know, Herkus used to be a Teutonic Knight," his father informed him.

"H—He did?"

"Aye," Sarginus said. "But these are his roots. He's Natangian at heart." Sarginus smiled. "When he was young, he was captured and brought to the Holy Roman Empire. There, he learned their tactics and language. But his Prussian roots called him back to our side."

"Fascinating…" Gailimantas took another drink. "Is that how he knew that they would split into two groups?"

Sarginus nodded. "The gods have given us a gift," he said. "This is just what we needed to defeat these people once and for all."

"Sarginus!" called another soldier. "Nice save today!"

"Ah Schadeus! You did very well."

"Yes, but unfortunately, my brother, Abgautis, was slain in battle."

"Oh. I'm sorry."

"I know. But alas, we cannot change the gods' decisions. His widow is distraught, but she'll find a good place in my household."

"Speaking of widows, how is Nomedas doing with his brother's widow?"

"Ah! She is expecting his child! It should be born slightly after Myre's child…"

Gailimantas left his father to chat. He didn't want to get dragged into that conversation. He knew it would end up being about how Gailimantas was 14 and hadn't thought about taking a wife yet, while others his age were planning to buy a wife soon. Though he wasn't a prince, his father was part of the warrior elite that was highly valued in Prussian society. People of his status were expected to have at least a few wives, but he knew he wouldn't have too many, as his brothers were dead, so he wouldn't take in any of their widows. He knew war was another way to obtain a wife, as raids would often bring back several women. But the war had been endless and throughout the back-to-back battles, Gailimantas simply had no time for a woman, much less one who couldn't understand what he was saying. Then there were bride markets where he could buy a Prussian girl, but Gailimantas still considered himself too young. He wasn't even done growing yet.

Gailimantas sighed. A wife would be nice. He could imagine settling down and having a family when he was older. When all the fighting was over. He imagined coming home from a long hunt or a border skirmish, probably spattered in blood, to find his wife making dinner and five of his children running to greet him. Then he would go and greet the shy one all the way in the back, like his father did to him when he was little. And then after his father's new wife would put the kids to sleep, he would spend the evening with his own wife. Though she would probably scold him for being covered in blood and tell him to rinse off in the creek. Gailimantas smiled, replaying his earliest memories in his head, putting himself in his father's place. *Times were simpler back then. Back when we lived in the countryside. Back before the war forced us to hide in the fortress. Back when we were still a family. I've been to so many places… It's cool to see so many cities, but I'm getting tired. I want to just rest for a little bit...*

Gailimantas went to the clearing to watch the dancers. He knew this dance, but wasn't sure how far into the song the group was. He wanted to finish his drink anyway.

Gailimantas saw someone next to him out of the corner of his eye. "Ah," said the man, "I wish I remembered how to dance to this song…"

"This one is pretty fast," Gailimantas said.

"I remember this from when I was a child," the man said. Gailimantas recognized the man's voice. He looked at the man next to him and did everything he could not to gape in awe. There stood the legend himself, Herkus Monte. He sipped his drink, casually watching the dancers with a reminiscent smile on his face. He had fought on the battlefield with this man, but he had never been this close to him. Gailimantas wasn't sure what to say to this hero. This gift from the gods. But he had to say something. He had the chance to talk to *the* Herkus Monte.

"So… Kreuzberg..."

"At last, our efforts were worth it," Herkus said. "I can't imagine how little food they had left. They looked so frail. They must have been eating their horses." Herkus turned to Gailimantas. "One day, you too will know the thrill of the battlefield." Gailimantas felt dejected.

"I—I was at that battle…" Gailimantas said to correct him. "I fought with you, sir."

"Really?" Herkus raised his eyebrows in surprise. "How old are you?" "Fourteen summers," Gailimantas replied.

"Really?" said Herkus. "I thought you were a tall child. You look very young. Your voice is still changing." Gailimantas felt his face turning red in embarrassment. "What is your name, boy?" Herkus asked. Gailimantas's heart skipped a beat.

"G—Gailimantas, son of Sarginus."

"Well, it is nice to see a young, able boy willing to fight for our people," said

Herkus, smiling.

"Of course. It's the least I can do for my family…" Gailimantas said. "Except for my father, everyone else perished because of the Teutonic Order. I was very young when they first attacked us…"

"Ah. My condolences," Herkus said. "It gives you the will to fight, doesn't it? When you fight, they fight with you." Gailimantas gave a nod. "One does not easily forget the oppression of their people. I rejected their ideas of civilizing the other. I went along with it all to just get back home, but I would never work for them. I could never forget how they treated our people." Herkus sighed. "They don't wish to convert us anymore. They wish to destroy us now. When Prussians actually started converting to their religion, they invited some of the Prussian chiefs to negotiate with them. But when the elders arrived…" He pounded his fist into the table. "They slaughtered all of them. Then they set fire to the banquet hall. No one survived." Herkus pushed aside his cup. "Even if we do convert like they want, it is never going to be enough for them. This isn't about religion anymore." Gailimantas remained quiet. "You would understand more than anyone, wouldn't you?" Gailimantas nodded along.

"Well, if the Lithuanians can beat them, so can we," replied Gaili-mantas. Herkus smiled.

"Ah yes," Herkus said. "The Lithuanians… I admire them. They gave us all hope that these Teutons could be defeated." The song then changed to something more lively. "This song… I love this song."

"Let's dance then," Gailimantas said. "I'll teach you how if you don't know." Herkus gave a smile in return.

"I suppose I cou—"

"May I have your attention please?"

A loud shout came from the entrance of the camp. An unfamiliar man sat on his horse. He dismounted as a couple of people from the village led his horse to safety.

"I have a message for Herkus Monte from our leader!" he announced.

"I am Herkus Monte," said Herkus. "State your business."

"My leader Glande asks for your assistance in battle as soon as possible," the messenger informed.
"Glande?"

"The leader of the Sambians," clarified Herkus. "What are the details of his condition?"

"The Teutonic Knights have defeated us and forced us to retreat to Kalgen," said the messenger. "The last battle saw thousands of our men dead. We tried starving out the garrison in Königsberg, but a spy amongst our ranks ratted out our strategy. We need reinforcements as soon as possible!"

Herkus thought for a moment. "We must help our comrades out," he declared. "But first, let us ask the gods for guidance."

"Shall I prepare a sacrifice?" Stantiko asked Herkus.

"Yes," Herkus said. "Bring us the first prisoner that we caught to-day." Stantiko nodded. Gailimantas's heart sank. Just when he thought they would be getting a break. He was tired and slightly sore from the months—no, years—of staking out that fortress. Well, at least he had tonight. Maybe tonight would be enough.

Soon, two soldiers led a struggling man out to the clearing past the large, sacred tree in the center of the town. Gailimantas knew that they were leading him to the forest. Behind the men were two people with torches and an archer. Gailimantas followed the ever-growing crowd of people out to the forest. Two of the soldiers led the man to a tree not far from the entrance of the camp. The soldiers tied the man, who was still struggling and begging, to a tree. The priests then began to chant their prayers to Potrimpo.

Gailimantas watched as the archer approached the tree. He took an arrow from the quiver and loaded his bow. He then released the arrow, shooting the man in the heart. The man gasped a few dying breaths and let out a few last desperate cries of help, but soon, the light in his eyes faded. The blood from the wound ran freely down his bare chest. Herkus turned to his men.

"The blood runs freely!" he announced. "As the gods have predicted our success, we shall attack!" The soldiers cheered, Gailimantas with them. He had faith in his leader and in his gods. Surely they knew what was best for them. If that meant more fighting, so be it. Anything so that they could live in peace again. Herkus turned to the messenger.

"Tell them we will be there as soon as we can," said Herkus. "As many of our men are weak and tired, we will leave in the morning."

"Thank you, sir!" said the messenger, smiling.

"My fellow men, prepare for battle," announced Herkus. "Tomorrow we head to Twangste!"

Sparks flew as Friedrich's sword clashed with his enemy's. He put his heart into every swing, each shockwave resounding with his drive, spurring him on. Friedrich loved the battlefield: the pulsing adrenaline rushing through him, the feeling of power every time he swung his sword, the feeling of justice every time he inflicted a wound on the enemy, and of course, the sweet, sweet victory at the end of the battle. When he wasn't tethered to his mentor, he felt so free, finally getting the chance to use his skills he had been honing for years.

Friedrich and his brothers thought they had bested the Sambians months ago. The snow had long melted and the summer sun was sinking lower on the horizon. Everything was fine for months until the Sambians decided to block the Pregel River once again. Not that Friedrich minded. Just sitting in that castle and training was boring. Friedrich lived for the thrill of crushing his enemies in the name of God. But for that to happen, there needed to be some heathen to fight and enough chaos for his knight to send him into battle.

Friedrich stared the enemy dead in the eye. He scoffed. These stupid heathens didn't even have armor covering their face. Their swords met again, both bodies pushing closer and closer to each other. Friedrich then kicked the man in the stomach. It wasn't too powerful, but powerful enough to take him off guard. Friedrich then slashed at the enemy's face, leaving a large cut over the enemy's eyes. The man cried in pain as Friedrich quickly stabbed him in the face. Next.

Friedrich looked over to see Simon in a fierce duel with another pagan. He ran forward, seeing the man had no leg armor, and slashed at his legs, causing the man to fall to the ground. Next.

Out of the corner of his eye, he saw a pagan trying to sneak up behind him. *Nice try.* Friedrich spun around and swung his sword. He missed, and the enemy kicked him with such force, he fell backwards onto his posterior. But it wasn't enough to take him out of his zone. Friedrich waited for the enemy to come to him. The enemy swung down at him, but he spun out of the way, rising back to his feet and stabbing the heathen in the side where his armor was loose. Next.

Friedrich looked next to him and dodged a sword just in time, blocking the next swing with his own sword. Friedrich noticed that the enemy was pushing closer. He hit the enemy with his shield, causing him to fall backwards into the mud. The enemy was sprawled out on his back. Friedrich stomped towards him, pressing his feet into the remaining mud so he wouldn't slip. By the time the Prussian realized what was going on, Friedrich was ready for the killing blow. But before he could strike, a large force knocked him sideways, sending him hurling through the air. Friedrich landed on his back, the mud breaking his fall.

As soon as Friedrich realized what was happening, he saw the soldier on top of him swing at him. He rolled out of the way just in time, but was met with a stomp to his stomach. His armor mostly blocked the pain, but that move had cost him his sword. The enemy struck him with his own sword, but Friedrich hid behind his shield. Friedrich couldn't see, but he kicked upwards, hitting the enemy in the leg. While his foe recoiled, he tried to use the shield to push the enemy off him, but couldn't see his direction. Friedrich heard something land in the mud a bit past his feet, but still felt the heathen on top of him. At least he had knocked the sword out of the other's hand. Friedrich felt the enemy's limbs tense up, ready to bolt after it. *Oh no you don't!* Friedrich sprung to his feet with his enemy, grabbed the other by the back of the tunic, and pulled him back with such a force that caused the two to slip and tumble down the side of the hill. Friedrich felt his helmet come off in the sticky mud as he rolled along.

When they finally stopped rolling, Friedrich instantly hopped up, ready for action. But he couldn't see the enemy. He couldn't see any soldiers at all. Had he landed somewhere else? Could he not see him due to the mud? His hair and face were now splattered with mud, the stains dying his white uniform a dark brown. He whipped around when he heard the mud squishing. His enemy stood a meter higher than him and was looking around. Friedrich was instantly struck with nostalgia. Bells were ringing in his head but he couldn't figure out why. He did find it odd that this man lacked facial hair, but was too tall to be a child. *I thought these heathens didn't shave.* When the foe noticed Friedrich, his eyes gave an intense glare as he pulled out a dagger and charged towards him. Friedrich, still in possession of his shield, prepared to body check him, but he saw his enemy slip on the mud. Friedrich prepared to charge when the pagan slid downwards, in between Friedrich's legs, slashing at the inside of his thigh. Friedrich yelled in pain as the enemy knocked him over and resumed his position on top of him, slamming him into the grassy field. The two locked eyes with one another. This pain in his leg. Those green eyes. That hairless face. Was this the man from the Battle of Pokarwis the previous year? The one that got away because his commander forced them to retreat?

Gailimantas stared at the man beneath him. He knew he had seen this man before. Those fiery amber flecks that popped against that icy blue iris. He had definitely fought this man in the past, but he didn't have time to think. He had to fight to kill. The Teuton was prepared for an attack to the head. Gailimantas knew this. His eyes scoured the man's body for another opening. But to throw the man off, he went for the neck.

Friedrich blocked the attempt. *How stupid is this guy?* The Prussian kept stabbing around the facial area, each attempt blocked by Friedrich's shield. Sometimes he just stabbed into the shield. Friedrich moved his shield in different directions, trying to block the different angles that the attacks were coming from. He was about to knee the enemy where it hurt, but before he could, he felt a sharp pain in between his stomach and his pelvis. The sharp pain then stretched across his stomach until he finally kneed the enemy in the solar plexus.

Friedrich sat up to survey the damage. It was too painful for him to sit up. He screamed as fiery pain spread across his lower abdomen. Blood began to stain his uniform and soon, the grass. *No. No! Oh God no!* The wound stretched from his lower left hip to the middle of his lower stomach. Friedrich began to feel sick. He then heard footsteps running away.

"Coward," he growled. "Didn't even finish the job…" Friedrich hunched over, starting to spew his own blood. He then collapsed onto his stomach.

Friedrich laid on the ground, blood pooling at his side and from his mouth. *I'm going to die… I mean, I knew it was going to happen but… I didn't think it would be so soon. I'm only 19 years old. I thought I would at least get to defeat this tribe. And become a Ritterbruder. And be a holy hero. Maybe even be canonized as a saint. I haven't even become a full knight yet!* He laid there for a while, thinking about all the things he hadn't done yet.

He threw up again, the metallic taste of blood washing over his tongue. He stared at the tissue, staring into the red pool now covering the grass. Red. The color of the blood he shed, the blood he spilled, and the color of his family. The color of the honor he brought to his name and the honor he had brought to God. He flopped back down, a smile on his face. *I suppose I've lived an awesome life. I helped put those heathens in their place. I've sent many of them back to where they came from. I've done the Lord's will. And that's all that matters to the Lord. I am a holy hero. Surely, I will be a martyr.*

He laid there for what seemed like an hour. He felt his body growing colder and colder. Waiting and waiting.

Ignoring the pain, he flipped himself over so he could look at the grey sky above him. It was darker than before. *I'm ready for paradise,* he thought. *I've fought a hard battle. And now I'm ready to see my father again. I can't wait to see the look on his face. Especially after I'm celebrated as a martyr. And my brother and mother… They're going to be so proud.* He chuckled a bit, but stopped when blood rose in his throat again. After spitting up again, he laid back, folded his hands, and closed his eyes. *I'm ready, Lord.* Suddenly, Friedrich heard soft footsteps coming towards him. He opened an eye.

Before him stood a beautiful young woman wrapped in a white cloak. Her skin was almost as white as snow. Long, tight black curls peeked out from behind her veil. The grey clouds behind her made her seem even more radiant. He stared at her in awe.

"…An angel," Friedrich sighed. *She must be here to escort me to Heaven.* The woman stared at him, a slight smile on her face. Friedrich held out his hand. She took it and knelt down to him. She then wrapped him in her embrace. He rested his head on her shoulder, tired from the pain, submitting to the heavenly beauty. She then leaned in and kissed him on the neck. Shortly after, Friedrich's vision became darker and darker. *It's finally time…*

# Chapter 5: Angel

Gailimantas pushed his way through the scattered crowd of people around the infirmary tent. This couldn't be happening. This couldn't be real. There was no way his mighty commander had been slain in battle. The sounds of a drum and of the praying priests were muffled by the murmurs of those around him. Whispers and rumors had spread amongst the soldiers, some saying he was still alive, some saying he was dead. All Gailimantas knew was that he was forced to retreat due to his commander's injury. When he returned to the battlefield after that duel with the strange man, orders of retreat were echoing everywhere. Apparently Herkus had been grievously wounded by one of the sergeants after severely injuring one of the Teutonic commanders. He had been in the dark for two days, worrying about his commander's condition. Seeing a crowd of people around the tent this morning gave him a bad feeling. He didn't know what his people would do without Herkus. He didn't know what *he* would do without Herkus. Herkus was not just his commander. He was his idol, the hero of the Natangians, a prophet sent by the gods to save their people. If he were to disappear, his life and hope would vanish with it. But as he pushed forward, the crowd began to disappear. Voices were not panicked, but they were calm, simply murmuring. Gailimantas's expected grief was replaced with confusion as he heard the commotion amongst the people scattering from the tent.

"What are we going to do now?"

"Who knows when they'll attack us next?"

"It's true! I saw it myself! The bastard pierced him with a small lance!"

"Peckols really scared us today."

"Who's going to replace him? What can we do now?"

"I'm just happy the gods kept him alive."

"He's alive?" Gailimantas interrupted.

The soldier turned around. "Yes. The injury is pretty bad, but he's still alive," he replied. Gailimantas felt a weight lifted off of his chest.

"Oh praise Deywis! Praise the gods!" Gailimantas exclaimed. He couldn't believe it. The spell he had casted worked. His commander, no, *his savior* was alive.

"I'm not sure if he's awake right now, but he's in rough shape," said the soldier. "So don't go playing around the tent, kid." Gailimantas felt his mouth hang open for a moment.

"I am 14..." he reminded the soldier. "I fought on the battlefield with you."

"Oh. In that case, go on in. He may be resting though. He's all the way in the back. He has his own area."

Gailimantas stood awkwardly outside of the tent, feeling nervous about going inside. Then he remembered, there were others inside the tent as well, so it wouldn't be too awkward to just walk by and see Herkus. Gailimantas entered the tent, passing by the other injured soldiers, searching for his commander. *I'm just going to see how bad his injury is. That's it,* Gailimantas assured himself. *I'm just going to walk in, see how he is, and leave. He probably has had a swarm of people around him and wants his privacy.* Gailimantas stopped at the back of the infirmary where a long cloth hung down, separating part of the tent from the rest. He smelled the incense as he got closer. He stalled for a bit, nervousness still swirling around in his mind. *You've talked to him several times before! You shouldn't be so nervous! But he probably doesn't want to see anyone right now… Just a check up.* Gailimantas poked his head behind the curtain, only to be met by the intimidating gaze of his commander. His heart jumped, eyes widening in surprise. He didn't expect him to be awake. He didn't expect him to be staring directly at him either. Herkus was just laying there, a blanket covering all but his head. Gailimantas couldn't see where he was injured.

"Sorry!" Gailimantas said. "I must have the wrong room!"

"Wait!" said Herkus. Gailimantas pulled back the curtain again. "Could you get me some water, please?" Gailimantas nodded, dashing off to the other side of the tent where the water was kept. He quickly found a cup and poured some water from the pail before rushing back to his commander, being careful not to spill any. He slipped through the curtain and handed the cup to Herkus. "Thank you," Herkus rasped, clearly parched. "Gailimantas, right?"

"Yes sir!" he replied, excited that his commander remembered him. Herkus sat up to drink his water, wincing in pain. His chest was heavily bandaged.

"Yes," Herkus said. "I remember you. Your face is easy to remember." Gailimantas couldn't hold back his excited smile. Herkus Monte knew who he was! Herkus put down his cup. He let out an aggravated sigh. "I was so focused on taking down Ulenbusch… I didn't see that other one coming. I'll be more careful next time." Gailimantas assumed he was talking about the Teuton's general. The man who wounded his hero.

"I'm just happy you're okay, sir," Gailimantas said, kneeling to be at his commander's eye level. "I prayed and cast a spell for your health. I was about to sacrifice one of my eyes as an offering to the gods."

"Please, don't offer yourself," Herkus advised, slowly shifting back down to a lying position. "We need young, healthy soldiers like you. You haven't been in this tent before, have you?"

"Only once when my father was injured," Gailimantas answered. "I've been in the healer's house when I was younger, but that was back when my brothers were still around."

"Your brothers?"

Gailimantas proceeded to tell Herkus about how the Teutonic Knights attacked his village, how he lived in the forest for about a month, and how he came to Swintamīstan.

"Your story seems to be the opposite of mine," Herkus said, smiling. "While I was captured and taken to the Holy Roman Empire, you escaped from the Teutonic Order."

"Why do they capture children and take them to the Holy Roman Empire?" Gailimantas asked.

"Their plan is to educate them in their ways, so that when they return to Prussia they can teach the gospel and the German practices to their 'inferior' brethren," Herkus explained. "I worked hard to become a soldier. The Order took a liking to me and deployed me as soon as they could. I have to admit, I learned a lot from my time there." Herkus looked up at the ceiling. "Most of our soldiers on the frontlines have perished in these past few battles. That or they have been injured at some point," he added. "The fact that you haven't been injured on the battlefield yet shows that either you have good defense or are a coward. It's pretty hard to be a coward on the front lines, so I'm going to assume the former."

Gailimantas bowed his head. "Thank you," he said. "That means a lot coming from someone like you." Gailimantas returned to standing upright and alert. "Is there anything else you need, sir?"

Herkus gave a slight smile. "You want to be like me someday, don't you?" he said.

Gailimantas was quiet for a moment. "I wish…" he scoffed, kneeling again. "There's no way that I can be like you. I'm not smart, I'm not educated, nor am I an incredibly skilled soldier. I am just a boy. I've only ever slain four soldiers, and I'm on the frontlines. One of those was two days ago." He bowed his head. "You were blessed with the enemy's knowledge, trained amongst their ranks, and have returned to share that information with us. You have led us to numerous miraculous victories. Our tribe thought the gods had forsaken them, but then they gave us you." Gailimantas knew he was rambling, but he couldn't help himself in the presence of his idol. "I… I hold so much admiration for you. You are a hero from the gods, sent here to save us. And I will lay down my life to protect you if I must." It was quiet for a while.

"Gailimantas, lift your head," Herkus said. Gailimantas obeyed, staring into the eyes of his wounded leader. "Only bow like that before the gods. I am not one of them." Gailimantas was silent for a moment. "You have your own experiences that aid you in battle. And I am sure that you will come to use them someday. I—"

A soldier entered the room, a plate of deer meat in hand. "Herkus," he said, "we have slain a large deer. We have prepared your dinner." Herkus smiled.

"Gailimantas, can I ask a favor?" Herkus asked.

Gailimantas looked up. "Anything, sir," he said.

"Tell my men that I'll be back on the battlefield before they know it," Herkus said. "I'm not going to let those Teutonic Knights savor their victory for long."

Gailimantas smiled proudly and nodded. "You have my word, sir!" said the boy.

"Brother Friedrich! Brother Friedrich!"

Friedrich opened his eyes to darkness. *Am I in Heaven?* He slowly sat up, noticing that he was still on the hill, but it was after sunset. He heard footsteps racing towards him. He turned around to see two of his brothers rushing towards him.

"He's alive!"

"It's him!" they called. "We found Brother Friedrich!" Friedrich was confused when he saw his comrades' relieved faces.

"Brother Friedrich! How did you end up over here?" Tomas asked.

"We thought you had been killed on the battlefield!" cried Franz.

"Dear Lord! Your mouth is covered in blood!" David gasped.

"I'm…alive?" Friedrich questioned. *The cold, the pain… It felt so real. It couldn't have been a dream, could it?* Though only half of the moon illuminated the night, Friedrich could still see the large bloodstains on the ground. Friedrich felt his stomach. The wound was gone. But yet the blood, the evidence, was all around him. Friedrich's eyes widened in shock.

"Brother Friedrich?"

"That angel… She healed me…"

"What are you talking about?"

"I was supposed to die. I was about to die, but then…I saw an angel…"

"An angel of the Lord?"

"She embraced me and…she healed me…" Friedrich explained. "The Lord used His divine power to heal me of my injuries! Look at this blood! This blood was once mine! But the Lord sent an angel to heal me!"

"By God! Friedrich has witnessed a miracle from our Heavenly Father!" Brother Tomas proclaimed. Friedrich smiled, frozen in awe and wonder. "We have to tell the Komtur. No, the pope!" Everyone began instantly chattering about the miracle.

"Can we talk about this inside?" David suggested. "Brother Friedrich probably wants a bath." Friedrich didn't realize he was covered in blood and dirt. He scraped off a bit of dry mud that flaked off of his palm. David handed him a handkerchief.

"It's going to take more than that," Friedrich chuckled as the group began to walk back. "What of the pagans? Did we win?"

"We were victorious!" proclaimed Brother Tomas. "Their army tried to block our ships, but thank God reinforcements came! And one of the great leaders, Herkus Monte, was injured in battle. Now that such a large threat is out of the way, our job is going to be so much easier…"

*It's not my time yet,* Friedrich thought. *God still needs me on Earth. I promise, I will not fail again.*

"By the way, Brother Friedrich. You have something on your neck," David pointed out.

"It's probably just blood spatter. I'll clean it later."

# 1263

"Forget the others! Find the generals! I want to make them suffer!"

Gailimantas ran alongside his comrades, following his commander's instructions. Being sure to dodge the bodies of the enemies that had been massacred by their surprise attack, Gailimantas began the search for the enemy's leader, who was still alive and trying to flee. The orders were to bring him back alive, but to kill the others on sight. Gailimantas relied on the moon and his torch to light his way through the forest. He had two other men with him, but the trio were horseless. They had been searching for hours, but so far, not a sign of a living Teutonic Knight.

"Maybe they already captured him," his comrade guessed.

"We have to keep searching," Gailimantas said.

"Maybe we should just head to their camp and join the rest. Or at least find the others," another man suggested.

"We may be wasting time. We should report back to the others. Because I don't see or hear a single sign of life out here."

"Okay, fine," said Gailimantas, giving in. "We'll look for another troop."

The group entered the clearing where the river and the ravine were. Arrow covered bodies still littered the valley. Gailimantas felt a strong sense of pride staring at the aftermath of his leader's glorious plan. Earlier, they had led the enemy into a trap, luring them into the ravine with small numbers while archers were waiting to ambush them from above. Their archers tried to fire back, but it was hard to hit something they couldn't see. Then, a brigade of mounted men charged in and massacred the rest of the Teutons. Very little of their white uniforms were left unstained. Gailimantas smiled at the hours-old memory. It would be a scene he would replay in his head tonight.

"I think the camp is this way," pointed the other soldier. The group then began to head in the suggested direction.

"I think it's safe to say that there's going to be a nice celebration after this," the older warrior said. "Don't you think so, Naleyks?"

"I don't know," Naleyks replied. "Herkus hardly holds rituals anymore."

"We can't afford to host celebrations," Gailimantas lectured. "We're in the middle of war. We can't afford to let our guard down. Not even for a minute."

"But we should give thanks to the gods for our victory," Naleyks said.

"...I guess that's true," said Gailimantas as he took off his helmet, collecting some water to drink.

"For someone so young, he acts like an old man," Naleyks muttered under his breath. "He's only 15." He then realized that the other soldier didn't respond to his joke. "Hey Wissegar, did…" Naleyks's words caught in his throat as he realized that his partner was no longer there. "Wisse—" Naleyks was cut off by a flash of white.

"Naleyks?" said Gailimantas as he whipped around to see both of his comrades, lying on the ground, their blood clouding the river crimson. Standing next to him was a Teutonic Knight. His white uniform was stained a pink color from the carnage. His helmet was missing and his chainmail slumped haphazardly around his shoulders. His strawberry blonde hair was caked with blood, probably from his comrades. Judging by his clothes, he was an average soldier, but still a full-time soldier. He wasn't the target that they were looking for. However, he had just killed or severely wounded the others in his patrol, so Gailimantas had to take care of him. Gailimantas drew his sword, ready for the soldier's attack, but instead the soldier stood still, squinting at him, as if trying to confirm something.

"*Well I'll be! God has been gracious to me today,*" said the soldier, speaking in a foreign tongue. Gailimantas raised an eyebrow and stepped backwards, confused. The soldier stepped forward, close enough for Gailimantas to see his facial features. "Remember me?" the soldier smirked, switching to Prussian. As there weren't any other soldiers around them, it was easy to hear. Gailimantas halted his actions, a surprised expression on his face. Did this warrior just speak to him in his own language? Could he be a Christianized Prussian? Or maybe he was a Prussian spy amongst the Teutonic Knights. That would be strange if he was, since he just killed two members of his squad.

"How—How do you know my language?" Gailimantas replied, putting his helmet back on. "Are you one of us? Or are you a traitor to your people?" The man scrunched up his face. He clearly didn't know what Gailimantas was talking about.

"I am a German man of God!" the soldier proclaimed. "I am not scum like you!"

"Then who are you?" Gailimantas asked. "And how do you know me?"

"I am Friedrich von Rotenkreuz. And I am taking my revenge."

"For what?" Gailimantas asked. "I don't even know who you are! Why me? What did I do to you?"

"Is your pagan mind that small?" Friedrich scoffed. "We have met multiple times in the past!" Gailimantas looked into his eyes. He remembered those eyes. The flecks of amber that popped before their blue background, like a ring of swirling fire on a bright blue day. He remembered killing this man last year, so how was he still alive? "I never thought I would see you again," Friedrich continued. "Last time you managed to beat me when you stabbed me in the stomach. And to think that you were not even a real man yet. I was bested by a boy! But you are a man now. So I won't hold back on you." He charged at Gailimantas again, Gailimantas blocking his swing with his own sword. *He probably just recovered from his wound. But I left him badly wounded. How did he recover so well? Could he be a reanimated corpse that wasn't buried properly? No. He can't be a demon. Don't be so childish, Gailimantas.*

"I—I thought I killed you last time," Gailimantas stammered. "H—How are you—"

"I was saved by a miracle," he said. "A miracle from God." Friedrich smiled. "My Lord helps me in times of trouble. He has a destiny for me. And that destiny is to annihilate you worshippers of the devil until you finally submit and pray to our one true God!" The two broke out of their stalemate, stepping backwards.

"Wh—Why are you doing this?" Gailimantas asked. "Why do you attack our people?"

"You send your prayers to Hell and not God," Friedrich said, stumbling with his words, as it had been a while since he had spoken this language. "The church told us to bring the word of God to this unholy land. When you all become Christians and stop your sinful lives, we will leave."

"…Sinful?"

"All that you do is an act against God," Friedrich elaborated. "Praying to multiple gods, making idols and praying to them, drinking, lusting, thievery, witchcraft, having multiple wives… These are all sins. And you will go to Hell if you don't stop doing them."

"We have to give thanks to our gods," Gailimantas said. "We need to show our thanks for their creations, or else some of them might get angry. We're not going to stop worshiping our gods. They have given so much to us!"

"Then you can join the demons you worship in Hell," Friedrich growled, charging at Gailimantas. Gailimantas blocked the diagonal attack, feeling his shield take damage from the heavy blow. Even though Friedrich was five years his senior, Gailimantas was about the same size as him. He swung back, but Friedrich was too fast and dodged him. The two were constantly weaving back and forth, never a moment standing still. Friedrich unleashed a barrage of attacks, swinging from every direction. Gailimantas kept stepping back, his shield taking numerous brutal hits and becoming further and further damaged. Out of the corner of his eye, he noticed the forest behind them.

*You have your own experiences that aid you in battle. And I am sure that you will come to use them someday.* Hearing Herkus's words echo in his head, Gailimantas knew what he had to do. He took the chance to dash away from Friedrich when he had the chance, tossing his torch into the water, running along the ravine and towards the trees.

"Hey! Coward! Don't you dare run away from me again!" yelled Friedrich, chasing after him. Gailimantas continued running until he reached the trees. He ran until he was sure he was deep enough and until he found a tree that was easy enough to climb. He quickly sheathed his sword and picked up a few rocks from the base of the tree, stashing them away in his pocket before climbing the oak. When he was sure that he was out of sight and well hidden by the leaves, he sat there silently, listening. Just like he used to do when he was hiding from hostile animals or when he didn't want to sleep on the ground. Moments later, he heard the rattling of Friedrich's metal armor and the leaves crunching under his feet.

Friedrich was having fun, but he was not a fool. He knew that the Prussian was waiting to ambush him somewhere. He scanned behind the tree trunks, looking for a glint of silver armor, or at least a splash of reddish-brown. But the darkness of the night made colors fade to monochrome and the shadows that the trees cast shrouded the forest in an extra layer of thick shade. Friedrich flinched at the sound of rustling leaves, feeling his body becoming tense. He continued to look around for his target, but it was incredibly hard to see.

Gailimantas smirked, seeing his enemy in his line of sight. He was getting close to his tree, as expected. Gailimantas tossed a rock across the forest, where it landed directly across from Friedrich. Friedrich looked in that direction and began to run towards the sound, disappearing into the shadows. Gailimantas, listening to the sound of the leaves crunching beneath his enemy's feet, slid down the tree as quietly and quickly as possible. He slipped behind the tree immediately after he hit the ground, brushing the shoulder length, russet hair out of his face. He heard his enemy's tracks stop short for a moment before continuing to walk away from him. Gailimantas then took the rest of the rocks out of his pocket. He then began to hurl them in scattered directions.

Friedrich looked around in panic. Leaves were rustling in many different directions around him. Were there more soldiers hiding in the forest? Had the pagan led him into a trap? He looked around to try to find an exit, but nothing but trees surrounded him and he couldn't recall where he had entered. *To the devil! I'm surrounded! What should I do?*

Gailimantas heard his enemy running away from him. It would give him time to think of a plan as this man was clearly stronger than him at the moment. As he listened to the enemy's footsteps run further and further away, he couldn't shake the feeling that something was wrong. He had this strong, stomach-churning feeling that sent shivers pricking at the tip of his skin. The feeling that he was being watched. He quickly peered over his shoulder just in time to see a figure in a cloak standing a meter away from him. But the cloak wasn't a bright white like his enemy's. It was a darker color. Gailimantas wouldn't have seen the figure if it weren't for its ghostly white hands. It wasn't dressed in armor and was currently frozen as Gailimantas stared at it. *What is a civilian doing so close to the battlefield? What is his business here? Is he from one of the tribes? Is he from the Order? His cloak isn't white, so I doubt he is a Teutonic Knight.* Before Gailimantas could ask a question, the figure lunged at him, slamming him into the tree, nearly knocking him over.

Friedrich stopped running and gripped his sword tightly. *I have no choice. I have to fight. I'm not running away from these bastards!* Friedrich turned around, ready to strike, but saw no one there. He didn't even hear anyone behind him. Not a single figure could be seen in the darkness. Friedrich stood there confused until he heard a yelp in the distance. Was another one of his allies in the forest? Who else would be fighting? If he was indeed surrounded by the Prussians, Friedrich ought to flee, but if he had at least one other comrade, the two would have a chance at taking on at most four of them. It didn't sound like there were more pagans than that. *I can't just leave a soldier behind. God would want me to try to save him. And if it's one of the higher soldiers… If it's a Ritterbruder…* Friedrich sped towards the opposite direction, intent on saving his comrade.

Gailimantas spun out of the way before the figure could inflict any damage. He reached for his sword, but the cloaked figure's cold, bony hands gripped his arms. A bit of moonlight shone through the trees, illuminating Gailimantas's opponent. The shriveled, red skin and the festering, rotting sores brought back illusive memories. The deranged man stared at Gailimantas, revealing his long, sharp fangs with a threatening hiss. Gailimantas's heart began to race faster. A demon. Just like the one he encountered as a child. No one believed him when he told the story of being attacked by a demon while he lived in the forest for a moon. For the longest time, he wondered if it was all a dream, just a childish fantasy. But here he stood, a grown man, staring at the creature who had fangs longer than acorns and skin covered in green mold. It wasn't a dream. This was real. He may have been easy prey for this demon the first time, but he was a man now. Not only a man, but a soldier. Gailimantas struggled with the demon, who kept snapping his jaws at him, and pushed back against him. He felt his enemy struggling to fight against him. He then delivered a sharp knee to his stomach causing the monster to recoil. Gailimantas stood up and grabbed his sword, ready to finish it off, but the creature was suddenly gone. Gailimantas looked around him, confused. *How could he just vanish? How did he get away without me seeing or hearing him?* In his confusion, Gailimantas stayed put, back against the tree, scanning the area for both of the men he was fighting.

Friedrich slowed down as he heard the sounds stop. All of the fighting stopped. Not even a cry of victory or pain could be heard. The entire forest was silent, spare the flutter of some small winged creature. *What is going on?* Friedrich stiffened as he heard crisp footsteps behind him, getting closer and closer. *There you are.* Friedrich turned around to face his enemy. He could see the silhouette of the person coming towards him. The figure was not in the shape of his enemy and it was not charging towards him. It was someone in a cloak, slowly stumbling towards him. A dark cloak. *A grey cloak! An ally!*

"Brother!" Friedrich greeted. "Thank God I—" Friedrich was interrupted when the stranger pounced on him, pinning him to the ground. Friedrich, still confused that a fellow brother would do this, struggled with the mysterious man, trying to push him off. "Brother, it's me. A fellow brother. A fellow Teu—" Friedrich was taken off guard when the figure bared his fangs and hissed. Friedrich's heart jumped into his throat. *This is no man! This is a demon!* Friedrich screamed in terror as the creature lunged for his neck, sinking his teeth into the soft flesh. He began to feel woozy, his energy slowly draining away. But Friedrich wasn't going down without a fight. He kicked and struggled as much as he could.

Gailimantas was taken aback when he heard his enemy screaming in terror. A string of what he could only assume were German curses followed. He wasn't messing with him anymore, so why would he be screaming? He heard the leaves rustling, as if prey was caught by a predator, desperately trying to escape the jaws of death. Gailimantas snuck out into the clearing. He kept his sword unsheathed, prepared to take on any monster as he crept in the direction of the scream.

Realizing his hands were free, Friedrich quickly reached for his sword. His energy had drained significantly and to him, the sword weighed as much as a horse. Friedrich hoisted whatever strength he had left and swung the sword sideways, hitting the demon in the side. The demon screeched in pain and released Friedrich. Friedrich felt the weight of the creature disappear off him. He scrambled to his feet, but his energy was almost gone, and he could barely keep his eyes open. He stumbled forward a bit, slowly losing consciousness, tumbling to the forest floor and rolling down the slight incline of the hill.

The screaming came to an end shortly before Gailimantas arrived at the scene. Nothing was there. He jumped when he heard movement from the leaves. It sounded like something had fallen. Cautiously, Gailimantas began to tread back to the entrance of the forest, keeping an eye out for both of his enemies. He then felt something under his foot. He picked up the sword from the ground. Examining it, he noticed the cross decorating the end of it. It was the same cross that decorated the uniforms of the Teutonic Knights. *This must be his sword. So that means...* Gailimantas decided to bolt back to camp, leaving the creatures of the night and his imagination behind him.

# Chapter 6: Nightmare

"You know, when I signed up to be a knight, I didn't expect to be stranded, starving, and looking for dead bodies."

"We are Diendebrüdern, mind you."

"What is so special about these nobles anyways?"

"They're trained professionals with years of experience. They know what to do next. They're all that we have left now that our leader is dead."

"They were probably captured by the pagans."

"We need to find other bodies because we're running low on supplies. Especially after our loss yesterday. You know that."

"I know. You don't have to be a buzzkill, Clovis."

Friedrich awoke to the sound of chatter. He cringed at the sunlight shining on him. *Oh God, the sun is so bright.* As he sat up, he noticed that his back was stiff and sore, especially his side. *Ow! Lord in Heaven, I slept with a tree in my side last night… I'm used to sleeping on the ground but how in Heaven did I end up in a place full of so many twigs?* Friedrich then remembered what happened the previous night. How his troop had been called to Kulm due to repeated attacks there. Trying to save hundreds of captured men from the pagans. Getting knocked off his horse. Getting separated from his knight and the other squires and frantically trying to find them again.

He remembered the ravine. The horrific ravine with red stained water, littered with white corpses. Friedrich ran into *him* again. The pagan with the young face and lack of facial hair. The one that got away. Friedrich growled, scratching his beard. *That bastard got away… But how did I end up here?* He sat up, wobbling a bit as he was on a slight hill. He heard the chatter again. People were speaking in Low German.

"Whoa!"

"Are you alright, Brother Rudegerus?"

"Just tripped on a stupid rock. Why are there so many rocks everywhere?"

"Let's just hope we don't run into any heathens."

"We can take them!"

"There's only four of us, Brother Gilbert."

"That doesn't mean we can't send them back to Hell!"

"Look at what they did! They killed more than half of our finest knights and that doesn't even include the Diendebrüdern. I'm starting to think this is a lost cause."

"Me too."

Friedrich stood up. Could it be? Other members of the Order had come to find him? Sure enough, Friedrich looked over the hill and saw the black uniforms. These were Diendebrüdern, or servant brothers, the non-noble volunteer knights. It would explain their vernacular. *They're speaking Low German, so they may be from a totally different troop. But brothers are brothers. They are the only ones who can help me.*

"What was that?"

"A deer probably."

"Maybe a hidden pagan who was waiting to ambush us."

"No worries," said Friedrich. "It's just me." Friedrich looked at the surprised faces of the men staring at him. Some of the men looked slightly scared. "Thank the Lord I ran into you all. I got stuck in quite the situation."

"Another member of the Order!"

"Are—Are you from Master Helmrich von Rechenberg's regiment?"

"Yes. I am."

"How did you… You're ali—"

"We'll ask questions later," interrupted the more serious brother. "What is your name?"

"Friedrich von Rotenkreuz," Friedrich answered.

"Brother Friedrich!" one of the brothers gasped.

"You recognize me?" Friedrich asked.

"Is it true?" said a brother who looked at him in admiration. "Were you really saved by an angel on the battlefield?"

"An angel?" said another brother.

"Would I bear false witness?" asked Friedrich.

"No, I'm not doubting you," the brother replied. "I just… Rumors tend to get overexaggerated."

"So it's true?" asked another soldier. Friedrich smiled with pride. So the news had spread all over the empire. He was famous within the Order now.

"We'll take you back to our camp," said a brother, smiling. "Heinrich will be happy that we found such a legend. It'll give us hope. We could really use some hope right now." The group began to head off in another direction.

"Where are you going?" asked Friedrich. "Löbau is that way." He pointed in the opposite direction.

"Löbau?" said a brother. "Löbau is gone."

"Wh—What do you mean—"

"Löbau is gone. The Prussians have it."

"Why do they have it? " Friedrich asked. "What happened? Did they win?"

"What happened? Herkus Monte is what happened!" scoffed another brother. "The bastard bested us once again."

"The Prussians took a lot of captives and ransacked Löbau," explained a brother. "Destroyed and burned everything. Killed and captured everyone, including Master Helmrich and Marshal Dietrich. It's a miracle that we managed to flee." Friedrich's heart sank. *Löbau was captured? Everyone is gone? It can't be.* Friedrich started shaking in both fear and anger, afraid that his friends and his mentor may have been captured or killed, and enraged at those that had done this. "We're planning on going to the next major city after gathering up what's left of the soldiers. We'll probably head to Sautenburg or Soldau since they're close."

"I don't believe you told me your names," said Friedrich.

"I am Clovis, and this is my brother, Gilbert," a soldier said. "With us are Brother Rudegerus and Brother Bastian."

"Good," said Friedrich. "Nice to see there are other survivors." Friedrich put on a confident smile, hoping to alleviate some of their worries. "It is time for us to find a new regiment. I'll be sure to speak good of you four." The four men looked ecstatic, grateful that they had met Friedrich. "Are there any others that you know have survived?"

"Yes," said Rudegerus. "The camp isn't too far away from here. We're residing in a nearby village called Prandnitz."

"How many are there?"

"When we left, it was around 20, I think," answered Bastian.

"Lead me there then."

"Right this way."

Entering the church, Friedrich could see numerous brothers of varying ranks. Diendebrüdern, Halbbrüdern, novices, even some squires. Friedrich saw no Ritterbrüdern in the church. There were at most 30 of them. Löbau was a pretty populous city. With all the reinforcements called, Friedrich felt a bit crushed that such a minuscule number survived. Half of them were clean and freshly bathed, while the other half were still smudged with blood, sweat, and grime. Friedrich then realized that he probably looked even more disheveled than the rest of them. He did fall into the bloody river when he was looking for his comrades. That was probably why he was already receiving wide eyed stares from other brothers.

"We have found another living brother!" announced Bastian. Nearly everyone in the room turned to look at Friedrich. Friedrich bowed his head in greeting.

"Brother Friedrich von Rotenkreuz," he said, walking to the front of the church to join the other brothers. He heard whispers and murmurs as he joined the crowd of brothers. Whispers revolving around his current claim to fame. "Is there a Ritterbruder or higher official of any kind here?"

"Yes. We have one Ritterbruder. But he's talking to the head of the town right now."

"He's been gone for a while…" commented another brother.

"Alright. At least we have some authority figure," Friedrich replied.

"Brother Friedrich," said a young squire who came up to him, eyes wide in awe, "is it true? Are you the one who was saved by an angel of God?"

"Why yes. I am ind—"

"Fritz!"

Friedrich turned around, hearing brisk footsteps coming towards him. He gasped at the sight of the man who had just yelled out his name.

"Simon!" Friedrich winded his way through the people he was talking to and hurried to greet his best friend. Simon was part of the freshly bathed group, his dark red hair washed and clean. "Thank the Lord you survived!" Friedrich realized something. "Wait, how *did* you survive? Weren't you in the ravine with me?"

"The ravine? Is that where you were?" Simon asked. "We were wondering where you went after you gave Herr Heinrich your horse. I was worried you died. I suppose we were in a crowd. But we left with another group of brothers to pursue another pack of heathens."

"So that's where we got separated."

"Then Heinrich told me to get another horse for you but we couldn't find you," Simon explained. "Then he said to get another horse anyways. When I came back, I couldn't find him, so I rode around all night looking for him. Then I ran into someone else who said that Löbau was ransacked so I took him and rode to here. How did you make it here?"

"I was fighting an old friend. A pagan I had battled before. I chased him into the forest and then…" Friedrich thought back to what happened. "I…I can't remember."

"You can't remember?"

"I remember being surrounded by the pagans," Friedrich recounted. "I could hear them all around me. I was ready to fight but then…" Friedrich closed his eyes. "I'm trying to remember what happened. I just remember waking up next to a tree on a hill and being very stiff. Luckily these guys showed up or I would have walked right into the enemies' hands."

"Maybe a bath would help," suggested Simon. "There's a nice bathhouse in town. You should wash up. You deserve it more than the rest of us." Friedrich caught a glimpse of his appearance in the golden tabernacle. His short, strawberry blonde hair and his neatly trimmed beard were decorated with powdery dirt and small leaves. His white uniform had a reddish tint from falling into the bloody ravine and was spattered with mud from sleeping on the forest floor. There was a leaf caught in his chainmail and another hanging on the edge of his cloak. His uniform had a few small holes in it and reeked due to the carnage. Most unusual of all was his neck, which had freshly smeared bloodstains surrounding two small marks the size of peas on the side by his jugular. He touched the marks, feeling that the texture of the marks was similar to a scab from a small wound, giving off a sting when he tried to brush them off like dirt. He looked ten times as messy as everyone else here. *And I thought people were staring at me because of the rumors. I look like I've been living with wild dogs for weeks! Worst of all, I'm in a house of God looking like this…* Suddenly feeling self-conscious, especially being in a church, Friedrich nodded, agreeing to the offer.

"That's a good idea," Friedrich accepted. "Where is this bathhouse?"

"It's right around the corner, right next to the bakery," Simon directed. "I can walk you there—"

"Brother Friedrich?" Friedrich turned around to see a familiar face at the entrance of the church, putting his hood down. His eyes lit up when he saw his mentor.

"Herr Heinrich?"

Heinrich looked like he had just come from the bathhouse as his uniform and hair were clean.

"Dear Lord, I can't believe you made it…"

"I can't believe it either," Friedrich said. "What are you doing here?"

"I saw everyone else fleeing so I assumed that we had been called to retreat," Heinrich explained. "Imagine my shock when I saw Löbau on fire. So I walked until I came across this town. Fortunately, I found other brothers here too." Friedrich was curious how his mentor got here before he did by just walking. But he smiled and nodded, ecstatic to see his mentor alive. The knight stared at him for a while. Friedrich was quiet, trying to figure out what exactly he was staring at. He then remembered that his appearance at the moment wasn't the prettiest.

"Oh. I know I'm all filthy. It's a long story," Friedrich said.

"What happened to your neck?" Heinrich asked. Friedrich touched the marks again, feeling them once more.

"I actually don't know," Friedrich admitted. "I don't remember how I got them… I was chasing after this pagan, and I was in the forest. He led me into a trap, and I heard all these people coming towards me. Then I heard someone yelling for help. I ran, thinking one of us was in danger. But then the shouting stopped. Then, I saw this figure in a dark cloak. I remember it approaching me and then… I don't remember anything from there… I just remember waking up to these brothers' conversation. They really helped me out."

"A cloaked figure?" Simon said. "You didn't mention anything about that earlier. You must be remembering things."

"Why don't you take a bath?" Heinrich suggested. "The bathhouse is nice and warm. Maybe you will remember what happened after that."

"Will do!" said Friedrich. "The angels in Heaven can probably smell me right now…" The group laughed at his joke. Friedrich began to head outside. He touched the marks on his neck once again, feeling the slight sting of pain.

*How did I get these?* he wondered.

"I can't wait to get back home. My wife will be excited to see me."

"We were trying for a child last time. She was pregnant when I left. Now I can see my son or daughter."

"Last time I visited home, I had a surprise son. It turns out my wife became pregnant right before I left and when I came back, there was my son! It was my favorite trip home."

Gailimantas strolled along next to his comrades through the town. They had stopped in a small town on their way back to Sambia. The Sambians needed help in the North so they were on their way to help them again. The Sudovians and Lithuanians were raiding Kulm, so there wasn't really any reason to stay. They did not want another fight with them, especially since their relations were not the greatest with some of the other Prussian tribes. Although his men were camping in the forest, he and another group of soldiers were patrolling the town, looking for supplies and booze. But they had to journey incognito. Even though members of the Order were not visible when they arrived, there could be some undercover. People of this town spoke Prussian, albeit in a strange dialect that was nevertheless understandable. From the other tribes Gailimantas had heard, he figured that they were Warmian, or at least of Warmian origin, since this was a very Germanized town. There were a lot of German speakers here, more than Prussian speakers, so they had to be on their guard.

"Are you excited to see your wife again, Gailimantas?" Wudewuto asked.

"Oh," said Gailimantas. "I don't have a wife."

"You don't have a girl you're interested in?" Sandwers probed.

"No," Gailimantas admitted.

"Gailimantas, how old are you again?" asked an older soldier.

"Fifteen summers," Gailimantas replied.

"Why don't you have a wife?" said Widewuto, laughing. "I know you're a little young, but we've conquered so many cities, surely one of the women must have caught your eye."

"This is Mantas we are talking about," scoffed Pomeus. "Remember the last time, when we took him to a bathhouse?" Gailimantas felt his face turn red.

"I wasn't there for that," said Sandwers. "What happened?"

"Please don't…" said Gailimantas, covering his face.

"First, the woman saw him and said 'I think you're too young for this,'" laughed Pomeus. The entire group of men laughed with him. "Then, the poor kid got nervous and couldn't even finish the job."

"That was almost a year ago!" Gailimantas snapped. "And I don't need facial hair. Herkus said that the Teutonic Knights aren't allowed to shave, so it's a symbol of defiance."

"Don't get so worked up! We're just teasing you, Mantas," said Pomeus with a smile, messing up his hair.

"Hey, do you think there's a good tavern around here?"

"It's a bit early to be drinking, Dargel," Sandwers replied.

"Says who?" Dargel asked.

"Said our commander! We have to be alert in case of an ambush."

Gailimantas's mind drifted away from the conversation as a song entered his ears. The song was soft, but the voice was clear and high pitched. Gailimantas realized that he recognized the words that were being sung. This was a song in his own language.

"Gailimantas?"

Gailimantas realized that his group was a few paces ahead of him. "Someone is singing in Prussian," he said.

"So?"

Gailimantas didn't respond and followed the voice around a corner, easy to distinguish in a small, quiet town. His breath caught in his throat when he saw the singer in an alleyway. She was counting the fruit in her basket, sitting against a building. Her long dark hair was covered by a thick brown veil. A spray of freckles dusted the light skin on her nose. Her dress was a uniform, dark brown color and looked like it had seen better days. She looked rather dirty, smudged in ash. But the way the dark material smudged her face made her more endearing to Gailimantas.

"Mant...as?" The rest of the group finally saw what he was staring at.

"Wow. What a beauty," commented Sandwers.

"Mantas?" Pomeus called, tapping his shoulder, receiving no response. "Are you—"

"She is the most beautiful woman I have ever seen…" sighed Gailimantas, an infatuated smile on his face. Pomeus raised an eyebrow. "Never before has my heart beat so fast just by looking at a person. And her voice is like a clear little bell." The friends turned to each other.

"You want her?" Pomeus smirked.

"If not, I'll take her for myself," Sandwers said. Gailimantas finally recognized the others standing behind him.

"I think I found my wife…" said Gailimantas. "I want her."

The group gave each other smiles.

"Looks like Mantas finally found a girl he likes," remarked Pomeus.

"I told your father that I would try to talk you into getting a wife. Now I don't have to," Schadeus chuckled.

"Well, go get her before she gets away," nudged Sandwers.

"What? What do I do?" Gailimantas asked.

"Just talk to her. Don't worry. We'll find out where she lives," said Pomeus.

"Okay then," Gailimantas said, hesitantly stumbling his way into the alley. He shuffled up to the fair maiden in front of him. The young woman, noticing him, stopped her singing and instantly stood up.

"*Can I help you?*" she asked, her demeanor changing completely to a sour mood. She spoke to him in German, so Gailimantas had no idea what she was saying.

"I, um…" Gailimantas cleared his throat. "I don't know any German." She blinked, surprised he responded in Prussian. "I know you can speak Prussian." She was quiet for a moment, her sour mood dissipating slightly.

"What do you want?"

"I just…um." Gailimantas cleared his throat again, hoping to clear his nerves as well. "You are a Prussian, yes?"

"Why do you ask?" She raised an eyebrow. "What does it matter to you?"

"I didn't think there were many left here," Gailimantas replied. "You know, after the Crusades…"

"Did you need something?" she asked, a bit annoyed that he was straying from the topic.

"Ah. Of course," he replied. "My name is Gailimantas. And I have to say that you are the most beautiful woman I have ever laid eyes on." Her annoyed expression swiftly dropped. "I want you to become my wife." The girl was quiet for a moment. "I am willing to pay your parents any amount of money they want for you."

"That's not going to happen," she answered.

Gailimantas blinked. Was this how it was supposed to go? He expected her to at least say something along the lines of meeting her parents. He even expected his buddies to swoop in and just take her. He didn't expect her to simply say no to him.

"Why not?" he asked.

"I am not a woman who will become someone's wife. Have you been living under a rock for the past few years?" she snapped. Gailimantas tilted his head, confused. The woman's demeanor changed again. "Now that I think about it, you have an unusual accent. And I've never seen you around before. So you must not be from here. Where are you from?"

"I'm Natangian," he replied.

"Oh I see," she said. "You're one of those soldiers that's fighting the Teutonic Order."

"Why yes, I am," he smiled proudly.

"Well, that settles it," she said, a sly smile coming to her face. "The chances of me ever being your wife are now none." Gailimantas's heart sank.

"What?"

"Even though God has forsaken me, there is no way my parents would ever hand me away to a devil worshiping pagan like you," she remarked. The woman then spun around and walked briskly in another direction. Gailimantas froze. He could hear his comrades whispering behind him. He ignored them and began to run after her.

"Wait!" Gailimantas called out. "I don't even know your name! If this is truly the last time we meet, at least give me the name of the woman who breaks my heart." The woman turned around. "I am Gailimantas, son of Sarginus."

"Gailimantas?" she said. "That's an unusual name for a Prussian."

"My parents named me after the Lithuanian soldier that saved my father's life on the battlefield," he explained. "And your name?"

"Annuse," she replied. "I'm sure you'll hear my name a lot around this town."

"I'm sure I will," he said with a slight smile. "Such a lovely maiden must surely be the talk of the town." She turned around to look at him. She was clearly annoyed, but there was a hint of sadness in her eyes.

"I am, but not in the way you think."

"What do—"

"Don't talk to me again, heathen!" she snapped. "I may be an out-cast, but I will not stoop so low to converse with a pagan. My reputation is terrible enough! Now leave me be before I tell the church what you infidels are up to!" She briskly walked away. His friends instantly began talking over each other.

"Crap! She's a converted Prussian!"

"Christians… This won't be easy…"

"We may just have to take her ourselves…"

"Let's just do a wife raid throughout the town. I could use another wife."

"The Teutons are here. That would not go well, Sandwers."

"Don't worry, Mantas," Pomeus said, putting an arm around Gaili-mantas. "I have a plan to get her. I guarantee that you will leave this village with a wife."

Friedrich's troop had made it back to Soldau where they waited to be reorganized. They would probably be lumped into one regiment and go to Königsberg or something. But for now, they lived with the church there, living comfortably as they waited to be reassigned. His Komtur had perished in the battle, so they would be appointing a new one. Ru-mor had it that his mentor was one of the candidates, which made Frie-drich very proud.

It had been about two and a half weeks now, and he was starting to like this town. Though he had been pretty tired as of late. He felt drowsy during the day, but at night, he was plagued by insomnia. His nights consisted of lying awake on his mat for hours before finally sleeping for about five hours. The drowsiness subsided, but he still had many sleepless nights. He had tried praying and going to church, but nothing worked. He dreaded going back to the room where they slept and lying awake for another long, silent night. But that was only one of his many issues.

Women in this town kept trying to seduce him, especially in the bathhouse, but Friedrich resisted diligently. The temptation of women was always easy for him to resist, as he never understood what was so appealing about them anyways. Women were frail, useless creatures that honestly annoyed him. They couldn't fight for themselves and always relied on the men to do so on their behalf. All they did was stay home and watch children, and yet they constantly cried and whined. Nuns were different. Their weeping was replaced by song, they had no children, they relied on no one but themselves, and they actually did something useful.

Today, Friedrich woke up with an aching pain in his mouth. He managed to eat breakfast, but the pain just worsened throughout the day. He tried to ignore it and go on with his duties, managing to make it through most of the day.

"The last defeat at Löbau has made news all around the empire," Tomas said.

"It's so humiliating…" groaned Brother Ludwig. "I don't want to think about it."

"Brothers," Kennet spoke up. "Something has been on my mind since our last defeat."

"What is it Brother Kennet?"

"I've been thinking… Well, a terrible thought has crossed my mind as of late," Kennet began. "It's just… I'm starting to think that maybe this Crusade against the North is hopeless."

"What?"

"I don't know! I'm not sure why I feel this way but—"

"We're all thinking it, Brother Kennet," interrupted Franz. "But no one wants to admit it. Now it's out in the air."

"What? I wouldn't dream of giving up!" Simon said. "So we lost a battle. So what? We'll learn from this and fight back harder."

"*So what?*" repeated Franz. "They slaughtered 40 of our finest knights and some of our best commanders! Not to mention all the service brothers and volunteers they killed. As long as that traitor is around, they can predict every move that we make! It's hopeless!"

"Brother Tomas, you have the most religious education out of all of us," said Simon. "Talk some sense into him!"

"Never before have I lost faith in my Lord," Tomas said. "But after our last defeat, I'm starting to lose hope in our cause..."

"Brother Tomas, even you…" Simon trailed off. "Fritz?"

"Even if I'm the only soldier left, I will never turn back," Friedrich growled. "Whether it be God's mission or mine, I vowed that I would dispose of every last demon worshiper I can find. It's the least I can do for my brother and my father."

"Thank you, Fritz."

"I know you have a personal vendetta against the pagans, Brother Friedrich, but with the numbers that we have, there's no way we could even have a chance," Franz said. "You saw their troops! How can we compete with that?"

"We recruit more!" Simon argued. "We should focus our efforts on recruiting others into our cause. We should do as Brother David did: recruit those who may not be of noble birth. The peasants, the beggars, the scoundrels… In honor of his memory, I think we can give his idea a shot." Everyone was quiet for a moment, honoring the death of their fallen brother.

"I wasn't saved by God for you all to just quit on us," Friedrich growled. "The Lord sent an angel to save me from death so I could keep fighting. Surely that is a sign to keep going! How dare—"

Friedrich was cut off by another wave of pain in his upper jaw. He clasped his hands over his mouth, groaning.

"Fritz? Are you okay?" Simon asked.

"It's this cursed toothache," grumbled Friedrich. "I have suffered through it all day. I have prayed for healing, but it hasn't disappeared."

"Perhaps you should go to the infirmary," suggested Kennet. "Maybe they can help."

"With the nuns? We aren't supposed to interact with—"

"Brother Friedrich, these are nuns. Fellow sisters," assured Franz. "If anyone knows how to help, it's them."

The nuns looked at Friedrich and said that they couldn't see a problem with Friedrich's teeth. Friedrich insisted that they do something, so they spread this bittersweet mixture on his upper row of teeth and had him pray to St. Apollonia before seeing him off. They offered to take him back if the pain worsened, worried that it could be something demonic. Friedrich felt a bit better, but the pain would throb every once in a while. Friedrich thought if there were more monks at the infirmary, they would have done a better job. However, in a small town like this, he needed to be grateful for what there was. At dinner, he didn't bother with eating bread and stuck to eating nothing but soup. He chewed the carrots with his back teeth as it was his front teeth that hurt. His brothers could only watch him silently suffer. The pain had mostly subsided after dinner.

After evening prayer, the brothers returned to their mats, lit a single candle, and fell asleep one by one. Friedrich, feeling exhausted, began to drift off to sleep, grateful that he wasn't plagued by insomnia for once. But as he was dreaming, the stinging pain in his jaw pulled him out of his sleepy comfort. Friedrich stifled a yell, not wanting to wake his brothers or break the nighttime silence. *Are you kidding me? Now of all times? I'm finally tired!* The pain was worse than ever before. He bit his lip, trying to hold back a scream, but flinched when he felt a sharp pain in his lip. He let out a soft groan, sitting up and covering his mouth with his hand. When the wave of pain subsided into throbbing, he pulled back his hand. He froze when he saw the smears of crimson on his hand. Blood. He was bleeding.

Warning bells were chiming in Friedrich's head, telling him that something was very wrong. As silently as possible he swiftly danced around the others in order to sneak out of the door. He meandered his way through the halls, sneaking by as fast as he could. Friedrich ran outside, trying to get as far away from the building as possible. The pain in his jaw was increasing more and more. He began to panic, not knowing what was happening to him, terrified it might be something life threatening or demonic. He ran to the church, hoping to find someone there, but it was empty. Of course, it was so late at night. Evening prayer had already been conducted. He ran up to the altar and bowed.

"God, I know I'm not supposed to talk after evening prayer, but please, help me," he prayed. "Relieve me from this awful pain! It hurts! God, it hurts so much…" He lied there, praying the Lord's Prayer as many times as he could. He then took out his rosary and began to pray some more, even though it hurt for him to speak. Soon, the pain became so unbearable that he prayed silently. He was halfway through the rosary when he felt another strong wave of pain. He stood up and began to pace around the church. He halted when he came to the tabernacle. He looked at his reflection, moving closer to see his face. He could see that his lip was bleeding, blood smeared on both sides of his mouth. He pulled back his lips, trying to see what was happening inside his mouth. The sight made him stare at himself for a while, blinking his eyes, trying to make sure this reflection was correct. He felt his breathing speed up as he began to panic again.

"Wh—Wh—This can't be…" he gasped. Inside the golden tabernacle he saw the reflection of what appeared to be two wickedly pointed teeth. He shakily ran a finger along his upper teeth. The reflection did not lie. He felt a stinging pain on his finger and quickly looked at it. There was now a small cut on it, slowly beginning to bleed.

*No… God, please forgive me! Why is this happening? Am I possessed by a demon? I am one of your most devout followers, I can't possibly be a demon! I can't! What is the meaning of this? Why do I have teeth like a wild animal?* Friedrich felt one more wave of pain, this one more powerful than the rest. He began to groan, but that groan quickly became a cry of agony. *God, please save me! Of all things, I don't want a demonic possession to be my downfall! Please! God save me!*

After a few minutes, the pain subsided. Friedrich laid on the floor of the church, just catching his breath, waiting for the throbbing in his jaw to fade away. He eventually pulled himself up, facing the tabernacle once more. *Do I dare take a look at myself?* He checked on his teeth, which were longer than before. He ran his tongue along the front of his teeth, desperately hoping that this reflection was fake. Suddenly, he heard the church bell clanging loudly. Friedrich looked around, his eye stopping at the clock. Three in the morning. In another two hours, the clerics would be awake again. *What do I do?* Friedrich thought. *Do I tell the Order? Should I wait for the priests to wake up and exorcize me? But what if I can't be exorcized? What if I am truly a demon? What if they try to kill me? I have to get away from here, but where do I go? Where can I hide? This town is so small! I don't want to hide in the forest. Pagans may try to kill me. What do I do?* He then saw the ladder to the bell tower out of the corner of his eye. *Maybe I don't have to leave the church. I just have to hide and wait for these things to go away. But the bell tower is loud. And people check the bells. Maybe if I go to the infirmary? No. They'll check my teeth there. But perhaps if I sneak in, they won't. They will just assume I'm sick and that I've already been there.* Friedrich sped towards the infirmary. He pulled his lower lip over the new fangs to hide them. He crept into the building, trying not to be noticed.

"And who are you?" Friedrich halted when he heard words that cut his plan short. He slowly turned around to see a young nun glaring at him. *Curses! The wench caught me!* Her expression changed when she saw his face. "Ah, someone from the Order. What ails you, brother?" *God, what do I say here?* "Oh wait, you were the one with the toothache earlier, right?" Friedrich nodded, rubbing his jaw. "Has the pain come back?" He nodded. He put a hand over his mouth.

"It can wait for tomorrow," he said. "I know it is early in the morning." Friedrich noticed that he had a lisp now. "I wish to not disturb my brothers in their slumber." Friedrich cringed. This was getting annoying. The sister nodded.

"Alright. You may stay here. If you find an open bed, go ahead. Your previous bed should be free."

Friedrich nodded a thank you. He continued through the infirmary, returning to the bed he was in earlier that day. The pain that he had dealt with all day was now gone, but his mouth was still sore. Friedrich felt exhausted after the whole ordeal, but his worries began to swirl around inside him again. He tried his best to be optimistic. *What shall become of me now? I highly doubt I am a demon. I can say the Lord's prayer easily. This is probably just some form of possession. I just need to be exorcized and things will return back to normal. But to be safe, I should talk to someone else in person. Someone I can trust. I've come so far. God himself sent an angel to save me from death. There's no way I can be a demon. Maybe this is all a dream! Yes! Just a very painful dream...*

Friedrich's conflicting thoughts swirled around in his head, slowly lulling him to sleep. He clutched his rosary tightly and eventually drifted off, hoping that this would all be a mere nightmare when he awoke.

# Chapter 7: Bloodletting

Friedrich spent the morning in the infirmary, mostly hiding. What he had hoped was a terrible dream turned out to be a living nightmare which he couldn't wake up from. He didn't feel sick, he didn't have any sinful urges, nor did he have trouble praying. He just had long, sharp teeth and a slightly sore jaw. That was all. Well, he was also very hungry. The stew he was fed wasn't very filling. All morning he took care to hide his teeth, mostly by pretending to be asleep whenever the nuns came to check on him. No matter how much he debated himself, he couldn't figure out a proper solution to this. Every time he was about to reveal his problem or ask for a priest, his heart began to race when he saw the nuns come over, afraid that they would burn him at the stake or something. He had seen an exorcism before. They just chained up the person, said a few prayers, and threw some holy water on them. That wasn't so bad. But the reputation… He kept his eyes closed, knowing the nurses were right next to him, but something else made him break his cover.

"Fritz! There you are! I was wondering where you went." Friedrich glanced over to see a deeply worried Simon. He hid his mouth under the sheets, turning away from his friend. He groaned. *Oh great. The last thing I should do is talk to someone. But maybe I can trust Simon. Maybe he could help me.*

"You're still suffering from that toothache from yesterday, huh?" Simon said.

Friedrich tried to say Simon's name but ended up lisping the first syllable. *Looks like I'll have to choose my words carefully.* "I need your help," Friedrich stated.

"What do you need?" Simon asked. "I'm willing to get you anything you need."

"The other night, something unbelievable happened to me…" Friedrich explained, giving up on hiding his lisp. "My toothache is gone, but I have a new ailment. An ailment that I can't even begin to understand. I don't know what's wrong with me now. I'm honestly worried about what's going to happen to me…"

"It's not smallpox, is it?"

"No," Friedrich replied. "It's not painful, but…"

"You sound kind of weird. It's hard to hear you when you're covering your mouth," Simon pointed out.

"Sorry…"

"If it is worse than smallpox, then what is it?"

Friedrich checked that there was no one else in or near the beds next to him. It was just him and Simon. He uncovered his mouth.

"I need you to promise me something," he prefaced. "Please don't tell anyone about this until I know for sure what is going on…" Simon nodded. "Late last night…I grew these." Friedrich then pulled back his lips, revealing his teeth. Simon's eyes widened in shock, his body recoiling back slightly. He was frightened by the sharp canines, but seeing that this was his best friend kept him from running away in terror. This creature looked, sounded, and behaved just like Friedrich. It couldn't be the devil, could it? "I—I think I'm possessed by a demon or something," said Friedrich. "I don't feel it trying to take over my body, but I don't know how else to explain this." Simon swallowed his fear and decided to trust his friend. After all, if he were in a situation like this, he would want help too. As a member of the Teutonic Order, it was his duty to help out others in need.

"I've never seen a possession like this one before," noted Simon. He stared at Friedrich, absolutely perplexed. "Normally people just shake and convulse. I have never heard of anyone growing animal teeth."

"Do you think I should be exorcised?"

"Are you having sinful thoughts?"

"N—No..."

"Do you have any urges to abandon God and worship Satan?"

"Absolutely not!"

"Say the Lord's prayer for me."

Friedrich instantly obeyed. "I've prayed the rosary three times," he said. "Nothing has worked."

"You don't *seem* possessed..." Simon noted.

"Maybe the demon is dormant. Maybe it is just waiting for its time to strike!"

"If that's the case, you need to strike it first! We need an exorcism as soon as possible!"

"Right!" Friedrich agreed.

"I'll go find a priest!" said Simon, as he began walking towards the door. "Don't worry Fritz! I'll make sure you're saved!"

Friedrich smiled. *I knew I could trust Simon. But I've never experienced an exorcism before. I've seen a couple of them, but the people were always convulsing and shaking and looked like they were on the brink of death. I don't want to go through that. But if I want this to go away, I have to go through with an exorcism.*

Simon soon returned with a priest. Friedrich had a mix of nervousness and hope clouding his brain. He looked up at the priest, hope in his eyes. The priest took a step back in shock at the sight of Friedrich's teeth.

"I know. It's terrifying, isn't it, Father?" Friedrich said.

"Wait, you are aware?" the priest asked.

"I told you that this is an unusual case, Father Albert," said Simon. "He doesn't feel ill. He can say the Lord's prayer without any problem. He doesn't have any demonic signs other than this."

"This is the strangest possession that I have ever witnessed," Father Albert admitted. "Honestly, I'm not positive on what to do. I don't even know if this is a demonic possession at all." He thought for a moment. "Perhaps this was a curse set upon you by a worshiper of the devil."

"A curse?" said Friedrich, his voice wavering.

"Maybe it was cast upon you by one of the Prussians," guessed Simon. "Maybe it's a demonic curse."

"I honestly don't know that much about them," admitted the priest. "They don't come up very often. I have never seen this kind of curse before… I honestly haven't seen a curse take place at all."

"Maybe we should try a prayer first?" suggested Simon.

"I've prayed the rosary three times," reminded Friedrich.

"Then this must be a powerful curse. Maybe it is indeed the work of a demon. A demon that is laying dormant for now. I suppose Father Nathaniel can perform an exorcism, but he is going to need some time to prepare. He needs to have permission from the bishop." Friedrich nodded. "We shall set something up this evening. Let's hope that it doesn't worsen during that time."

"Thank you, Father," said Friedrich, bowing his head.

"I will ask around if anyone has heard of a curse like this," the priest added. "God bless you. We will meet later on tonight." The priest then left the infirmary.

"A curse from those pagans," growled Friedrich. "I should have known."

"An enemy that can harness Satan's powers is a fearful enemy indeed," Simon said. Friedrich sighed. Nothing else appeared to be wrong about his appearance. He just had weird teeth. He closed his eyes and tensed his body, desperately putting his heart and soul into his prayer. He tried to imagine his body free from demons, wishing he could just move these teeth somewhere else. Suddenly, he felt another pang of pain and let out a groan. "Herrje!" Simon exclaimed. "Fritz, they're gone!"

"Huh?" Friedrich ran his tongue along his teeth. Sure enough, his mouth was back to normal. "Bless the Lord! He has answered my prayer! Now I don't need to be exorcized." He rejoiced that his prayer had succeeded, however he had this strange feeling that they weren't really gone. He felt that they were still there somehow, but just hidden. But Friedrich didn't care. His problem was solved, and his curse was lifted as far as he was concerned.

"How do I look?" Gailimantas asked.

"A bit thin, honestly," admitted Dargel. "You look a bit pale too. I hope you're not getting sick."

"I feel fine."

"Mantas, yesterday you ran out of breath after five trips up the hill," Sandwers pointed out. "Normally, you can do seven."

"Maybe I should see a healer when I get back…" Gailimantas conceded.

The group stopped in front of a small wooden home. There seemed to be a red stain on the door that was washed off, which Gailimantas found peculiar.

"Are you sure this is the right house?" Gailimantas asked, going up to the door.

"We asked around. This is where she lives," assured Sandwers.

"She seems to have a negative reputation," added Dargel. "Are you sure this woman is the one you want?"

"Yes. Absolutely," said Gailimantas.

"Well then, go get her," Pomeus said, patting him on the back. "They're still Prussian, right? They shouldn't be too unfamiliar with our customs."

"Okay then. I'm ready," Gailimantas said before knocking on the door. "By the way, thanks for all your…" Gailimantas then realized his friends were gone. "Hey! Don't just leave me h—"

*"Can I help you?"*

Gailimantas looked down at a short, mustached man. Gailimantas was taller than him, but he still managed to be intimidating somehow. Gailimantas took a deep breath.

"I—Is this the home where Annuse resides?"

The older man blinked, surprised that this man spoke Prussian.

"Annuse is my daughter, yes," the man affirmed, switching to Prussian.

"What is going on?" asked an older woman who came to the door.

"Um…" Gailimantas's brain was at a loss of what to say for a while.

"Are you one of those Orthodox Christians?" the man asked.

"What? No, no!" Gailimantas replied. "I'm just a traveler from out of town."

"I can tell," said the woman.

"If this is about something else our daughter did, we were planning on—"

"Your daughter is by far the most gorgeous woman I've ever seen," Gailimantas spilled. "If you would be so kind, I would like to have her as my wife. I will pay whatever you would like for her—"

"We only have 300 marks," called Pomeus from down the road.

"I will pay 300 marks for your daughter," Gailimantas offered. The father looked astounded, however the mother was enraged.

"*Our* daughter?" he said. "Are you serious?"

"You simply want to pay for our daughter like a cow?" the woman spat. "No matchmaker, no proposal, just a price?"

"Jaune, remember what our daughter has done," her husband reminded her.

"You—You're one of those polygamous heathens, aren't you?" she snarled. "I can tell by your accent! You're going to get us—"

"Jaune," her husband stopped her. She reluctantly gave in. "You want to marry our daughter?"

"Yes."

"You do know our daughter is impure, right?" said the father.

Gailimantas blinked. "What do you mean?"

"She gave away her virginity to another man without marrying him," he clarified.

"Does she have any children?" asked Gailimantas.

"Of course not," said the father.

"So, can I marry her?" Gailimantas asked again. The man's eyes were wide, surprised at Gailimantas's offer. "I mean, a virgin is nice, but it doesn't really matter. Some of my friends' wives weren't virgins. Some of them were Christian at one point too. They're still good wives."

"Māts? I heard yelling. What's—" Annuse stopped when she saw Gailimantas. "You! What are you doing here?"

"This man wants to marry you," informed the man.

"What? This man is a Natangian pagan. You're not—"

"Let us talk for a bit about this," interrupted her father.

"What?" said her mother. "You can't actually be considering marrying her off to a—"

"I never thought anyone would ever want to marry my daughter," the father said. "Besides, this man is willing to pay us instead of us giving a dowry." Annuse's expression softened slightly. The mother looked around, suddenly fearful.

"But what if the Teutonic Order finds out?" the mother whispered.

"Then we'll do this in secret. There will be no gathering or anything," said the father. "Alright," he said to Gailimantas. "Meet us at the river at sunset. We will be ready then."

"Thank you, sir," Gailimantas said, kneeling at the man's feet. "I promise that your daughter will be safe and happy. And she can keep her faith if she wants. I won't tell our leader."

"We will meet you at sunset," the father said, closing the door. Annuse just stood there, frozen in awe. "Well, go get your things." Annuse shook herself out of her trance.

"This is heresy," said her mother.

"It's the only way we can improve our reputation without harming our daughter," hissed the father. "You heard what happened a week ago. She was almost killed! It's for the best, Jaune. Whether we like it or not." Annuse hurried to her room and started to pack the few things she had. She was silent, not knowing what to think of the situation. Tears blotted her eyes. Tears full of not only fear of the future and change, but joy and relief. Sure, she was terrified to be surrounded by pagan barbarians and what they might do to her, but she couldn't help but feel excited about starting a new life and moving away from a place that shunned her. This was a chance to restart her life. Perhaps it would be a better place. She wiped away a tear.

"I—I'm actually getting married..."

Over the next few days, Friedrich felt himself becoming sick. For a while, he just assumed it was because he was traveling all the time, but when he was back in Balga, his condition did not improve. No matter how much he ate, he always felt like it wasn't enough. Even when he felt satisfied and had a large meal, a part of him still felt hungry. The first week, it was merely an annoyance. On the eighth day, he began to have constant hunger pangs and feel nauseous. Two weeks after leaving the infirmary, the pangs became slightly painful. When he worked, he kept feeling dizzy and sick. His brothers told him he looked pale and sickly, as if he were starving. As the days progressed, Friedrich felt worse and worse. Every time he stood up, the room began to spin, and he always felt exhausted. After a bit over a month, he finally returned to the infirmary after he fainted.

Friedrich rested on the bed, wanting to just doze off, but the nausea and the cramps made it difficult. He groaned as another wave of pangs hit. He ate a decently sized meal this morning, but it felt like he hadn't eaten in weeks. He begrudgingly dragged himself to the bowl of water laying next to him. He squinted, hoping he could see his reflection, and what he saw shocked him. He wasn't just thinner, he was emaciated; his face looked gaunt and paler than normal. Looking at his hands, he realized they had become bonier. He looked like one of the starving soldiers at Königsberg, which was currently being sieged again. He sighed, laying back down. *What is wrong with me? It feels like I'm slowly starving again, even though I eat daily. Is it some kind of plague? I've never heard of any disease like this. I can't die of disease! I have to die a noble death on the battlefield! I can't die like this! I won't die like this!*

"I have never seen an illness like this before," the doctor analyzed. "You said you constantly feel hungry?"

"Yes," Friedrich replied. "But I'm also dizzy, nauseous, and incredibly tired."

"Perhaps it is bad blood," suggested the doctor. "Too much bad blood must be building up. Perhaps we need to get rid of it." The doctor left to go prepare the ritual. He sighed. *Just some bad blood. I just need to go through this, and I'll be fine.* The doctor returned with a blade and a bowl. He took Friedrich's arm and rolled up his sleeve. Friedrich watched as he cut behind his elbow, wincing slightly at the pain. He watched the cut slowly turn red as blood began to spill out slowly at first, but then turned into a steady, ever flowing trickle. The bad blood was leaving him so he could feel better. But Friedrich wasn't feeling better at all. In fact, he was feeling increasingly worse. As more blood drained out of him, he felt as if his body was falling, sinking into space as his vision became cloudy and blotted by dark spots. Friedrich had felt this feeling before. He knew what was happening to him. *This is just like that time on the battlefield. When I was on the hill, lying there dying… I'm dying!*

Friedrich tried to let out a scream, but it only came out as a weak groan. Friedrich saw the doctor look over at him with a scared expression on his face. A ringing in his ears prevented him from understanding what the doctor was saying, but it was something about demons. The last thing Friedrich saw before his consciousness faded was his mentor rushing into the room. He heard the knight's harried voice fade as everything became dark and silent.

# Chapter 8: Afterlife

Gailimantas sat in the cart in silence. The sun was setting and soon they would have to set up camp. His comrades were laughing and joking around, talking about visiting Swintamīstan. Gailimantas was excited too. He couldn't wait to see his father again. Most importantly, he couldn't wait to introduce his new wife. She was sitting next to him in the wagon. These past few weeks of traveling had been long and boring. They even had to go a day without food here and there. Normally Gailimantas wouldn't have minded, but he was trying to prove to his new wife that he could support her and that she would have nothing to worry about for the rest of her life.

Throughout the entire trip, she had been mostly silent. She only spoke when spoken to and her answers were short, blunt, and sometimes rude. She was always in a sour mood and muttered something in German every now and then. He looked at the road and realized that there was a sign with a bunch of strange symbols on it. The first symbol looked like a snake. Like most of his comrades, Gailimantas was illiterate, so he had no idea what the sign said. He then turned back to Annuse. Gailimantas tried to talk to her again, "I heard that we are getting closer to Swintamīstan. That's the town I live in. It's probably quite different from your town." Annuse looked out at the forest surrounding them.

"Swintamīstan… Even though I speak your language, I can't help but feel so alien," she remarked.

"We'll get to meet my father. He'll be so happy that I finally found a wife." Gailimantas smiled. "He used to be a soldier like me, but he's getting old, so he just stays home with his wife."

"Won't your mother be angry that you brought home a Christian woman?" she scoffed.

"My mother is dead," he replied. "And people bring home wives from all over. An unconverted woman isn't the same as an unconverted man." Annuse put her head on top of her knees, curling up into a ball.

"Why?" she said, slightly muffled. "Why are you so nice to me?"

"What do you mean?"

"Don't ask me that!" she snapped. "You know what I mean! I'm a disobedient, troublesome woman who mouths off to people, I'm not of your religion, I'm not even a virgin. So why? Why on Earth would you pick me to be your wife?" Her head returned to her knees, hiding her face. "Aren't you supposed to be a barbarian? Aren't you supposed to take me against my will and give me to your comrades to have fun with? You bought me like I'm a slave, but yet you treat me so gently. Why?"

"Because I want to. Being rough with someone so delicate as you wouldn't be right." Gailimantas brushed his hand against her cheek softly, feeling warm tears against his hand. "I don't care about your background. You make my heart beat like it never has before. That must be love, right?" She looked up at him, her face red from crying.

"Love?"

"I chose you because you caught my eye and made me feel things I never have," Gailimantas elaborated. "I'm excited to be with you and to make you a part of my family."

"I…I was told you people couldn't experience love," she admitted. Gailimantas chuckled. "I was also told I should be stoned to death and that I was going to Hell."

"Well, then screw that town," said Gailimantas. "If they are willing to shun a beauty like you over something so silly, then they don't deserve you." She looked down.

"I thought my Lord had forsaken me after what I did. I thought I was to be eternally punished," she continued.

"Well, my gods haven't forsaken you," added Gailimantas. "In fact, I'm grateful that they have brought you to me." Annuse smiled.

"I suppose your gods are more forgiving. Or at least, your people are." Annuse had a slight smile on her face. This was the first time that Gailimantas had seen her smile. Annuse closed the uncomfortable distance between her and him, their arms now touching. They paused when they heard a shout.

"What was that?"

"It sounded like someone was shouting military orders."

"What's going—" Suddenly an arrow whizzed out of nowhere, barely missing Gailimantas's head. Annuse screamed. The two heard galloping and looked to the right of them. In the distance, they could see white uniforms parading towards them. The cart's passengers gasped and began to panic.

"Teutonic Knights?"

"Oh give me a bloody break!"

"Are you kidding me?"

"How did they get out here?"

"*To the left! Shoot at them from the left side!*" called a voice from outside the cart.

"Everyone on the left, duck!" Annuse said. "They're going to fire from the left!"

"What? How do you know?" asked a soldier.

"I understand German," she said. Everyone in the cart ducked. Shortly after, a barrage of arrows flew over their heads. Another shout came from the German commander.

"Now what did he say?" asked Schadeus.

"He said he's going to cut us off at the front," translated Annuse. She tapped the driver's shoulder. "Turn this cart around as quickly as you can. They're planning on barricading us at the front."

"I have a better idea," said the driver. He then snapped the reins and the horses turned off the path into the woods. The horses picked up speed, dodging trees and rocks as the cart jiggled and bounced everywhere. Everyone held on for their lives.

"Not exactly how I expected to arrive in Swintamīstan," Gailimantas said, clinging onto a beam for dear life. "Please Deywis, just make this stop."

"It doesn't seem like they're following us," noticed Annuse.

"I think another cart is following us," noticed Pomeus. "Hey, that wife of yours is pretty useful, Mantas." Gailimantas would have smiled and taken pride in his wife, but right now he was trying his best not to throw up. "Mantas? You don't look so good."

"Maybe we could use her as a spy. To gather information on the Teutons," suggested Schadeus.

"You picked a good girl, Mantas," commented Sandwers. "I have to admit."

"I think I'm going to be sick…" Gailimantas groaned.

Friedrich opened his eyes. He looked around the infirmary, feeling lithe and energetic. He didn't feel hungry or sick anymore. If anything, he felt full. Next to his bed sat his knightly mentor and soon-to-be Komtur of Balga on a stool, reading the Bible. He put it down when he noticed Friedrich staring at him.

"Komtur! What are you doing here?" Friedrich asked.

"I'm not Komtur yet, Friedrich," reminded Heinrich. "That has yet to be assigned."

"Yes sir."

"I heard about your…illness," Heinrich explained. "I knew that the worst was going to happen so I came here as soon as I could. You almost died as a result of that bloodletting. Thank God I managed to arrive in time."

"I was about to die?" Friedrich asked hesitantly. "What was wrong with me? Am I cured now?"

"Unfortunately, Brother Friedrich, this is an ailment that has no cure," Heinrich answered. Friedrich felt his body lock up after he heard those words.

"…No cure?" Friedrich's voice started to shake. "Am I going to die?" Heinrich shook his head. "Then what's wrong with me? What's going to happen to me?" Heinrich let out a sigh.

"Brother Friedrich, it's time that we had a talk," Heinrich began.

"What kind of talk?" Friedrich asked. He felt better knowing he wasn't going to die of disease, but now he felt like he was going to die nonetheless, of confusion.

"About what happened to you," Heinrich replied. "I know that we should have had this discussion sooner, but I didn't think that you were already on your second bite. Then I heard something from Father Gerhard about a curse back in Soldau, and I knew I had to see you as soon as possible."

"Second?" Friedrich asked. "What do you mean? What are you talking about?"

Heinrich sighed, thinking about how to craft his words and explain this to Friedrich.

"You are no longer human, Brother Friedrich," Heinrich stated.

"No longer human? What am I if I am not human?" Friedrich laughed it off, believing his mentor was making a joke or a metaphor.

"You are on your way to becoming a demon," Heinrich replied grimly. Hearing the word "demon" again made Friedrich's easygoing mood drop and shatter like fine glass.

"…A demon?"

"You are not created by Lucifer himself," Heinrich explained. "This is just a curse that he has inflicted upon mankind. Unfortunately, God cannot directly cure us of this curse. However, what we can do is dedicate our lives in the church and serve God's will to make up for the terrible things that we must do." Friedrich reflected for a moment. It was hard to comprehend all this information that was just dumped on him. He had so many questions. He didn't know where to begin.

"What kind of curse is this?" Friedrich finally asked. "What's wrong with us? What terrible things must we do?"

"We are cursed to drink the blood of others for our survival," Heinrich explained.

"Blood?" Friedrich began to shake.

"You can still eat normal food to keep you somewhat full. As for me…" Heinrich drew his fangs. Friedrich flinched in response. *They look just like the teeth I had that night. Is this why…* "I need to consume blood instead of food to survive. As a result of this, we cannot die naturally."

"We…can't die?" Friedrich asked.

"We can," Heinrich replied. "I have seen it before. Not of natural illnesses, however."

"C—Can we not go to Heaven?" Friedrich trembled.

"That is yet to be known," answered Heinrich. "Most don't think so, but I believe that if we do the Lord's will for however long we may live, we will most definitely see the Lord in Heaven. Converted heathens can go to Heaven, so why can't we? It will just take more suffering for us on Earth in order to get there." Friedrich felt like the room was going to start spinning. This all sounded so crazy to him. Eating blood? Being immortal? It sounded like a children's story. But the knight's fangs were very real.

"How old do you think I am Brother Friedrich?" asked Heinrich, shaking Friedrich out of his daze. He examined Heinrich. His dark brown hair was almost black in color and shined in the last rays of the setting sun. His mustache and beard were even darker and neatly trimmed, unlike his hair that looked like it hadn't been cut in a while. Dark, bushy eyebrows lined his sky blue eyes, but Friedrich noticed that his pupils were not completely dark. Maybe it was the sunset, but it appeared that his pupils had a reddish tint to them. Not a wrinkle lined the Ritterbruder's face. He looked like he was in his 20s and hadn't aged a day since Friedrich first met him. But he knew that he was older. He didn't realize until now just how handsome Heinrich von Andernach was. If he was a woman, he would be all over him.

"Um… 39?" Friedrich guessed. Heinrich chuckled a bit.

"I am 150 years old," Heinrich revealed. "Today is actually my 150th birthday."

"Impossible," Friedrich gasped. "Only those in the Bible that were—"

"It is a result of this curse," Heinrich interrupted. "I do not age. My senses have been heightened. I do not get sick. It is harder for me to become hurt in battle. As a result, I have lived on this earth for many years." Friedrich stared at his knight in awe, finding his words hard to believe. "But as miraculous as that sounds, there are many negative effects. My skin burns and my vision becomes weak in the bright sunlight. I have a terribly strong sense of smell, I am awake at night, and I must consume blood every day." Friedrich thought for a moment. He could have sworn he saw Heinrich in the sun before. Maybe he was misremembering things. If he really thought about it, almost all of his conversations with the knight had been in the evening. Whenever they had to travel, he always kept his armor on or had his hood over his head.

"Is it the same for me?" asked Friedrich. "Am I…Am I what you are?" Friedrich felt his mouth becoming dry. "What even are you? What are we?"

"I understand that you have many questions, Brother Friedrich," said Heinrich. "I assure you I will answer them all." Friedrich nodded, understanding. "Many call us demons or monsters or the cursed ones. In the North, people call us draugrs. As of late, people here call us nachzehrers."

"N—Nachzehrers?" Friedrich repeated. "After-living?"

"When I first became one, there were very few in the northern Holy Roman Empire—where I am from," Heinrich explained. "Now, however, they seem to be more common around the Prussian coast. Ever since the Crusade started here, I've seen many attacks. It's frightening how many I have encountered since I've been here. And far too many of them are feral. Absolutely uncivilized creatures. They live in the forest and attack anything with a pulse. Those are the real demons."

"How did this happen?" Friedrich asked. "How did you…How did we become undead? I don't remember dying…" Friedrich trailed off, having answered his own question. Being stabbed in the stomach on the battlefield. Being attacked by that demon in the forest. Almost dying just moments ago from having his blood drained. *I've been on the brink of death three times…*

"Nachzehrers become what they are by being bitten by another nachzehrer and surviving," Heinrich answered. "Normally nachzehrers go after the weak and vulnerable. Often that means those that are alone in an unfamiliar environment, or the sick and dying. Their bites often save the latter's life, which is why they are undead. It took three bites for me to become a nachzehrer. I see you haven't had a third bite yet, as your eyes are not red."

"So the thing that attacked me…"

"That 'angel' that saved you probably was a nachzehrer too," added Heinrich. "He was probably a man of good faith, saving you out of the kindness of his heart."

"Saving me?"

"A bite from a nachzehrer has healing properties," Heinrich explained. "Some believe it is holy, some believe it is satanic, some believe it is witchcraft. If you survive an encounter, whatever sickness or injury you had is cured. Which is why many nachzehrers are priests and healers, using their powers for good rather than their own selfish purposes. This is why some of us have concluded that this curse may not be demonic after all, but a test from God. These powers give us the chance to either help others or help ourselves."

"Some of us?" Friedrich questioned. "How many of you are there?"

"More than you think," smiled Heinrich. "We are few, but we know who we are. At least, those in the Order do."

"What about you?" Friedrich asked. "You aren't a healer or a full-time member of the clergy."

"My duty is—or was until recently—to help those on the battlefield," explained Heinrich. "I was the one who helped lead the night attacks. I save those who are dying on the battlefield when I see them. It also keeps me fed so that I don't have to turn to other means to feed."

"So why not just turn everyone into nachzehrers?" Friedrich asked. "Why not have everyone become these immortal, supernatural healers? Wouldn't it be easier to defeat our enemies?"

"I would not wish this curse upon anyone," replied Heinrich sternly. "There is still so much that we don't know—not even I know everything about myself. One thing we know for sure is that we can not feed on each other. If all of us were to become nachzehrers, there is no doubt we would all starve. Many would turn against our Lord for their own selfish desires. This curse has corrupted many. It can turn a man into a bloodthirsty beast. Not everyone can handle the responsibility of this curse. That is why I refuse to bite you again unless you are on your deathbed. Our numbers are few, but we need them to be. Both for our sake and the sake of others." Heinrich stood up. "I have to go pray. Rest up and get well."

"Wait! One more question," Friedrich halted. "How am I still alive after the bloodletting? What did you do to save me?"

"I told them that you had a curse that could only be cured through ingesting holy blood," he said. "One of the priests gave some of his blood. I know I had to lie, but I did so to protect you. People will not understand what we are. It's a sacrifice we have to make." Friedrich sat there silent for a moment, processing all this information. *Heinrich lied for me. He went against the rules of the Order—the rules of God—to protect me...*

"Do not be afraid, Brother Friedrich. You do not have to go through this alone," assured Heinrich. "I will make sure that you are safe and that this doesn't happen again. I will be there to educate you on everything you need to know and prepare you for the future. I wish I had someone like that when this happened to me, so I'm going to give you what I can." Friedrich felt his fears and worries evaporate with Heinrich's words. Something about the knight's promise told him that everything was going to be okay. He sighed away his current fears and put on a brave face.

"Thank you, Herr Heinrich."

"Ah! It's great to be home!"

"Don't get too comfy. We have to go off and fight again soon."

"Ugh! These Sambians are a pain in the ass! I can only imagine what stupid situation they got stuck in this time…"

"We have to go all the way to Twangste. Again."

"Didn't we already do that?"

"The Sambians are still fighting there…"

Gailimantas helped Annuse out of the wagon. He looked around the town he called home. Swintamīstan had expanded a bit since he was last here. There were more houses than last time, and the town was a lot busier. Annuse was instantly drawn to the large tree with the statues of the gods nestled into the branches. He smiled as he approached her. He planned to convert her eventually and was glad she was already taking an interest in his gods.

"Ah. These are the three main gods: Peckols, Perkūnas, and Potrimpo," he explained. "Peckols is the god of the underworld, Potrimpo is the god of the earth and seas, and Perkūnas is the god of the sky." Gailimantas pointed to the bonfire and the two vases that sat in front of the tree. "This is the sacred fire that we keep burning for Perkūnas."

"What's in the two jars?"

"In this jar is oil for Peckols," he explained. "And in this one, for Potrimpo, is a live snake." Annuse shivered.

"How do you remember all these gods?" Annuse asked. "How many do you even have?" Gailimantas thought for a moment counting the gods in his head.

"Honestly, I don't know how man—"

"Gailimantas! You're home!"

An older, blonde man with a full beard jogged up to Gailimantas and Annuse.

"Trenis! Nice to see you again," Gailimantas greeted.

"I have important—Who is this?" Trenis pointed to Annuse.

"This is my new wife, Annuse." Gailimantas's smile grew as he introduced his wife. "This is Trenis, son of Nubraus. We were neighbors growing up." Trenis raised his eyebrows.

"Oh. Congratulations, Gailimantas. I was worried you would never find a wife. Or rather, your father was." Trenis's expression suddenly changed as if he remembered something. "Oh! Gailimantas, you came back just in time. Your father needs to see you."

"Of course, I'm going to see my father. I was planning on seeing the new parts of the town first, and we are really tired from travel so maybe—"

"You need to see him immediately," Trenis interrupted. "I don't know how much longer he is going to last."

"What do you mean?" Gailimantas asked.

"He's been suffering from an illness for months now," Trenis explained. "It isn't looking good. He's prayed for your return soon so he could speak to you." Gailimantas's joy flipped to panic. His father was sick? He looked so well last time he saw him. He couldn't be. Gailimantas had to be sure.

"Lead me to him," Gailimantas said, keeping a brave face. Annuse looked at him with worry. Gailimantas swallowed his fear to keep brave for his wife.

Gailimantas followed closely behind Trenis to his home, Annuse trailing behind him. He wasn't even gone for a whole year. How could his father suddenly become sick? His heart was racing with panic as he tried his hardest not to let the tears forming in his eyes spill over. When they entered the small home, the first thing he noticed was an unfamiliar older woman in the cooking area. Gailimantas assumed that she was a healer and hurried to where his step-mother was sitting next to his father. His heart dropped when he saw his father. He looked frail and sickly, coughing and rasping as if the air was being slowly choked out of him. The sickly old man that had been fighting on the battlefield a couple of years ago looked up at Gailimantas, his eyes filled with joy.

"Thank Deywis," he smiled. "My son has returned to me." It took everything that Gailimantas had not to cry at that moment.

"Tāws!" Gailimantas dashed to his father's side. "Tāws, what happened to you? You were well when I left. What—"

"Peckols always comes to claim what is his," Sarginus said. "I didn't listen when I was told to take it easy." He broke out in another fit of coughing. "I guess I should have retired a while ago. I ended up just like my father."

"Tāws, you can't go. You're strong. You can pull through this if you just pray—"

"I've done everything I could, Gailimantas. I have been suffering for…months now. I think it's finally time I join your mother and your siblings. I'm not sure if I told you…but she was my favorite wife, your mother. And you…you are so much like her… After all these years…I can finally tell them…" Sarginus trailed off when he saw the woman standing at the entrance of the room. "Who…Who are you?" Gailimantas then remembered why he was so excited to be home in the first place. He took Annuse by the hand and led her over to join him.

"Oh. Father, this is Annuse. She is…my new wife," he said.

"Nice to meet you," Annuse said, bowing. Sarginus's face suddenly filled with life that had been absent from his body when Gailimantas first saw him. He beckoned Annuse to come to him. She slowly obeyed, and he took her hand in his.

"You…are a lovely young maiden," he rasped. "Where did Gailimantas find you?"

"In a village in Warmia," Gailimantas answered.

"Please do me a favor, Annuse," Sarginus rasped.

"Yes sir?"

"Please take good care of Gailimantas. He's all I have." He coughed. Annuse smiled.

"I will."

"I prayed and prayed, Gailimantas, but not for me," Sarginus said. "As I knew the end was near, I had two wishes." He coughed again. "The first was to see you one last time. And the second…" Sarginus hacked again, this fit lasting much longer.

"Tāws?"

"The second was for you to find a wife," he answered. "The gods have answered my prayers. I can now leave this life in peace."

"Tāws…" Gailimantas took his father's hands. "There's still so much to tell you. I'm not ready for you to go. Please!"

"I'm…very tired, Gailimantas…" Sarginus whispered. "Please, let me rest… I have fulfilled my duty in this life. You'll be fine on your own… You've been doing fine ever since you became my only son. Gailimantas…" A smile came to his face, his eyelids starting to close. "I'm so proud to have you as my son," Sarginus said with his last breath. Gailimantas knelt there, frozen. Grief washed over him, but at the same time, he felt a sort of resolve. His father's last wishes were granted, but Gailimantas now felt so alone without his father. He felt Annuse put her hand on his back. He felt his sorrow start to melt as he looked at the blurry form of his new wife, providing him comfort, letting him know that he wasn't going to be alone.

"Annuse…could you give me a moment alone?"

"Of course." She nodded before disappearing into the next room, where conversations with the other women in the house arose. It was only then Gailimantas began to sob, grieving the loss of not only a father, but a friend.

# Chapter 9: Anew

# 1264

The door to Komtur Heinrich van Andernach's office opened a crack, an eye peeking inside. A voice that usually resounded with confidence and pride was instead small and nervous.

"Hein–Komtur?"

"Brother Friedrich, why do you stall outside?" Heinrich asked. "Come in." Friedrich scooted into the office, staring at the floor, shoulders hunched in nervousness. Strangest of all was the ball of sheets bunched above his head. "Land sakes alive, Brother Friedrich! Why are you holding that ridiculous sheet on your head?" Heinrich scoffed. "We have servants to wash the clothes."

"Um, I have a problem… A big problem," said Friedrich, sounding defeated, as if he had lost a very important battle.

"Is it a combat related problem? Or is it a nachzehrer problem?" Heinrich asked.

"Well, I was going to head out tomorrow night for my night watch mission and I was going to talk to you about it but… I came across another problem," Friedrich explained. "A nachzehrer problem."

"What is it?"

"Well, I tried turning into a bat and…" Friedrich mumbled. "It's so embarrassing…"

"Just show me what happened."

Friedrich took the sheet off of the top of his head, revealing large, pointed bat ears that stuck out on top of his head. He looked at the ground, even more embarrassed.

"Herrje, Friedrich!" exclaimed Heinrich, putting his palm over his face.

"I know," Friedrich said. "I don't know what to do."

Heinrich sighed. "Sit down, Brother Friedrich." Friedrich obeyed, his head down in embarrassment. "Just relax and close your eyes. Now, imagine yourself retracting those ears like you retract the fangs." Friedrich closed his eyes and did as Heinrich told him, imagining himself retracting the large bat ears on his head like he would his teeth after a meal. "There. They're gone." Friedrich felt the top of his head and sighed in relief. "Please don't do that again without my supervision. Someone could have seen you."

"I know," Friedrich growled. "Ugh! Why can't I do this? I've only managed to transform once and that one time I got stuck and couldn't transform back! What's wrong with me?"

"It will get better with time…"

"It has been six months."

"Nothing is wrong with you. This is normal. Besides, right now your transformation is incomplete. Your body is in an unstable state between man and demon. Which is why your powers fail you so often," informed Heinrich. "It's why you can survive the sun and why you can still be somewhat satisfied by normal food. Why are you so focused on this anyways?"

"Because it would be such a useful skill on the battlefield."

"But I do not use this ability often though," added Heinrich. "It is only to be used as a last resort."

"Why?"

"Not even I can get it right most of the time. A big weakness that we have is that we can't control certain aspects of our powers." Friedrich felt slightly relieved knowing that the Komtur had similar issues. "In addition, we are men of God. The bat is an animal associated with witchcraft and Hell. So we must abstain from that form as much as possible. It also leaves us exhausted and hungry. In addition, when we transform back we're…" Heinrich hesitated as he tried to formulate his words. "We don't have any clothes when we turn back." Friedrich blinked.

"Maybe the infidels will be taken off guard by my nakedness?" Friedrich wondered.

"They are infidels, Brother Friedrich," Heinrich stated. "They know not what dignity is. You should enjoy your years in this stage. You won't have them for long."

"What do you mean by that?"

"You can't live with a foot in each world forever, Brother Friedrich. Your body and soul can't handle it. The most you will have is ten more years, and that's if you are blessed by God," Heinrich added. "Most likely it will be five or six more years."

"Why? What happens after that?" Friedrich asked.

"If you are not bitten, you will die," answered Heinrich.

"What?"

"You will become suddenly ill first so it's easy to spot. I'll be there when the time comes," said Heinrich.

"How do you know that?" Friedrich asked, now worrying. "How do you know that you'll be here? What if you're in Livland? What if I get sick and die before then? Why not just bite me now and get it over with?"

"I can't. You don't want to rush into this, Brother Friedrich," Heinrich snapped. "You still have a much greater chance to get into Heaven and meet the Lord. You can still get injured and die. You still have a chance at a somewhat normal life where you can spend some time in the sun and feast on normal food. You don't want to sacrifice that." Heinrich sighed. "I never had the chance to have what you have. I didn't have a choice. You told me long ago that you see me as a father that you never had. Let me be one." Friedrich was quiet for a moment.

"Can I ask you something?"

"Go on."

"How did you become a nachzehrer?" Friedrich asked.

"Ah. That was many many years ago," he began. "I don't remember my first bite, but I remember the second. I was a young soldier fighting in the Wendish Crusades."

"The Wendish Crusades?"

"It began over a century ago," Heinrich explained. "Our job was to convert the infidels in the Holy Roman Empire. We were working with some Danes."

"So you fought in another Crusade?"

"Yes," Heinrich continued. "During a battle at Dobin, I was fighting next to this Dane known as Arne. We had become quite friendly. Even though he was a foreigner, his German was perfect. He claimed he had traveled here a few times in the past. But it was more than a few times. He had been traveling here for hundreds of years. But I didn't know that until much later." Heinrich closed his eyes. "During the battle, I was wounded by a pagan. I fell to the ground. I just remember all of the blood. And all the red snow around me. And then Arne came over to me and just bit me. From then on, the rest is history."

"What was your third bite like?" Friedrich asked.

"I… I wish not to talk about that," Heinrich replied. "But speaking of nachzehrer issues, there is something very important that I need to teach you. You may be a knight now, but now I must teach you a new lesson."

"What is it?" Friedrich asked. Heinrich stood up from his desk and beckoned Friedrich to exit the room.

"Come. And grab your coat," he said. "It is time I taught you how to survive."

"I don't know about this…"

"You have to learn how to do this."

"But the rules say I'm not allowed to eat or drink outside of mealtimes or be outside of the Komturei at—"

"Friedrich, I'm the Komtur now. I grant you permission."

"But what if I kill him?"

"Every feeding is a test of temperance, Brother Friedrich. It is up to you to decide whether or not to give in to gluttony. You cannot live off of sheep's blood your whole life. You will face situations where you have to feast on a human."

"I see. This is a test of God."

"Many like us just devour all the blood like an animal. But we are men of God. We must have temperance and cut ourselves off before we kill anyone."

"Understood."

"Now, that man is alone. Beckon him to this alleyway and do as we rehearsed."

"Yes sir."

Friedrich stepped out into the street that was lit only by the flickering candles encased by lanterns hanging above the shops. At this point in the night, shops were beginning to close. Stumbling down the street was his target: a sloppily dressed drunkard who was singing a song about his favorite hobby. Friedrich stepped out and beckoned the man over.

"Excuse me sir. Could I see you for a moment?" Friedrich asked. The man blinked in surprise.

"Oh! A Teutonic Knight!" The man stumbled over his words. "What do you want?"

"Come with me," Friedrich beckoned him over.

"Am I in trouble?" the man slurred. "I'm sorry. I'm a member of the church, but—"

"You should know that drunkenness leads to sin," Friedrich began to lecture once the man was in the alleyway.

"I'm sorry," the man grumbled.

"Pray the Lord's prayer thrice and twelve Hail Marys and your sins will be forgiven," Friedrich continued.

"I'm sorry…"

"Now, for your punishment…" Friedrich approached the man closer.

"P—Punishment?" the drunkard stammered.

"Don't drink to excess again," Friedrich warned, drawing his fangs. Before the man could react, Friedrich sank his teeth into the man's neck and began sucking the blood out of him. Friedrich felt a heavenly feeling wash over him. It was as if he was surrounded by warmth, like he was being hugged by his mother. His hunger was fading away with his exhaustion, replaced with energy and power. The taste was nothing like animal blood. It felt far more satisfying and tasted completely different. Blood didn't taste like it did when he was human. It was a whole new, indescribable taste that surpassed anything he had ever eaten.

"Brother Friedrich!" Heinrich warned. Friedrich then remembered that he was supposed to stop. He reluctantly pulled away from the man. He felt the man's body go limp and gently set him down. "Don't give into the temptation!" Heinrich reminded him.

"Forgive me," Friedrich said, bowing his head.

"It was your first time," Heinrich said. "It is to be expected. I am surprised that you went so long without drinking another human's blood. Now, let's take this man to shelter." Friedrich picked up the man and slung him over his shoulder, following his knight.

"By the way, what happens if we don't drink blood?" Friedrich asked. "Do we starve?"

"I believe so," Heinrich answered. "Blood is our main source of life. Our bread and water. But as we starve, demonic, animalistic urges become stronger. If we do not feed, the demon will take control and make us attack innocent people."

"By God…"

"This is why it is important to bite as few people as possible," Heinrich explained. "If we all become nachzehrers, we'll all become animals and descend into madness."

"By the way, how did you know that man wasn't already bitten? If we're not supposed to create new nachzehrers, then how do we know who not to feed on?"

"You must not have the skill yet. I am able to smell who has been bitten and who hasn't," explained Heinrich. "Our sense of smell is heightened for that reason." He pointed to a nearby church. "He will be safe here." The two entered the building and gently laid the man inside. "By the way, how have things been since your knighthood?"

"It's boring watching over all the Halbbrüdern," replied Friedrich.

"You'll thank me later," said Heinrich. "Just be thankful that I'm Komtur now. On that note, there's something I need to talk to you about. You have been a prominent figure on the battlefield for a while, Brother Friedrich. And I believe that you have what it takes to be a leader." Friedrich looked at the knight brother in front of him. "With that in mind, now that you're 21 and an official knight, I believe it's time you have your own squire."

"My own squire?" Friedrich laughed. "I just graduated from being a squire! Now I have to teach one?"

"It comes with the duty of being a knight."

"Shouldn't you be giving the squires to the Ritterbrüdern instead?" Friedrich asked. "They probably need them more."

"Friedrich, I think it's about time you become a Ritterbruder either this year or next year," Heinrich said.

"You—You think I'm ready to become a Ritterbruder?" Friedrich had waited for this moment for years. Finally, years of being a draper, fighting heathens on the battlefield, getting lost in the woods, and risking his life on the frontlines had led him to this moment. He didn't expect for it to come so soon though. "But I just became a full knight. That would make me pretty young for a Ritterbruder."

"Well, given our hardships with the Prussians, I'd say you've taken the role of a knight for a while," Heinrich said.

"But don't I need to slay 50 soldiers in battle? And have five years of service?"

"You'll get that 50th kill this year. I have strong faith in you," Heinrich answered. "You have been with the order since you were a boy, Friedrich. You are without a doubt one of the most talented soldiers that we have. I believe you deserve that role."

"Oh thank you, Komtur! Thank you so much! I promise, I will not let you down!" Friedrich celebrated. He felt giddy and excited, his body feeling loose and relaxed. It was similar to how he felt after drinking wine. He just felt buzzed.

"I know you will take the position seriously."

"Yes sir." Friedrich felt like laughing, feeling pumped and energized. *Strange… I feel like I'm drunk. But I haven't had a drop of wine in weeks.*

"There are talks of forming a union for those who are like us," Heinrich said. "Within the Order, I mean. Since I'm Komtur now, maybe I will be the one to do this. There has been a great increase in nachzehrers in the past few centuries. Before, meeting one or two was incredibly rare and they were almost always traders from the North or the Southeast. But now, I know at least four in this area alone."

"But we aren't supposed to keep secrets from the Order," Friedrich reminded.

"Brother Friedrich, in this case, we do not have a choice," Heinrich said. "We must remain in the shadows and do our work in secret. We do not take credit for the good we do, nor do people know who we are. They just wouldn't understand beings like us." Friedrich nodded. He felt a sense of guilt going against the Order, but he knew it was for the best. He was cursed now, and this was how he had to live his life from now on. "With our vast powers comes great sacrifices, Brother Friedrich. That is just how our world is."

"Anything else I should avoid?" Friedrich asked. "Any other weaknesses we have?"

"Silver," answered Heinrich. "Silver is a metal of purity and we as demons should not touch it."

"But it doesn't hurt when I touch it," Friedrich said, feeling a bit more out of it.

"It isn't a matter of physical harm. It's a holy law we must follow," Heinrich explained. "We as undead have a few rules that we follow to keep peace with God."

"There are rules?" Friedrich questioned.

"Oh yes," Heinrich continued. "We are cursed beings. We cannot equate ourselves to humans. Therefore, we must follow a set of rules to even ourselves with the untainted man."

"Well what are the rules?"

"As we are impure, we are to avoid touching holy items and symbols of the Lord unless we are told to do so."

"Does that include my rosary?" Friedrich asked, holding up the item in question.

"You may continue using that, as it keeps the demon inside you at bay," Heinrich said. "Keep a cross around your neck as much as possible. Just don't touch a crucifix without permission. We are no longer worthy of such a privilege. Another thing that we are not allowed to do is enter any home or church without being invited in at least once."

"Will it hurt if I do?"

"No," Heinrich replied. "But God will look down upon you in shame. It is to keep things fair and we religious nachzehrers follow these rules to appease the Lord so he may seek mercy on us."

"I can't enter a house without being invited inside first, no touching silver or holy items…" Friedrich felt even stranger. He was having a hard time following the Komtur's words.

"I think I will write a list down for you," Heinrich said as the two exited the church. "The only thing that can actually hurt you is the sun, but you still have some tolerance to it. And of course, losing blood."

"Komtur?"

"Yes?"

"Is there any way that we can die?" Friedrich asked. "If these things hurt us but don't kill us, then what can?"

"I…I don't know that yet," admitted Heinrich. "I've only seen it happen once. It was a long time ago. I was with my friends in a forest, and we encountered a demon. But not just any demon… I never thought that they really existed. I've heard rumors and folk tales but…" His former mentor sat down, troubled.

"What was it?" Friedrich asked, sitting next to him.

"A werewolf," Heinrich answered. "It killed some of the people I was with, tearing them to shreds. It was so terribly gruesome. May their souls find peace in Heaven."

"A real werewolf..." Friedrich couldn't believe what he was hearing. "Those exist?"

"Indeed they do," Heinrich replied. "They are large, terrifying creatures."

"What else exists? Ghosts? Changelings? Moss people?"

Heinrich laughed. "I haven't heard of such things existing," he replied. "I have met a werewolf though. And from that I learned that while it may be harder for us to be killed, it is still possible."

"How did you escape?" Friedrich asked. "How did you survive the monster?"

"I flew away," Heinrich replied.

"Flew away?" Friedrich repeated. "Wait, we can fly?"

"We turn into bats, remember?" Heinrich said.

"Oh. Right. That."

"Though sometimes it doesn't work, as I've told you before. It took me years before I could figure it out. It's like playing an instrument. It requires lots of practice," Heinrich said.

"What other abilities do we have?" Friedrich asked, getting excited in his drunken state.

"I'm not even sure that I know everything that we can do," Heinrich admitted. "I'm pretty young compared to the others I have met."

"You're 150 years old!"

"I met one man who was in his 500s."

Friedrich's mouth hung open. "That's so...extraordinary... Whoa..." Friedrich stumbled on a cobblestone. Heinrich barely caught him before he hit the ground.

"Brother Friedrich, are you alright?"

"I don't know, Komtur…" Friedrich replied. "I'm feeling a little woozy, honestly. It's like that time we were surrounded and had excess wine, but little bread to eat… But I'm not drunk. I haven't had any wine today." Heinrich stared at Friedrich for a moment, perplexed, before a look of realization came to his face. He covered his face with his hand.

"Ah. You drank the blood of a drunkard. Perhaps that's the reason why," concluded Heinrich. "I assure you that this is not a normal occurrence."

"Oh. Okay…"

"You may lean on me, Brother Friedrich," Heinrich suggested. Friedrich accepted Heinrich's offer.

"Thanks. Komtur…"

"This is my fault. I should have guessed that this would happen."

"Did you really meet a guy that was 500 years old?"

"Indeed. He was from the North. Sweden I believe."

"I guess that makes sense," said Friedrich. I heard from Brother Petra that there isn't much sun up there during the winter. Speaking of which, the last of your rash seems to be gone."

"I hope you learned your lesson."

"I know. I know. I'll keep you out of the sun…"

# 1268

"How is your arm doing?"

"Pretty well," Gailimantas replied. "It's a bit sore, but I rarely feel its pain anymore."

"That's good. Maybe next time you'll pay more attention on the battlefield," Annuse teased.

"I'm just happy I'm alive. Many of our troops were captured and even Herkus Monte was injured."

"Well, it gave you an excuse to come home. Speaking of whom, where is he now?" Annuse asked.

"I honestly don't know. He's probably hiding or talking to the other tribes. Every Christian in the world is probably looking for him." Gailimantas opened the windows to let the pre-summer breeze in. The summer solstice would soon arrive. It was a special day for Gailimantas, as he was born on the summer solstice. It always made him feel special since most children were born in spring. Every time he celebrated, it made him grateful that he was still alive. The fireflies would light up the trees and bushes as if they were decorated with flickering golden stars. Annuse put her arms around her husband, careful to avoid his bad arm.

"You should be asleep," murmured Gailimantas.

"So should you," she said. "You've been tense as of late. I know you're worried about Herkus, but there's nothing you can do right now. You're injured." Gailimantas looked at the cursed sling around his arm that prevented him from fighting alongside his comrades, keeping him at home. "Besides, you don't need to be fighting right now. You'll actually be able to see the birth of your first born," she added. Gailimantas turned around, smiling at his wife. She was due any day now, and Gailimantas was one of the privileged few who would actually be there for the birth of his child.

"You're right," he sighed, "I guess I should just enjoy the summer."

"Let's just—" A high pitched scream cut Annuse off. It sounded like a woman was in terror.

"What was that?" asked Gailimantas.

"Did someone scream?" asked Annuse.

"I'm going to see what's going—" started Gailimantas.

"No! Don't go out there!" said Annuse, clinging to Gailimantas's undamaged arm tightly.

"I have to protect the town," said Gailimantas. "It's my job."

"I just…have a really bad feeling," said Annuse. "Please just stay inside."

"A bad feeling?"

"Something… A spirit is telling me not to go out there," she said. "I don't know why, but I have some intuition that there's something horrible outside." Annuse then rushed to the windows and shut them.

"What are you doing?" Gailimantas asked. "Don't you want to let in the cool air?"

"I have a really bad feeling," Annuse repeated. "Something is telling me we need to stay inside. Mantas, please. Besides, you're injured."

"I can still wield a sword."

"Mantas…" Annuse looked at him, her eyes beginning to cloud with tears that sparkled in the candlelight. Gailimantas was surprised she wasn't yelling at him by now. Maybe she was genuinely scared. He sighed.

"Alright," he conceded. "I'll stay inside. Let's go to sleep. I can see you're tired." Taking his wife by the hand, he led her to the hay-stuffed mat the two slept on. Next to it was a small wooden cradle that Stantiko and his wives made for them. Gailimantas was about to blow out the candle when he heard another low rumbling sound. He paused for a moment, listening as the growls turned into animalistic snarls.

"Animals?" Annuse asked, her grip on him tightened. Long howls could be heard in the distance.

"Wolves," Gailimantas concluded. "Someone must have seen wolves and got scared. Not sure how wolves got inside the walls though."

"Just wolves…" Annuse sighed.

"Well, I might as well help out the guards before they eat the—"

"Please, don't go," Annuse begged, holding on to his arm tightly, refusing to let him get out of bed.

"They're just wolves—"

"But what if they aren't?" Annuse cut him off. Gailimantas looked at her confused. She sighed. "When I was young, I had this dream where I heard howling. So I looked out my window. And outside I saw…" She was interrupted by a loud bang. It was as if something had slammed into the wall of their house, making everything on the table and shelves clatter.

"Wh—What was—" started Gailimantas. Another bang cut him off, followed by several others. It was as if someone who was huge and bulky was slamming into their door, trying to force their way in. "By Peckols…" Annuse's grip became even tighter. Gailimantas squeezed back, becoming more and more worried as the banging continued. Soon the banging stopped, and a moment of peace came with fading snarls. "That was a huge wolf… If it was even a wolf…" He looked over at his wife. "Are you feeling okay?" She nodded.

"The baby is moving again," she replied. "It's kicking me a lot." Gailimantas smiled. "When I was a girl I had this dream of this…terrifying beast," Annuse narrated. "It was like a large wolf on two legs. And it was roaming through the village, chasing after people. I remember the people screaming and getting killed. They were so terrified and… It all seemed so real… I was so scared, my mother called a priest to try to vanquish my thoughts since I refused to leave the house for two days."

"It's okay," Gailimantas said. "We're safe inside this house. You have a warrior to protect you. You're one of the safest people in the world." Annuse's hand intertwined with Gailimantas's, her small, thin fingers interlocking with his long ones. Gailimantas turned to his wife. The way she smiled almost made Gailimantas wish his arm would never heal so he wouldn't have to go back to war. He couldn't imagine what grief she would have if he didn't come home from battle one day. Or if the battle came to them… "Annuse, I have a request," he stated.

"Hmm?"

"If the day comes that I don't come home…"

"Mantas…"

"It's very possible. Please just listen to me," he began. "I want you to follow my customs and stay with Pomeus's or Trenis's family. Besides you, they are the closest thing to family that I have." Annuse was quiet. "Annuse, please promise me." She hesitated before silently nodding. "If I have to go into hiding, and the knights come…"

"I won't say a word about you."

"No," argued Gailimantas. "You have to protect yourself and whatever children we have."

"But I can—"

"Please," he said. "If it means keeping you safe, my life matters less. If it comes to that, choose your children over me. You know their language and their culture. You can blend right in and keep them safe." Annuse was starting to get emotional again. She had been a lot more emotional lately, as expected.

"It would be hard for me to rat you out," she scoffed. "Don't bring up things like that. We're about to have a family. You're supposed to be happy." Gailimantas felt a slight smile scrawled across his face. He found it cute whenever she called him an idiot. Her cheeks would turn slightly red, and she would have this adorable look on her face. He couldn't see it now because of the darkness, but he could picture it clearly in his head. Even though women in Prussia could be severely punished if they defied, insulted, or struck their husbands, Gailimantas found it charming when she protested him and just couldn't be mad at someone so captivating.

"I suppose. I have a while before that happens, depending on what happens to my arm," he said. She smiled, pulling him closer, mumbling something. "What was that?"

"I said thank you..." she murmured.

"What for?"

"Making my dreams come true," she replied. "I...I never thought I would ever get married, much less become a mother. I never believed that any man would want me but..." She smiled. "Thank you for being my husband."

Gailimantas returned the smile. "Thank you for being my wife."

Annuse shuffled her way back to the bed. Gailimantas remained where he was. *She's right. I should enjoy what I have now. Many men would kill to be in my position. As much as I'm itching to get back to the battlefield, part of me wants to stay here forever. I don't want my children to experience the heartbreak I had when my family was taken from me. They should have an amazing father like I did. And I want to be that father. I want to be their protector and their hero, like my father was to me.*

"Are you coming to bed?"

"Let me be sure the windows are secure, in case it comes back," he said.

"Don't take too long. You might have to sleep on the floor if you aren't here fast enough." He couldn't help but smile at her remark. She had a great sense of humor and Gailimantas loved her for that. Gailimantas hurried to the window, looking for something to keep the shutters closed. He felt a tickle in his throat, coughing into his hand. When he pulled away his hand, tiny red spots of blood were sprayed on his palm. He sighed. *Again? I thought I was done with this. I hope I can be healed soon.* Gailimantas then put a chair in front of the door and joined his wife in bed.

"That seems to be the last of them. The coast has been clear for hours."

"I think we've captured them all."

"We should still keep a lookout, just in case of a night ambush."

"It's going to be annoying to rebuild the fortress again."

"Good thing we captured a lot of Prussians. Now they can rebuild what they destroyed…"

"Königsberg has been under siege by the Prussians for years. Hopefully this will be the last time this city has to face such turmoil."

"Doubtful of that. These heathens just keep coming back for more."

Friedrich and his Halbbrüdern were on night watch duty for Königsberg. Nightly jobs were part of Friedrich's agenda ever since he became a nachzehrer. Normally his Ritterbruder duties were much more exciting, like charging into battle on his own horse with the finest equipment in the kingdom and making major decisions with the other Ritterbrüdern in his Komturei, which were few. But ever since he was called to Königsberg, he had mostly been stationed on defense, watching a bunch of lower knights, or he would be forced to train a bunch of young, newly recruited novices. Right now he was supervising a bunch of Halbbrüdern, or half brothers. These were knights that did not take monastic vows and had lives outside of the church. They weren't required to do military service, so they mostly stood watch. Friedrich, as well as the majority of full-time brothers, thought of them as lesser due to this.

"I hope this siege is finally over," said Brother Ruben in his Northern accent. "Then I can finally see my wife."

"Me too," said another brother named Christoph. "I haven't seen a woman in so long."

"I admire you Ritterbrüdern for taking monastic vows," said Georg. "I wish I could, but I love my family too much."

"I don't see how you can," Friedrich said. "Women aren't worth giving up service to God, in my opinion."

"You seem to be antagonistic towards those who settle down and take a wife, Brother Friedrich. Why so?" asked Ruben.

"Taking a wife is for the weak," he answered. "God gave me a mission, and I am fulfilling it alone. I am alone, I've always been alone, and I always will be alone. And that's how I like it. With no one telling me what to do except the Lord himself."

"But don't you feel restricted by the church?" Christoph asked.

"The church gives me freedom," Friedrich replied. "I am not bound to any woman nor child nor family. I live for God alone, with no one else in my life to distract me." The half brothers looked at each other for a moment.

"Maybe things will finally go back to normal after this," Georg said.

"What is normal at this point?" wondered Friedrich. "Even if we finish the Prussians here, there are still many pagans left in this area. The King of Lithuania broke his vow of Christianity, and the Livonian Brothers are now struggling against them. I say it's only a matter of time before the Lithuanians invade us as well." The Halbbrüdern began to talk amongst each other. Friedrich continued to watch the horizon, barely paying attention. He could hardly be bothered to remember half of these brothers' names anyways.

"I hear those Lithuanians are brutal. They even ransack other pagans sometimes."

"I hear the Livonians keep coming back defeated. I hope we never have to fight them in our lifetime."

"Hold on, I see something on the horizon," noticed Ruben, nudging the brother next to him.

"It's…more reinforcements!"

"They're a little late…" scoffed Christoph.

"I'll talk to them," Friedrich said, sighing as he climbed down the tower and crossed the moat to greet the incoming knights with blazing torches. Judging by their dark uniforms, they looked like they were almost all half brothers and servant brothers. *Great, more soldiers that aren't ready to commit full time. They wouldn't have been much help to us anyways.* A grey cloak dismounted and walked to greet Friedrich. He pulled off his helmet. He looked very young, like a fresh new recruit. But he had the expression of a fearless older man. He and the soldiers behind him were in full armor, prepared to fight, though they looked tired and distressed, as if they just came from battle.

"Greetings, Ritterbruder. We are reinforcements from Magdeburg sent to Königsberg to fight," proclaimed the brother.

"Where are your Ritterbrüdern and Komtur?" Friedrich asked.

"We were ambushed on the way here," he explained. "Almost all our Ritterbrüdern were injured or killed. The majority of our forces are Halb- and Diendebrüdern and we only had a few. The others didn't know the way to Königsberg, so I volunteered to lead the way. I grew up here, so I know the whole area."

"Well, we have already defeated the Prussians and chased them from the city," Friedrich answered. "Your services are no longer needed. But you may rest here for the night. We can see your journey was perilous."

"Thank you, brother," he said, bowing. "We thank you for your hospitality."

"Think nothing of it," Friedrich said. "We're always willing to help out our fellow brothers. You were brave today, brother. God would be proud that you led your troops to safety."

"Just doing God's will."

The soldier bowed, returning to his men. Friedrich couldn't help but smile. He had a strong feeling that this boy was going to go far. He would probably make a good Ritterbruder if he was ready to commit. Friedrich would hopefully be in a higher position by then. He planned on working with the Grand Master one day. Friedrich then thought for a moment. *Will Heinrich ever really retire? How long will he work for? He won't age, so eventually, people will get suspicious of him. Will he have to flee town? Change his identity? Will I have to do the same thing when the time comes?* Friedrich snapped out of his thoughts and saw that the knights had all passed the gates. Not a soul stood on the other side of the bridge. Friedrich shouted up at the young Halbbrüdern to close the gates as he returned back across the bridge. The door began to lift again, but over the metal clanking, Friedrich heard a shout.

"Wait!"

Friedrich paused when he saw a couple of men on the other side of the clearing. They were moving very slowly towards the gates. One man dressed in red and white seemed to be carrying a man dressed in white. As the two came closer, Friedrich could see the black cross on the Ritterbruder's white uniform as he was carried by the other knight.

"Oy!" Friedrich shouted. "Lower the gates again! We have two more!"

"Are you sure?"

"Does it sound like I'm unsure? Lower the gates!"

"Yes sir…"

Friedrich waited for the bridge to finish lowering before taking a closer look at the men. As soon as he could see the details, he instantly recognized the knight brother. Brother Franz had a severe wound on his arm, wrapped with white cloth. Underneath the cloth, the white uniform was stained entirely red. What looked to be the other knight's cloak was wrapped around his midsection. He looked semi-conscious. The bottom half of his uniform was stained in a grey-brown color, as if they waded in a dirty river. The other knight was wearing a uniform Friedrich had never seen before. He was covered in the color white, but he had a bright red cloak and his chest was decorated with his coat of arms, but he was so muddy, he couldn't make out what the symbol was. It looked like his armor was of very high quality and specially made for him. *A Preußenreiser! I haven't seen one of those in years!* The volunteer knight was limping and looked exhausted and pained, which made Friedrich wonder why Franz wasn't carrying him instead. When the knight made it to Friedrich, he looked like he was going to pass out from agony. His ginger hair was short and neatly trimmed like his facial hair, but they were smudged with blood and dirt. Part of his sleeve was torn off and his helmet was missing.

"Praise the Lord!" the Preußenreiser gasped in relief. "Thank you brother! This man needs urgent medical care!"

"Oy!" Friedrich called up to his men. "Get down here! We have two soldiers who are injured!" He turned back to the knight, who slowly lowered Franz to the ground, wincing in pain. "What happened to you two?"

"The knights I was with were ambushed by the Prussians. We were protecting the outside…" He leaned against a wall.

"We called all troops inside hours ago," Friedrich said.

"The Prussians slaughtered us all," he explained. "They got me pretty bad in the leg and then they knocked me out. Then, a few knight brothers showed up and they were chased elsewhere. When I woke up, I looked around to see if anyone was still alive… And I found him…"

The other brothers rushed to the scene.

"What's going on?" asked one of them. "Is that a Preußenreiser?"

"Is that Brother Franz?" asked another.

"Take Franz to the infirmary," instructed Friedrich. "He needs immediate care. Bring a stretcher back for this knight here. Brother Christoph, you stand guard."

"Yes sir."

"Thank you so much, brother," sighed the knight.

"I'll help you inside," Friedrich offered. "I see that your leg is injured." He let the volunteer knight lean on him as he brought him across the moat. "What happened after you found Brother Franz?"

"I saw that he was still alive and injured, so I brought him back to the city. It took me a while since he was so injured and halfway through he was hardly able to stand. I couldn't just leave him there to die. I… don't know what happened to the rest of my troop. I think most of them were slaughtered. Those infidels are so brutal…" Friedrich had him sit against the city wall.

"I know. I've dealt with them since I was a child," Friedrich scowled. "You did a noble thing today. I'm grateful that we have another experienced noble knight in our ranks. God will surely reward you in Heaven for volunteering your services to us."

"Thank you, brother," he sighed. "I also have a personal issue with the Prussians. They killed my family when I was young."

"Really?" Friedrich said. "They killed my father and my brother. My mother and I were rescued by the Order. We were enslaved there for years."

"How horrible."

Friedrich was surprised to find someone with a history similar to his own. Despite him being a knight from outside the Order, perhaps the two would get along well. Friedrich then felt someone tap on his shoulder. He turned around to see the young grey cloak from earlier.

"May I help you?"

"Yes. Do you know where I can find the Komtur of Königsberg?"

"Ah. He is probably within the castle with the other Komturs."

"Thank you sir," he said. "I don't believe I got your name."

"Friedrich von Rotenkreuz," he replied proudly.

"Thank you, Brother Friedrich." The young soldier dashed off.

"That young boy did something amazing earlier today—" Friedrich started.

"Pardon," interrupted the noble knight. "Did you say your name was Friedrich von Rotenkreuz?" The noble gazed intensely at Friedrich.

"Yes. It is. Why?" The knight's eyes widened, his mouth agape. His hand covered his mouth as if to keep his breath from escaping. "Are you okay?" Friedrich asked.

"The Lord has been so merciful," whispered the knight, slowly rising to his feet. "Every suffering in my life has led me to this miraculous moment." Friedrich was riddled with confusion as the knight hugged him. "It has been so many years, my dear brother." Friedrich squirmed out of the stranger's embrace.

"What are you doing? Who are you?" Friedrich raised his voice. The man smiled slightly, leaning against the wall again.

"Of course you don't recognize me. It has been more than 15 years, hasn't it Fritzi?" he said. "It's me, Wilhelm." Friedrich stared at the man again, locking eyes with those nearly identical to his. The man who looked so familiar was a person whom he had not seen in almost two decades. He felt tears welling up in his eyes.

"By God… I—I thought you were dead…" Friedrich swallowed back emotions, trying to save face like the elder brother he was, desperately fighting back tears while hugging one of the men that he had been trying to avenge for years. He thought he had been sacrificed to the pagan gods. He never expected to ever be reunited with Wilhelm unless it was in Heaven.

"I thought the same of you and…" started Wilhelm, his words getting caught in his throat. "For many years, I have lived with the guilt of abandoning you two and—"

"Brother Friedrich? What are you doing?" said a voice behind Friedrich. Friedrich turned his head towards the voice to see a few of the brothers had come back with the stretcher. A Ritterbruder had come back with them.

"Where is the injured knight?" Christoph asked.

"Is that a Preußenreiser?" Tomas asked.

Friedrich gestured to the knight next to him. "Fellow brothers, this is Wilhelm," Friedrich said. "My younger brother by blood."

# Chapter 10: Bonds

## 1252

It had been a bitter winter. The air was so cold and dry that just a few moments outside without gloves or a coat would make the fingers tingle in pain and numbness and dry the skin to where it cracked and bled like the skin on the back of a disobedient servant after a flogging. Friedrich had come to hate winter. It was a time of wondering if he and his family would survive. The only way Friedrich had survived was through sharing his body heat with his mother and brother. Sometimes there would be other slaves, but there seemed to be no room for him tonight, since he returned later than usual. Unless he slept on the cold, hard floor, but the hay provided him some warmth and comfort, unlike the floor that zapped the heat from him and gave him aches in the morning. He couldn't understand the other slaves anyways and they seemed to show no interest in him. No one was here to share body warmth tonight. He was surprised. He expected this from his mother, as she often worked very long hours. But his brother should be back by now. When his brother did come back, Friedrich was planning on sitting on him for the stunt he pulled today. Friedrich got a strong whack across the cheek with a branch because Wilhelm didn't show up to his post today. As soon as he walked in through that door, he was going to let Wilhelm have it. Normally Wilhelm was back before he was. Since he had been old enough to work, he had been given Friedrich's old job of menial house tasks, while Friedrich was promoted to cleaning and maintaining the stables. He missed when he was six and he wasn't cleaning horse dung and surrounded by smelly animals.

Friedrich looked in the wooden pail by the front door, which contained a half eaten leg of a bird and half of a roll. He smiled, thankful that his mother and brother would have something to eat when they returned. He returned back to the haybed, tucking his legs and arms into his garment, trying to keep his body heat. Friedrich was shivering so hard, he began to feel ill, and his body ached from shaking. He felt exhausted, but the biting cold kept him from drifting off to sleep. The one good thing about the stables was that it was always warmer than anywhere else during the winter. *Maybe I should just sleep there from now on. If only I was an older woman. They sometimes get to stay in the houses with their masters. Maybe that's where Mutti is tonight.* Half of Friedrich hoped his mother got the chance to avoid the cold tonight. But the other half hoped she would come back and share her warmth with him. *If I was an older girl, I wouldn't have to be scared of these barbarians suddenly sacrificing me one day. I would always have a nice warm place to stay and wouldn't have to worry about freezing during the winter. I wouldn't feel humiliated about my current situation. My entire life wouldn't depend on if I fled this place or not.*

He heard footsteps crunching in the thick snow outside, followed by the sound of the wooden door opening and a large gust of cold wind blowing in. He snapped his head around, expecting to see his brother, but was surprised to see his mother instead. She seemed to look a bit better than usual. Her long, sandy hair seemed to be a dirty and duller light brown now. She looked pale and thin, but fewer red and black marks covered her skin today. Her lips were cracked, bleeding slightly and there were dark rings around her eyes. He noticed that she had a newer looking cloak on. His mother always came back late. The men that made her work sometimes made her work until the early morning. He would often wake up to his mother holding him tight, sharing her warmth with him. Whenever Friedrich saw her lately, she always just sat there and stared. Her eyes always seemed to be void of life and hope. She used to cry a lot when they first got here, but over the years, she became silent, only responding to him and his brother with small sounds.

"Mutti," he whispered, grabbing the bucket, "I saved you some food." Her eyes drifted to the bucket before slowly reaching out her arm and grabbing some food and slowly eating it, not even looking at him. Friedrich sighed. If only he was bigger, stronger, and older. Then he'd be able to keep these men from hurting his mother every day. Just maybe he'd hear her say more than a sentence to him. Or maybe even smile. Friedrich could only recall one memory when his mother was smiling, and that was one of the few memories he had of his father. It was very faint, but he remembered first moving into their manor and being excited by a rocking horse made for him by his own father, who had whittled it while he was in the military. It was his earliest memory and one of the few of his father.

"The stable is very warm," Friedrich whispered. "It smells, but it's a nice place to be during the winter."

"Hm," she responded. She was usually like this. There were times where she wouldn't say a real word for months. Friedrich thought she would have more to say today. Especially since she was probably reprimanded for Wilhelm's disappearance as well.

"I got hit in the face because Wilhelm didn't show up to do his job today," said Friedrich. "I'm going to kick his butt when he gets back." To his surprise, his mother's expression changed, suddenly stopping her chewing. She didn't respond. She just bowed her head to the ground. Friedrich looked concerned, his thoughts about Wilhelm still nagged at him, going from angry to worried. "Mutti, where's Wilhelm?" Friedrich asked. His mother didn't answer. She just continued staring at the ground, slowly chewing her food. "Mutti?" With the last bite of meat, she finally looked Friedrich in the eyes.

"He never came home…" she finally said, her voice raspy. "Rudayko asked me where he was. I told him I didn't know. He went to the river to fetch some water and…" Her expression didn't change, but a single tear ran down her cheek. "He's…" Friedrich instantly felt guilty about what he was planning to do to Wilhelm if he returned. If his brother walked through that door now, he would squeeze him so tight until he folded in half.

"Did they… Did they find out?" Friedrich asked.

"I don't know…" she rasped. More tears began to fall. Friedrich hadn't seen his mother cry like this in years.

"But he's… He's dead?" Friedrich asked, getting emotional. His mother got down on her knees, looking her son in the eyes. It had been a long time since his mother had looked at him like this. It had been a while since he had seen any emotion from her at all. She put her arms around him, hugging him tightly.

"It's just you and I, Fritz," his mother whispered, holding him tight. Friedrich began to cry on his mother's shoulder. The three of them had suffered through years of hell together after his father died. Being treated as less than pigs for as long as he could remember was bearable with his brother by his side. Just talking with him about his day filled him with hope. He wished that he could take his previous thoughts of decking his brother in the cheek and turn them into a magic force that would bring his brother back. The back of his mind tried to come up with excuses and explanations to distract from facing reality, but produced nothing but empty pages. Wilhelm was gone. End of story.

Friedrich did miss his mother's warm hugs though. Feeling her warm tears on his shoulder reminded him that he still wasn't alone and that she was still alive. While she hardly ever talked anymore, he still had his mother. Seeing her cry like this almost made Friedrich happy in a way. He was happy to see her animated rather than the soulless husk she normally was. *Maybe I can talk to her everyday and try to get her to talk back to me. It's the only way we can keep ourselves patient.* He never wanted to break free from the hug. It was too warm and calming. *If only I was older and bigger. Then I could come up with a way to escape. Then I can stop those men from hurting my mother every day. Then I could lift a sword and strike down whoever killed Wilhelm.* He reluctantly broke free from the hug.

"Hey, Mutti?"

"Yes?"

"How about we sleep in the stables tonight? It will probably be warmer," Friedrich suggested. He looked at his mother for a response. She was just staring off into space again. "Hey, Mutti. Come on, let's sleep in the stables." She looked at him again.

"…Okay." Friedrich reluctantly opened the door to the hut, the freezing air greeting him. Crunching through the snow, he led his mother a few steps outside and to the stables. The moment they stepped into the barn, the atmosphere became much warmer. The horses and pigs would radiate heat. It smelled, but it was a small price to pay for such warmth. He led his mother to the sheep's pen, where the sheep were huddled together, attempting to sleep. He led his mother into the pen, trying to avoid stepping on feces based on what he could see from the moonlight. He led her next to the flock of sheep, gesturing her to lay down. She looked hesitant, so he took her wrist and brought her down to his level.

"Just lay next to the sheep. It's warm," Friedrich encouraged. She slowly kneeled down and laid next to the warm, wooly animal. Friedrich laid down next to another, his head across from his mother's.

"It's been a while since winter has been this warm…" his mother said. Friedrich wiped another tear as a smile grew on his face. Seeing his mother show signs of a soul gave him a bit of hope. Hope that one day they will be free. Hope that Wilhelm was still alive. Hope that one day, they will have their estate back.

"Maybe Willi just got lost. Maybe he will come back," Friedrich said. His mother just responded with a soft, sleepy noise. Friedrich smiled. The sheep radiated heat that made his numb fingers tingle and melted the icy chill on his skin, and the worries of his brother in his brain, with a homey embrace. He made a good decision to come here. Friedrich watched his mother slowly drift off to sleep. *If only our father were here. Then we would have escaped by now.* Friedrich sighed. He said that to himself every day. It never changed the fact that the patriarch of his family was dead. *It's up to me now, isn't it? I have to be the one who looks after her. I have to help us escape. I don't have time to mourn for Wilhelm. I need to look after the family I still have.*

"Someday, God will send someone to save us," Friedrich assured. "I know He will." Once again, he got only a small noise from his mother, letting him know that she heard him, but that she was tired. Friedrich felt sleep tugging at him too. Wrapping his arms around a fluffy sheep, he drifted off into a warm, wooly slumber, sleeping soundly for the first time in years.

# 1268

Gailimantas stared at the creature in his arms. He was absolutely enamored with the small, sleeping pink person. He stared at the tiny human being that was currently swaddled with a thick brown cloth. The life that he helped create. After months of waiting and hours of screaming and squeezing, he finally had what he wanted. He couldn't understand how other soldiers talked about their children so casually. It was probably because they never had the chance to be in his position. They would be gone for years at a time sometimes and would never get to hold their children like this or watch them come into the world like Gailimantas had. Things like this made Gailimantas never want to go back to war. *I made this. I helped make this. This is mine…*

"Mantas?"

Gailimantas dropped his attention from the baby and turned back to his wife, who was laying in bed. She still looked weak and tired, but the color was returning to her face.

"Oh. I thought you were asleep," he replied.

"I am tired," she said. "But I've been asleep for a while. How long have you been here?"

"I never left," he replied. "You've only been asleep for twenty minutes or so."

"Really? It felt longer…" Annuse looked up at him. "What do you think? I'm sorry I couldn't produce you a son."

"She's…absolutely beautiful," he said. He wasn't lying. She looked just like her mother probably did when she was born. He was not disappointed in his creation. He was proud of it. This was a part of him. A symbol of his success and his legacy. The infant then opened her baby blue eyes. Gailimantas felt his heart melt. Her charm was so powerful, it numbed the pain in his shoulder, making him forget that he wasn't supposed to be using his arm like this. She was so small. Surely he couldn't damage his arm more by holding her like this. Even if he did, all that would mean for him was that he would get to stay home with this tiny angel. Most would be upset to have a daughter instead of a son. Many Prussian girls were abandoned or sold into slavery. While Gailimantas would have been ecstatic to have a son, something inside him wanted to protect this precious little girl from all harm. "We made something beautiful."

"She still doesn't have a name," murmured Annuse.

"I've been working with nothing but men for months," he said. "I can't possibly think of a good name for a girl. I hardly know any women outside my family."

"I guess I have a few names that I like…" she smiled.

"What names do you have in mind?"

"Eimants, Melstis, Kirsne, Vudevutas, or Myre," she listed. "I don't know much about your naming customs."

"Four of those are male names," Gailimantas pointed out. "And those are all…" Gailimantas paused for a moment as he looked at his wife, who seemed to be proud of herself. "You want to name her after my family?"

"I think it would be a way to honor their memory," she said.

"Well, some of my siblings could still be alive," he said. "They were probably taken captive by the Teutonic Knights."

"What do you remember about your sisters?"

"I only had two sisters," he answered. "One was just a baby when she died, so I didn't know her well. My older sister, Kirsne, seemed to have her life together. She was about to get married at the time. My parents were looking for a suitor for her. She didn't talk to me much. She would mostly focus on herself and let my brothers push me around."

Annuse thought for a moment. "What about your mother?"

"M—My mother?"

"You told me a lot about your mother and how much you miss her and respect her. I think having her as a namesake would be a good idea," she explained. "What was her name?"

"Kaliste," he replied. "I believe that was her name."

Annuse paused. "Kaliste… That's cute. I like it," she said. "It just…fits her."

"It really does…" He noticed the infant had closed her eyes again. "She looks just like you."

"Does she now?" Annuse yawned.

"You should get some rest," he insisted, feeling something rise in his throat.

"Could I hold her for a moment?" Annuse asked. Gailimantas handed her the child. He began to leave the room. "Where are you going?"

"Just going to…get some fresh air," he replied, coughing a bit.

"Do you still have a cough?"

"I think it's getting better," Gailimantas replied.

"Are you sure?" Annuse gave him a look of disbelief.

"Annuse, I promise, everything is fine with me. My cough is going away. The blood is going away," he assured. "The evil spirits are leaving my body."

"Alright…"

"I can't let myself become ill. I have to stay healthy for my family," he smiled. Annuse became a bit less tense. "I'm going to tell the rest of the village the news."

"Alright. Be back soon," she chuckled.

Gailimantas exited his home. As soon as he was outside, he burst into a brief fit of painful coughing. By the time it subsided, he was gasping for air. *Hopefully I can keep myself healthy. But it seems to be going away. I shouldn't worry about it. Just focus on what just happened. It's time to celebrate, not worry.* He looked up at the beautiful houses surrounding him. Swintamīstan was as lively as ever today. Most of his friends were out at war, but he knew Trenis was around at least. Gailimantas rushed off to the center of the village, excited to tell everyone the good news.

Friedrich and Wilhelm were whittling together, talking about their lives since they were separated. It had been almost two decades since they last talked. The sisters and monks had been examining Wilhelm's leg for so long, so most of his time was spent in the infirmary. The nurses had been preventing Friedrich from seeing Wilhelm for almost three days at this point and gave him vague explanations such as, "He needs more rest." Today, Wilhelm was walking around perfectly and the two were finally able to sit down and talk about everything that had happened since they were apart.

"So what was wrong with your leg?" Friedrich asked. "The nurses said something about a really horrible curse set upon your flesh. I must have misheard because you're walking around perfectly fine."

"Oh no," Wilhelm said, sitting down across from Friedrich. "That was the person next to me. My leg was fine. I was just really sick. I had a fever, and my stomach was feeling so awful. I'll spare the details though, lest we lose our dinner."

"Are you still sick?"

"Yesterday morning, the nurses went to check on me, and I was perfectly fine," he answered. "My leg was healed too! It was like my wound never existed. The pain was gone, the fever was gone, the exhaustion was gone… I'm feeling just as good as normal." Alarm bells went off in Friedrich's head. Could someone have bitten Wilhelm? And why would they bite him? Perhaps it really was just a light illness. Maybe Friedrich was just worrying too much.

Friedrich changed the subject. "What were we talking about before?" he asked.

"I think we were talking about what happened after we were separated at the pagans' settlement," answered Wilhelm.

"Oh! Right! You were in the middle of your story!" Friedrich remembered.

"When they took me out into the woods, they were distracted by something, so I ran," Wilhelm narrated. "I ran until I was far away from them. I ran into the woods as fast as I could. I wandered for a couple days until I found a road. Luckily a couple of travelers saw me and picked me up. They took me to Gudensberg, and I trained to be a knight there. I trained under my adoptive father, Sir Johannes von Rickenbach, who fought in the War of the Lombards."

"What made you volunteer for the Order?"

"After fighting in the war in Thuringia," Wilhelm continued, "I decided to take a break, settle down, and I wanted to start a family. But… That's a long story. I heard that knights were needed to fight on the Prussian front. I was in a rough situation spiritually. But suddenly, here I am on the Prussian front. Honestly, I never expected you to be a full knight brother."

"When you last saw me, I was ten years old," nudged Friedrich.

"I know," Wilhelm said, "Wait. I'm going to be 24 soon. So that would mean you're…"

"25 years old."

"And I thought I was old," laughed Wilhelm. "You're pretty sturdy."

"I'm as fit as I was ten years ago," Friedrich bragged.

"You're a full brother. Meaning you took monastic vows…"

"And I am one of the best knights around."

"So you never started a family or married."

"No. Did you ever start a family?" Friedrich asked.

"Well, my luck has not been so favorable," Wilhelm began. "I was married to a lovely woman, Helena. She was the daughter of the Count of Joachimsthal, you know, our great uncle from our mother's side. I would have been married for six years by now. We had a hard time with having children. Every time we had a child, disease would always come in. We lost three children within five years. We prayed and prayed to God to let one survive. One made it to age five but…" He paused for a moment. "First it was my children. And then I lost my wife." Friedrich was heartbroken listening to Wilhelm's story.

"What happened?"

"Shortly after Helena gave birth to the fourth one, she became very ill and died within days. The baby became sick shortly after. So I was left alone, asking God why this had to happen. Why did I have to go through such heartache? I went to the local church and prayed as hard as I could for my son—the only thing I had left—to live. I promised the Lord I would dedicate my life to Him if my son would live. Sure enough, my son's illness passed and he was still alive. I took it as a sign from God that I was to join the Order. So I left my son in the care of his aunt and uncle in Joachimsthal." Friedrich smiled. He had been fighting for years and his little brother had grown up on his own. He had become an adult, got married, and started a family all while he spent his whole life traveling around the Prussian coast, killing pagans. He couldn't help but feel happy for his brother. Even though he saw that life as undesirable for himself, he respected Wilhelm for what he decided to do with his life. At least the family name would continue on. "When this is all over, I can't wait to spend time with my son."

"When this is all over…" Friedrich sighed. This crusade could take years at this point. He may not be alive by that time. Or at least, his brother wouldn't be. Friedrich felt his heart begin to tremble as he now realized that he would outlive his younger brother. He would watch him grow old and die while he stayed young forever. Well, that could be fixed, but did he want to subject his brother to this curse? Did he want to turn him into an undead demon just so he wouldn't have to watch him die?

"I've heard word about you being saved by an angel of the Lord. Is that true?" Wilhelm asked. Friedrich paused mid-stroke of his knife. He believed he was saved by an angel at the time, but now he realized that it was probably a nachzehrer like himself. Another question arose: should he even tell Wilhelm what happened to him? What would Wilhelm think if he knew that his older brother was now a demon? Would he tell the rest of the Order? Would he never speak to him again?

"I…I believe it was an angel of the Lord. But it could have been something else," said Friedrich.

"From the story I heard, there was blood all around you, but you had no wounds," he added. "That sounds like a miracle to me." Friedrich paused for a moment. This was his brother. His own flesh and blood. Surely he would understand.

"Well, I believed that it was an angel at the time. That—"

"Good day, fellow knights."

Friedrich snapped his head to respond to Heinrich, who was standing right behind the brothers.

"Komtur! What are you doing here?"

"It's a beautiful day. I thought I would step outside of the office. The Komturs have spent all day reorganizing troops since we had so many casualties…"

"But it's cloudy and raining," Wilhelm pointed out.

"Reorganizing?" Friedrich questioned.

"We're just going to have to move some soldiers around so we have more reinforcements at Balga. Königsberg and Memel seem to have soldiers to spare."

"Memel? That's the Kommende I'm at," Wilhelm commented.

"Oh! Wilhelm, this is the Komtur of Balga, and my former mentor, Heinrich von Andernach," Friedrich said. "Komtur, this my brother."

"Ah. Your brother has told me so much about you," Heinrich greeted the knight. "I didn't know you were alive."

"He's told me a lot about you as well," said Wilhelm.

"Please excuse my interruption but could I please speak to your brother for a moment?" Heinrich added.

"Oh. Not a problem," Wilhelm stated. Friedrich hesitantly stood up and followed the Komtur out of the room. Once the two were outside in the hallway, Heinrich looked around them, making sure that they were alone.

"Is there a problem, sir?" Friedrich asked.

"I had a feeling you would do this, Friedrich."

"Do what?"

"Be tempted to tell your brother about what you really are."

Friedrich stood there quietly for a moment. "How… How did you know—"

"I've been listening."

"Where? I didn't see you."

"That isn't important," said Heinrich. "I was originally going to tell you that I managed to relocate Wilhelm to Balga."

"Really?" Friedrich's eyes lit up. "Thank you so much, Komtur! You don't know how much this means to me!"

"He's an interesting soldier, and I want to see what he can do. The Komtur of Memel says he's exceptionally strong and experienced for his age. With all the fighting we do, we could use someone like him in Balga.

After all, it's not every day that a noble knight volunteers for the Order," he added. "That being said, I cannot allow you to tell your brother about your circumstances."

"But he's my brother. He would never—"

"You haven't seen him in decades, Brother Friedrich," lectured Heinrich. "You don't know what kind of person he is. Please. Before you even consider telling him, at least wait until you know him again. I have seen brothers betray their kin many times. I don't want to see that happen to you."

Friedrich sighed. "I have to tell him eventually though," he said. "I…can't stand the thought of outliving him. Watching him grow old and die while I live on. After all these years believing he was dead I… I don't want him to die on me again. He is the only family I have left."

"It's the price that we have to pay, Brother Friedrich," Heinrich said. "We are granted magnificent powers. But loneliness is one of the many consequences." Friedrich was silent again. "I know you are thinking about turning your brother," Heinrich said. "I know you are debating whether to give into your own selfish wishes or to let Wilhelm live his life the way he wants to. It's a natural thought to have. I would be tempted too if I were in your position. Let the sun warm his skin. Let him eat food that doesn't come from living beings. Let him live a life free from the carnage we must deal with. Let him live free from secrets and mystery. Let him be a man of God, free from darkness. Don't force this burden onto him just because you don't want him to die." Friedrich hung his head. "You had this forced onto you. Remember what you felt when you found out what you were?" Friedrich nodded, knowing that Heinrich was right. He didn't want to subject Wilhelm to that same experience. He wasn't even sure if he could turn him at this point, even if Wilhelm wanted it. Friedrich would just have to accept this fact of life. He was no longer human like his brother.

"Can I ask you something?"

"Go on."

"Do you know if someone… If Wilhelm was bitten recently?" Friedrich asked nervously, "Because his wound was suddenly healed, and his fever just miraculously disappeared. Do you think that… You know…"

"I thought he smelled off," Heinrich added. "I was afraid that it was you who had done it. I'm thankful that isn't the case. This makes it even more important that you don't tell him about this. The fact that he was left alive means someone deliberately was trying to save his life. Was his condition life threatening?"

"I don't know. It sounded pretty bad…"

"Perhaps one of the priests or doctors here is one of us. Quite the suitable place to be. He seems to be using his powers here for good at least. He shouldn't be a concern. Unless someone other than the priest or doctor visited him…" Heinrich pondered aloud. "Nevertheless, it would be nice to find out who this is. Hopefully it's not a rogue. If that's the case we may have to heighten security."

"But what will that mean for us?" Friedrich asked.

"You're right. We can't take that risk. It's probably just one of the doctors," Heinrich assured himself. "It won't even be a problem when we go back to Balga." The clock then began to chime, signaling that it was now two in the afternoon. "You should get back to your brother."

"Herrje! How long have we been talking?" Friedrich began to rush away from the Komtur, but suddenly stopped. "I have one more thing to ask you," he said.

"Make it quick."

"Do you regret being bitten?" Friedrich asked. Heinrich paused for a moment.

"I don't have an answer for you, Brother Friedrich," he admitted. "I miss feeling the sun upon my skin. I miss the days of not feeling ashamed for being what I am. I know that I am doing what I can to fulfill God's will but…" He sighed. "I don't know if it is enough." He put a hand on Friedrich's shoulder. "Your brother is waiting for you." Friedrich hesitantly stepped away before speeding up and dashing down the hall.

*Let him have his freedom,* Heinrich thought. *Let him have his humanity.*

# 1271

Gailimantas opened his eyes. There was a ringing in his ears and some spots in his vision that faded as the infirmary came into view. *I don't remember being in the infirmary. What was the last thing I did before coming here?* He rolled over on his side to see none other than his wife and daughter. His wife's face was red, most likely from crying. His daughter, on the other hand, had a look of curiosity. She was only three summers old, so she clearly didn't understand why her father had fainted in the kitchen. She looked just like her mother—mousy brown hair and fair skin with a spray of freckles. Her green eyes lit up with excitement as she saw her father awaken.

"Tāws is awake! Tāws is awake!" she exclaimed. Gailimantas smiled and patted her head. "Tāws is so silly to fall asleep in the kitchen like that!"

"I was just really tired," he said. "I wish I had your energy, Kaliste."

"Don't we all?" added Annuse. "Do you remember what happened?" Gailimantas then remembered him coming to help his wife who had spilled something on the floor so she wouldn't have to bend over. On his way to help her, he suddenly felt dizzy and tired. *I must have fainted. I wonder why.*

"Oy Mantas!" said Pomeus, who seemed to come out of nowhere. "I heard you had quite a fall. Did you overwork yourself again?"

"Maybe that was it…" Gailimantas thought out loud.

"Did you hurt yourself again?" Kaliste asked. "Does this mean he can stay with us longer?"

"Pomeus, could you watch Kaliste for a moment?" Annuse requested. "I need to talk to my husband." Pomeus nodded.

"Come on, Kaliste," said Pomeus. "Why don't you play with Tulne?" Pomeus led her out of the infirmary to play with his own daughter. Gailimantas was prepared for an angry lecture or even a slap from his wife, but was surprised when he was met with tears.

"You idiot! Do you want to end up like your father?" Annuse scolded before she started sobbing. Whenever his wife cried, Gailimantas felt worse than when she would scold him. Making her worry about him felt way worse than messing up and getting yelled at. Gailimantas sat up and put a hand on hers. "I don't want to bring another child into the world who never gets to meet their father," she sniffled. "I don't want to be alone in this so please… Please…" She knelt beside him, crying. Gailimantas put his arms around his wife, being as gentle as possible.

"I'm sorry. I promise I'll take better care of myself from now on," he assured.

"You better," she huffed. "Two young children are enough for me to take care of. I don't need a sick and dying husband to take care of as well. I'll need you to get another wife for that." She smirked at him. He chuckled a bit, but his laughter led to a fit of coughing. He covered his mouth quickly.

"I'm going to stay here for a bit. I'm not feeling all that well," he said, clearing his throat. "Maybe the gods planned this so that I could see my second child." Annuse smiled.

"They have been gracious to me then," she said. "As you have."

"I just returned from war and fell while I was off the battlefield," he sighed. "I'm not doing what a soldier is supposed to do."

"You're here to protect us, right? That's what a *husband* is supposed to do," she remarked. Annuse's response caused Gailimantas to smile.

"I guess so. I seem to have forgotten my duties," he said.

"I'll pray for your healing," she said. "May you get better soon." "I'll try my best to be out of here as soon as I can," he promised as he watched his wife leave. He sighed. *I really am ending up like my father, aren't I?* He looked at the blood on his hand. *Please Potrimpo, just grant me a bit more time.*

# Chapter 11: Revenge

## 1272

Friedrich surveyed the battlefield from his horse. Since he was a Ritterbruder, he had novices to command. Though Friedrich had been in this position for years now, he still had the urge every now and then to just throw his novices into battle like his mentor did for him. He preferred dismounted combat and always itched for it. It was boring sitting on a horse and being away from the direct thrill of the fight. Sure, charging into battle was fun, but he missed being able to use his legs and chase down infidels himself. When he felt like it, he would give his horse to a wounded soldier or a squire and have him relay the message of his victory while he finished the job. On this fine cloudy day, the Order had taken the infidels off guard with a surprise attack on one of their biggest strongholds. The pagans were unprepared, but they were putting up a fight. After all, this was a holy place in their eyes. Friedrich's Komturei had been planning on attacking this town for years. Every time they attacked, they would always be defeated since this town was so well reinforced. It was a Natangian town, so the Komtur hoped to find Herkus Monte or some of his adversaries here.

The Teutonic forces managed to back the heathens to the city gates, where another troop was able to penetrate the city walls. The Teutonic archers had eliminated most of the Prussian archers. It was now a free-for-all in ransacking the city. Friedrich smiled. He had been waiting for this moment. It was time to join in on the fun.

"Onward! Inside!" Friedrich commanded his novices. "Capture as many as you can! We need these men alive to build our new bathhouse!"

"But the Komtur wants them dead," one of his squires piped up.

"And I want a new bathhouse. Capture at least three of the men!" Friedrich ordered.

"Yes sir!"

Friedrich's novices charged inside, but the service brothers on the frontlines were met with a wave of thick black goo. Friedrich looked up to see heathens with large buckets of the black liquid. The Diendebrüdern panicked and scattered in multiple directions as molten tar burned their bodies and covered the holes in their helmets, obscuring their vision and blocking their means of air. *Well, there goes an entire line of troops...* Shortly after, a barrage of arrows flew at the heathens on the top of the gate. *When were those archers when we needed them? I swear Brother Peter's archers are so incompetent.*

Once the rest of the troops were inside the city, Friedrich could see that whatever soldiers waiting for them inside were currently being polished off. He looked and saw Simon and Tomas fighting three pagans at once. They seemed to be holding their own fairly well despite their lack of helmets. Perhaps their helmets were also covered in tar. They were Ritterbrüdern now, so they should be fine on their own. Friedrich was about to join the rest of the soldiers when he heard a voice.

"Fritz! Fritz!"

Friedrich turned around to see a soldier by the edge of the wall, limping towards him. It was Wilhelm. He was holding his left arm, which was bleeding heavily. After he pulled off his helmet, Friedrich instinctively rode towards his brother.

"What happened to you?" Friedrich gasped.

"It's not much. It's just a cut…"

"You're losing a lot of blood. What's wrong with your arm?" Friedrich asked.

"One of the Prussians got me in the arm. I can't move it without it bending…" Wilhelm winced. Friedrich dismounted and gestured towards his horse.

"Get on and get out of here."

"What? You can't be serious!"

"I'm not having my brother die in a place like this! Now hop on and get back to Balga!"

"But I'm not dying."

"Your arm is about to come off!" Friedrich protested. "And you're bleeding like a freshly slaughtered lamb. Now go!"

"Fritz—"

"As a Ritterbruder, and your superior, I order you to go!" Friedrich said.

"You're not my superior," Wilhelm protested.

"I'm your older brother. And definitely have a higher title. Also my mentor is the Komtur. So I kind of am your superior," Friedrich replied with a smirk. Wilhelm sighed and reluctantly got on the horse.

"I'm going to see if anyone else needs medical attention," Wilhelm said before he rode off. Friedrich sighed. He drew his new, freshly sharpened sword, a smirk on his face. He had sharpened it and cleaned it just for this invasion and was excited to finally use it. *It's showtime.*

Friedrich charged into battle, rushing to try to find Simon and Tomas. Out of the corner of his eye, he saw a pagan coming towards him. Friedrich blocked a swing from the infidel's sword. Parrying it, he managed to throw the enemy off balance and kick him to the ground. He hurried as he saw Tomas ahead. Simon was on the ground, injured, while Tomas was battling another bearded Prussian. Friedrich was about to hurry to his aid when out of nowhere, a sword went through Tomas's throat. Friedrich was bewildered. He hadn't even seen the second pagan come up from behind Tomas. He just saw his friend get stabbed in the throat. The pagan retracted his sword and ran off. He didn't even have a helmet and his armor was clearly meant for a smaller person. Simon got up again and began battling the same pagan as before. Friedrich chased after the other pagan. He wasn't going to let him get away with that. Who knows what a person like that could do? *Don't worry Tomas. I will avenge your death.* He realized how slow this man was. The man didn't even look behind him and seemed to be avoiding all conflict. Friedrich had him now.

"You! Stop right there!" he yelled. Friedrich tackled the Prussian from behind. The pagan was struggling, but Friedrich had no problem holding him down, as he was incredibly weak. The Prussian looked up at his captor. Friedrich's eyes widened when he saw the man's face. He felt a smile creep along his chin.

"Hello again, infidel..."

Rapid thumping sounds. High, shrill shrieks. Sharp popping, crackling. Clinking metal. Distant murmuring. A faint chorus of sounds echoed in Gailimantas's ears once again. His brain sluggishly processed the sounds, trying to connect the pieces surrounding him. He recognized these sounds. He had heard them numerous times in his lifetime. The smell of smoke made him reluctantly open his eyes. It looked to be around sunset. He pulled himself up and trudged to the entrance of the infirmary, his mind still muddled with confusion. Gailimantas stopped short of the entrance as he realized what was going on. His lethargy seemed to disappear as his brain finally connected the pieces around him, forming a picture that he didn't want to see. *Oh no. Please don't tell me…* Gailimantas peeked outside, witnessing the sight that he feared the most. Houses and trees were burning, dead people were lying on the ground, and men in white uniforms were battling everyday villagers.

Gailimantas knew he had to do something, but he knew his body was going to be uncooperative. Even though he felt drained, Gailimantas was tired of feeling useless. Swintamīstan was under attack and he was confined to the hospital; a sick old man at the age of 24. Every time he coughed, his body wracked in pain, and he spat blood. It was difficult for him to breathe. Every time he sat up, the world spun around him. Gailimantas had not been on the battlefield in months, but now his home was being attacked by the Teutonic Knights. He had something to live for other than his people now. He had a family: a beautiful wife and two daughters with another on the way. What kind of man would he be if he couldn't protect them?

Gailimantas grabbed a broom in the corner of the hospital, just in case he needed to defend himself, and dashed over to the smith's shop and burst through the door. As expected, supplies were low, so he had to make do. Supplies were always low since it was custom to burn deceased soldiers with their armor and weapons. Gailimantas threw on some ill-fitted armor. He didn't expect to be going out to the battlefield so soon. He didn't expect that battlefield to be his home either. So far, the battle was not looking favorable. He could not find a helmet, but he didn't care. He snatched the last sword and tightened his armor. *Time to defend my family. My town. My home.*

Gailimantas dashed out of the building and put his plan into action, helping out Pomeus by stabbing the man he was fighting in the back of the neck. He could hear the soldier gagging as the sword went through his throat. Blood stained the steel of his sword as he retracted it. Pomeus smiled a thanks. Gailimantas knew that his home was far away from where he was, so he dashed towards his home, trying to get to his family. He avoided the knights as much as he could, focusing on getting to his house and making sure his family was safe. The armor weighed his body down and his lungs kept reminding him to slow down, but he pushed through it. He was determined to fulfil his role as a soldier, a husband, and a father and protect his family. No illness nor Teutonic Knights would stop him from doing his rightful duty as a man.

"You! Stop right there!"

Gailimantas turned around at the sound of the familiar voice but was tackled to the ground and pinned from behind. He cursed himself for being too weak to free himself. He looked up at the knight. On top of him was a familiar blonde-haired menace. His fiery eyes seemed to glow in excitement as he relished in the destruction of Gailimantas's hometown. Friedrich von something. He remembered part of the strange German name from when he last saw him, but it had been nine years since then. This man took part in destroying his home 14 years ago, and now he was back to do it again.

"Hello again, *Ketzer...*"

"Shit." Gailimantas struggled in his grip.

"You've become weaker," Friedrich commented.

"Let me go!" Gailimantas yelled. "I have to get to my home."

"Not so fast!" Friedrich snarled. "Herr Friedrich von Rotenkreuz does not leave an enemy alive. For the longest time, you've been the exception. And now you've killed one of my friends. So I am going to finish you off right now…" Friedrich paused. "Um… You… I don't believe I ever learned your name."

"Why does it matter?" Gailimantas scoffed.

"I need to know your name before I finish you off," Friedrich said. "As much strife you have caused me, I have to say you're the most formidable opponent I've ever faced. Surely you have a name. You pagans have names, right?"

Gailimantas then wiggled out of Friedrich's grip and kneed him in the chest. "My name is Gailimantas, son of Sarginus. And I don't have time for you right now," he growled before dashing off towards his house.

"Hey! Come back here! I'm not done with you!" Friedrich dashed after him.

Gailimantas could see his house. The willow tree that hung behind it was still intact and unharmed. Its leaves were slightly draped over the roof. His daughter would tie little red strings around its branches to make it look pretty. The leaves always covered one of the back windows and provided nice shade during the summertime. But now it seemed like the tree was grieving over the ransacking of the city. He picked up his pace when he saw that the door was ajar. He burst through the door of the house.

"Annuse? Kaliste?" No response. Not a soul was inside. The house was in a state of disarray. Bowls of long cold stew were at the deserted table. A chair was toppled over. Blankets on the straw beds were scattered about. "Annuse! Annuse!" He ran back outside, looking around the perimeter of the house. "Annuse!"

"Nice place you have here." Gailimantas whipped around to see Friedrich leaning against the doorway, smug and confident, casually looking around his home, but not taking a step inside. "The willow tree really makes the outside look scenic. Not bad for a peasant," he commented. Gailimantas immediately charged at him. Friedrich blocked his attack with his sword.

"Where are my wife and daughters?" Gailimantas growled.

Friedrich parried Gailimantas's attack. "You have a wife and children?" he asked, raising an eyebrow. "Aren't you heathens polygamous?"

"Friedrich von Rotenkreuz, where is my wife?" he asked again, nearly shouting in rage.

"I don't know! I don't know who they are," scoffed Friedrich. "Maybe you should have protected them better. Where were you when they needed you?" Gailimantas charged at him again, but Friedrich stepped sideways and kicked him to the ground. Gailimantas instantly got back up and sloppily swung at Friedrich, missing every time. "Have you forgotten how to fight?" Friedrich kicked him in the stomach. Gailimantas slowly got up, leaning against a wall to support himself. He began to cough again, more severely than before.

"Oh. No wonder why you're so weak. You're ill…" Friedrich snickered, kicking Gailimantas in the side, making him fall to his knees. "What a boring way to die. I didn't expect this from you, Gediminas."

"Gailimantas," he growled. "And I don't care how sick I am. I have a wife and two daughters to protect. I will fight you to my very last breath. Even if that means dying. I'm not going to let you win!" Gailimantas spat blood onto the ground, pain ebbing from every cough. He knew he wouldn't stand a chance against Friedrich. Not like this. But nevertheless, he was going to fight until he died of his injuries or until he keeled over from his illness. He looked up at Friedrich, prepared to defend himself, but Friedrich looked totally off his guard. Instead he was staring at the blood on the ground that came from Gailimantas's insides. Gailimantas just leaned on the wall, catching his breath, spitting out blood.

"I just remembered how hungry I am," Friedrich smirked. "I suppose you'll do." Gailimantas managed to defend himself from Friedrich's attack, but was easily overpowered in a matter of seconds, receiving a strong blow to the stomach. Friedrich slashed his side, where his armor was weak. Gailimantas doubled over in pain, clutching his side and collapsing to the ground. He looked at the blood staining his hand, this time from an external injury. Friedrich chuckled in triumph. "Today is the day you finally die, Gailimantas, son of Sarginus. Today is the day I *finally* get my revenge," he said. "But while I'm at it, I might as well enjoy a nice meal." Friedrich drew his fangs, causing Gailimantas to scramble backwards in terror.

"An evil spirit?" Gailimantas gasped.

"It's been a while since I last saw you. A lot has changed since we quarreled in the forest."

"Wh—What are you?" Gailimantas stammered. He backed into his house, clutching his side in pain.

"I have been reborn as a nachzehrer," Friedrich explained. "Thanks to you leaving me there in the forest and running away like a coward, I was turned into this. And now you're going to pay."

"…A revenant," murmured Gailimantas before coughing up more blood. *I've heard of these creatures before. These monsters. A body that was not burned properly that becomes reanimated and terrorizes the living out of revenge. So I really did kill this man.*

"Committing ourselves to the church is the only way to redeem ourselves in the eyes of God," Friedrich said, now face to face with Gailimantas who was cornered against the wall behind his house. "It's the only way for us to go to Heaven. A place you will never get to see."

Friedrich then bit Gailimantas's throat. Friedrich hungrily sucked the blood out of Gailimantas, not holding himself back. He was going to kill him anyways, so he might as well make a meal out of it. Gailimantas tried to cry out, but Friedrich quickly covered his mouth with his hand. He felt his energy draining out of him, his body rapidly growing weaker and weaker. He tried his best to push him off, but Friedrich was just too strong. *I failed. I failed everyone because I'm so weak. I failed my wife. I failed my children. I failed my home. I failed my people. Am I really going to die here? At the hands of an evil spirit? I guess I deserve it.* Gailimantas felt his vision start to fade. *I'm such a failure...*

"Demon!"

*Klang!* Suddenly Friedrich was hit on the back of the head by something metal, causing him to fall to the side, unconscious. Gailimantas looked up to see Pomeus with a bulky shield. He grabbed Gailimantas, slung him over his shoulder, and began running as fast as he could.

"Don't worry, Mantas. I got you," he said, running to the forest.

"Annuse..." Gailimantas groaned. "I have to..."

"There's too many," said Pomeus. "We have no choice but to surrender the city and flee. We'll take it back another day. Right now we have to meet Herkus in Grewose."

"Not without..."

Pomeus gave a scoff and suddenly changed direction. Gailimantas knew he couldn't argue, but at this rate, he would rather die with his family than die out in the woods. If anyone was to live, it should be his family rather than him. He felt Pomeus shake him slightly and yell something to him, but his voice faded into the chaos. Gailimantas took one last look at his ransacked town. His burning home. Amidst all the chaos stood four figures near the entrance of the town. Two knights dressed in white and a woman with a small child. No. Two small children. She seemed to be looking at him. As his blurred vision came into focus, he gazed upon the face of his wife, holding their young daughter in her arms. She looked like she was about to cry, but she had a slight smile on her face, like she was trying to tell him things would be okay. That she would uphold her promise to protect their family. Her details faded as Pomeus ran further and further. Her beautiful blue eyes were probably sparkling with tears and her long brown hair was probably messy from the panic. Inside of her was what would be their third child. A child that he would never get to see. But she would be safe. They would be safe. He knew they would.

"Thank you…" Gailimantas tried to call to her, but he knew that she wouldn't hear him. Gailimantas smiled as he blacked out, knowing the most important people in his life would be okay. That was all that mattered to him. "Goodbye… I'll miss you…"

# Chapter 12: Revenant

"Mantas? Deywis, please don't die on me."

Pomeus continued running through the woods. He wanted to be sure that he was as far away from the knights as possible before checking on his friend. Gailimantas was in bad shape even before the Teutonic Knights attacked. Now his friend was covered in blood after being attacked by a monster. Pomeus never expected the Teutonic Knights to be full of fanged monsters, but he wasn't surprised. It would explain a lot about their tactics and technology. Pomeus was not exactly sure where he was going, but he knew that others were waiting for him somewhere in the woods. He hoped Herkus made it out alive at least. If Gailimantas didn't die here, he would want to if Herkus didn't make it. Without Herkus, the plight of the Prussians would be hopeless.

Pomeus didn't know where his family was, or if they were even alive. He had seen his brother on the ground, but he didn't have time to check on him. The Teutons would kill him anyways if he was alive. He didn't expect to see Gailimantas's wife so calm in the situation. She had her two children and was casually talking to the holy knights as if she knew them. He couldn't understand what they were saying, but he knew for sure that she and the children would be safe under their care. Being a former Christian, she would blend in well under the Teutons' rule. At least they would be safe and Gailimantas wouldn't have to worry about it. Worrying about his wife was all Gailimantas did whenever he was off the battlefield. When Pomeus finally believed it was safe, he stopped to rest. He gently slumped his friend next to a tree and began to examine him. Gailimantas had a deep cut in his side. It seemed to have stopped bleeding, but it was still very gruesome. He also had two wounds by his jugular with massive bloodstains surrounding the skin on his neck and around his mouth, from which a stream of fresh blood dripped. Gailimantas was still against the tree. His skin was pale, his chest was lifeless, and his eyes were closed.

"Please don't tell me…" Pomeus checked his pulse. Not a single beat of life. He checked again and again. Gailimantas's heart wasn't beating. "Damn it… Damn it!" Pomeus punched the tree that his friend was slumped against. "Deywis… Why, damn it, why the hell did it have to be him?" he shouted. "He's just a k…" He trailed off. Gailimantas was in his 20s now. He had a wife and two kids. He couldn't really call him a kid anymore, no matter how young he looked. At least he was able to honor his last wish. He went out of his way and almost got caught by a knight just so he could see his family one last time. Pomeus noticed that Gailimantas seemed to be smiling slightly, the last expression he must have made. That or it was his imagination. He must have been happy knowing his family was safe. Pomeus gave a slight smile. "You're a man now, Mantas." He sat there for a moment, staring at his friend, grieving his loss. Another thought came to his mind: How was he going to burn the body? If he didn't burn the body, Gailimantas would not be able to go to the afterlife. Even worse, he could come back as a vengeful spirit and haunt him. But Pomeus had no equipment with him that could start a fire to send him to the gods. He just sat there thinking. First his friend had died, now he couldn't even give him a proper cremation.

Pomeus shook his head. He was determined to give his friend a proper send off to the gods. If he didn't have the materials, he would find them. He didn't care how long it took. He would make sure his friend would see the afterlife. He knew there was a river nearby that had rocks that he could use. He could probably find some stones there to help start the fire. But first he had to tie up the body just in case it decided to become animate again and come after him. Legends said that without a proper send off to the gods, the corpse would become vengeful and come after the living. Pomeus knew it would be hard to find firestarters in the dark, so he knew he had to do it when the daylight came, as soon as possible. *Maybe I should sleep far away from the body just in case…* With the rope he had with him, he bound Gailimantas's arms and legs tightly so the body couldn't escape. With that, Pomeus left and began his search for shelter.

Gailimantas awoke, surrounded by green. He tried to sit up, only to realize that he was bound tightly with rope. Panicked, Gailimantas looked around him. *I'm in the forest? Why is there no one here? What happened? I remember being on the battlefield and fighting Friedrich… That evil creature. Maybe he has captured me and plans to kill me. Or maybe he's taking me to his commander. Whatever the reason, I have to escape from him before he can take me.* Gailimantas struggled with the ropes before realizing that he had a knife in his pocket and a sword at his side. He managed to slip his hand into his pocket and retrieve his knife. He then moved his knees to his hand that carried the blade and tediously began to cut the rope. Eventually, the last fiber broke, and soon he wiggled his way out of the loosened constraints. Finally free, he surveyed the empty forest. There wasn't any sign of human activity around him. There was no sign of Pomeus either. Confused, Gailimantas tried to understand where he was, but he was in unfamiliar territory.

*I guess I'm going to have to live out here for a while. I guess I should try to find water first.* He took a deep breath of fresh air. *Wait a minute. I'm not having any trouble breathing. I don't feel tired or in pain. Well, my arms and legs slightly hurt from the tight ropes, but I feel like I did when I was a child. I feel great!* A rush of excitement filled his veins. *I don't taste blood. My body feels as good as new. My sickness has vanished!*

Overflowing with a sudden pulse of adrenaline, Gailimantas suddenly took off running, something he hadn't done in a long time. The leaves crunched beneath his feet and the air painlessly rushed through his lungs, fueling his energy. Energy that he hadn't felt in years. He saw a pond ahead, little water insects making little splashes on the otherwise placid water. Gailimantas didn't slow down. He kept running until he reached the pond. He leapt into the air and broke the beautiful mirror of water by plunging into the pond. He let the water cool his skin, laughing as a refreshed feeling washed over him, washing his body of blood, dirt, and bodily fluids.

*I'm cured… I don't know how but I'm cured. Peckols has decided to spare me. The gods have granted me health… The gods have given me life again.* After spending so much time in the sick house and his own home, he finally felt free. He may have lost his family, but this was not the first time that he had experienced such a loss. At least his wife and family would be safe and would be able to live a long happy life without him. In fact, they would probably be safer without him. He then remembered why he was out in the forest in the first place. *I have to find Herkus. But I don't know where to begin to search.* He sighed. *Well, I made my way to Swintamīstan as a child. I know I can find Pomeus and Herkus as a grown man.* He stood up and climbed out of the pond, trying not to put too much pressure on the ground, knowing that the mud in the pond was sticky and would claim his shoes. After he was on dry land, he looked at the path ahead of him. Nothing but thick trees, ferns, and grass. With his new strength, he hiked on, a sense of hope in his heart. If his illness could be cured, surely anything was possible.

"So what is your status?"

"The doctors told me that I should stay off the battlefield for a few months," answered Wilhelm, looking at his bandaged arm. "How is your head?"

"I feel fine," Friedrich replied. "Just focus on getting better."

"I can kind of move my arm, but it's pretty painful," Wilhelm added. "I'm not supposed to move it for a while. Sorry I can't be on the battlefield with you."

"Just rest up. You'll be back on the battlefield before you know it," assured Friedrich.

"Brother Wilhelm?" said one of the sisters who approached the bed.

"Ah. Sister Zoe. You're back." Wilhelm smiled.

"I'm always happy to care for you," she cheered. "You're my favorite patient." This sister seemed like a bubbly person. Many Halbbrüdern talked about her. It was as if her aura itself numbed soldiers' pain. Friedrich never really knew her as he deemed himself to be too skilled on the battlefield to be seriously wounded. Looking at her, Friedrich had a feeling he would easily get sick of her. He didn't like the fact that these nuns were allowed to tend to wounded soldiers. In his view, it tempted the soldiers too much. However, he saw how busy these doctors were and understood the need for extra help. These were women of God. Surely they could be trusted not to tempt the men.

"I have to talk to the Komtur anyways," Friedrich said. "I'll see you around."

"I'll see you later, Fritz," Wilhelm said, waving him off with his good arm.

Friedrich left the infirmary and went to the Komtur's office. Friedrich was still in a bad mood. When he woke up, he learned that they had captured the city, but Gailimantas was gone. Vanished again like a deer in the woods. He couldn't help but worry that he possibly created another nachzehrer. If Heinrich ever found out, he would skin him. But he knew he had to tell him. It was against the code to keep secrets from one another, after all. Friedrich already lived in guilt knowing that he was lying to his brothers every day. If he couldn't tell the rest of the Order, he could at least tell Heinrich. He continued to the tall stone building where a rather fancy wagon with two horses stood. He looked at the two nearby knights. "What's with the carriage?"

"The Landmeister of Livland is here to talk to Komtur Heinrich von Andernach of Balga," replied one of the men.

"The Landmeister?" Friedrich questioned. "What would the Landmeister come all the way here for?"

The knight shrugged. "I don't know. Probably discussing the seizure of Swintomest or whatever it was called."

Friedrich continued inside knowing his conversation would be delayed. Friedrich had heard that the town they had captured would become a new established city. It wasn't far away from Balga, and they only had to build a church and convert the residents. When he was outside the room where Heinrich usually resided, he could hear voices. Friedrich knew it was none of his business, but he couldn't help but press an ear up against the door and listen in.

"So everyone in the city was captured?"

"Yes sir. A few may have escaped, but Herkus won't get far without his men—"

"Herkus escaped?"

"Yes sir, but—"

"Out of all things, capturing Herkus Monte was a priority, Komtur!"

"I know sir, but—"

"Do you have any idea what this means for us? He could be rallying up the Sambians as we speak…"

Friedrich listened as Heinrich was being chewed out by the Landmeister for failing to capture Herkus Monte. It wasn't the Komtur's fault. He had enough to do. Friedrich wrung his hands. How was he going to tell his commander that he had not only let the enemy know he was a demon, but accidentally cured him from a deadly illness and brought him back to peak fighting condition? On top of that, this man knew his name and would probably tell everyone he came across about what he saw. After a few moments, the Landmeister began to calm down, realizing that Herkus wouldn't survive without his army and would probably play into their hands anyways. He stopped criticizing Heinrich and instead began to congratulate him for taking one of the Prussians' strongholds.

"We also have a Christian woman from the town who knows both our language and theirs. She apparently had a husband who was very close to Herkus Monte."

"How can we trust her? How do we know she's not lying to save him?"

"She promised to give us answers if we didn't separate her and her children and didn't enslave them. She seems like a devout Christian woman and she speaks German too. She knows the Lord's Prayer and can pray the rosary. Lord knows how she survived under the pagans."

"Have you interrogated her?"

"We have asked a few questions. But right now she and her children are in captivity here in Balga."

"Go interrogate her now. Find out the name of her husband. Perhaps if we capture him, Herkus will fall into our hands as well."

"Will do, sir."

"Great job, Komtur. God bless you."

"God bless you, Landmeister."

Friedrich moved aside so that he wouldn't be seen immediately as the Landmeister and Heinrich left the room. Heinrich didn't seem to notice him at first until Friedrich called out to him.

"Brother Friedrich! Were you…listening in?"

"I was," he admitted. "I came to ask you about something, but I'm curious about this captive that was discussed."

"I am going to interrogate her now," informed Heinrich. "I want to interrogate her myself because I find the situation so interesting. What did you want to ask me?" Friedrich followed Heinrich down the hallway.

"It's not really a question," he began. "It's more of a problem. As I was fighting, I ran into that pagan that I have encountered repeatedly for years. The pagan that is the reason I was bitten twice."

"I remember."

"I had the upper hand," he explained. "And we were alone. And I was hungry, so I thought I would finish him off as a meal. But in the middle of my meal, something happened…"

"Did someone see you?"

The two continued to the other building where the prisoners were kept. It was a tall stone tower that was part of the fortress. Friedrich had only been there about twice.

"I don't know what happened," he continued, "but I was knocked out. When I woke up, he was gone. If he was gone when I awoke, does that mean—"

"He's still alive," finished Heinrich. "And he probably fled into the woods." He sighed. "Another one of Herkus's adversaries managed to escape…"

"I'm sorry!" Friedrich apologized. "I thought I had him! Now he's gone again. And he's still alive and stronger than ever!"

"It is just one pagan, Brother Friedrich," Heinrich said. "He won't be able to do much on his own. And this is still his first bite, right? He won't be any more dangerous to us than he was before."

"But—"

"Do not let personal conflicts get in the way of God's mission, Brother Friedrich."

Friedrich hung his head. "Forgive me. That was selfish of me."

The two entered the stone tower, the temperature dropping when they stepped inside. The building was dark, spare the two lone torches hung upon the walls.

"Komtur Heinrich! What can I do for you?" asked one of the Halbbrüdern on guard as the two approached.

"We are here to see the woman we recently captured from Swintamīstan," explained Heinrich. "The Christian woman."

"Ah. Right now, she is in a cell separated from her children," the guard reported. "The children are being looked after by Sister Julianna since they are very young."

"The Landmeister has ordered us to interrogate her," Heinrich stated. "Could you please accompany us to her cell?"

"Ah. Of course, Komtur. But I ask that you be gentle with her, as she is with child," he noted. "Right this way."

He led the two up the stone stairs to the highest cell in the tower. As they approached the top, Friedrich began to hear singing. It was an unfamiliar song, but he recognized that it was in Prussian. The guard gave Friedrich a torch. He then opened the wooden door and invited the two inside. Against the wall on the wooden bed sat a woman who abruptly stopped her singing. Her brown hair was covered with a grey scarf, but it was easy to tell that her hair hadn't been washed in a while. Her skin was pale from the lack of light, making the freckles on her face more defined. She was wrapped in a blanket, trying her best to stay warm. Friedrich was surprised that she was given a blanket in the first place. The room was fairly small and consisted of a wooden bed, a bucket, a torch, and some straw. On the wooden bed there was a rosary.

"Are we really talking to a peasant woman ourselves?" Friedrich whispered with a hint of disgust.

"I want to hear what she has to say."

The two approached the woman.

"Have you finally come to release me?" she asked. "I talked about returning back to my house in Swintamīstan. That is, if it's still—"

"We would like to ask you a few questions first," said Heinrich. "Then you and your children will be released."

She huffed. "About time," she grumbled. "It's so cold here. The nerve of you to have me stay here for three days with such little concern for my unborn child…"

"You were given extra rations and a blanket ma'am," said the guard.

"This is still no way to treat a woman of Christ," she huffed.

"If that is indeed what you are," said Heinrich. "You claimed your husband was close to Herkus Monte. Wouldn't that make him a pagan?"

"He is a pagan."

"Why are you married to a pagan?"

"She's probably a witch," Friedrich whispered.

"I was…sold by my parents," she said. "I didn't have a choice. I had to practice my faith in secret."

"I can't imagine how hard that was for you," said Heinrich. "You are in a safe place now."

"I certainly don't feel like I am," she grumbled.

"These peasants are so ungrateful," whispered Friedrich. "There's no way she's going to—"

"If you give us the information that we need, I will take care of your accommodations, ma'am," promised Heinrich. "You have my word." She sighed.

"Alright. What do you want to know?" she asked.

"Tell me about your husband," he said. "Preferably his name."

"If I do, it wouldn't matter," she said. "Prussians still only have one name. His name is not uncommon, so finding him solely on his name is useless."

"I knew you wouldn't talk," Friedrich piped up. "If you don't start telling us what we need to know, we're going to have to use other means of getting that information out of you."

"I will give information about my husband if you promise me two things," she said. "The first is that you let my children and I live out our days in peace. Give us our accommodations here and a means to support ourselves since my husband is missing."

"I already promised that ma'am," Heinrich agreed. "By the Lord's name, I promise that you and your children will be cared for by the church."

"Thank you," she said. "Now for my second condition…"

"Second condition?" Friedrich snapped. "You are not in a position to be negotiating with us, peasant!"

"I have vital information that you need," she said. "I have the upper hand here. Anyway, my second request is that you are not to execute my husband if you find him."

"What!" Friedrich scoffed. "That's absurd!"

"I cannot guarantee that, ma'am," Heinrich said. "If your husband has committed crimes against God, then he must be punished."

"Can God not forgive him?" she asked. "He is still an able-bodied soldier. We can baptize him."

"If you truly were forced against your will to marry him then why would you want to protect him?" Friedrich asked.

"If you truly are a Christian, why won't you just tell us his name?" Heinrich asked.

"Well, to be honest I'm still bitter about how I've been treated these past few days," said the woman. "And I still hold hope that my husband will convert to Christianity. My family has been torn apart, sir. Please, grant a Christian woman like me a chance to lead my husband down a righteous path if it's possible. Even though I was forced into the marriage, I don't want my children to be fatherless."

"Your husband was a barbarian!" started Friedrich. "Surely you can't possibly—"

"Fine," sighed Heinrich. "But only if you share whatever information I ask of you."

"Komtur, this is ridiculous," protested Friedrich. "We have the upper hand. We shouldn't conform to her stupid desires! Also, she's a peasant woman! What business does she have in talking to noblemen like this? And how do we know she's not lying? She may even be a witch!"

"Did I mention my husband knows Herkus Monte personally?" she added. Heinrich looked at Friedrich.
"Offering you and your children freedom is enough," Friedrich said.
"You are in no position to be negotiating, especially with a noble!"

"Fine then. Good luck finding him." Heinrich looked like he was about to give in, but Friedrich put a hand on his shoulder, assuring him that he knew how to handle this. "I don't like the way I was treated. Surely, you can't blame me for being upset," she said.

"Wait," Friedrich interrupted, "you said your husband is currently missing. How do you know that?"

She blinked. "What do you mean, how do I know?"

"You shouldn't know that information if you never told us to check for your husband," he noticed. "If you told us, we would have his name. How do you know that he isn't currently in captivity?"

"I…was told that no one was found in the hospital," she hesitated. "Which was where my husband was at the time of the attack."

"Why was he in the hospital?" Heinrich interrogated.

"He was ill," she revealed. "He had a horrible sickness. I was told that there were no ill people among the captives, meaning my husband is missing or dead."

Friedrich paused for a moment. *No, it couldn't possibly be…*

"A sickness…" Friedrich pondered out loud. "He could have rushed out of the infirmary and joined the battlefield. Have you thought of that?"

"He was horrendously ill for months!" she argued. "He was in no condition to fight! But there's a chance that idiot might have jumped on the battlefield anyways…"

"What kind of sickness was it?" Friedrich asked.

"Honestly, I have never seen anything like it," she admitted. "He was always tired, falling unconscious, and throwing up blood." Friedrich knew he was getting closer to the truth.

"You have children, right? Two of them?"

"Yes."

"Your husband was a soldier right? One who fought with Herkus Monte?"

"Yes."

Friedrich pondered for a moment.

"Brother Friedrich, is this going anywhere?" Heinrich asked.

"I may not need her to tell me his name or a description," Friedrich whispered. "I think I have an idea of who this man is." He turned back to the woman.

"Your house. Describe the house you lived in with your husband and children."

"My house? It looked like every other house in the city. Though our house was closer to the forest. It was made out of wood. A dark wood. There was a large willow tree behind it."

Friedrich knew he was close. Everything seemed to match. He just needed one more detail. But what could he ask her? *There has to be something I can ask that will confirm or deny my suspicions. I just need one physical trait. One unique trait. But asking her to describe his appearance would be too forward. She would never answer that. I have to be clever in how I ask this next question. What can I say to get her to tell me about his appearance? What is something unique about that infidel?* Friedrich's eyes suddenly lit up. He had the perfect question.

"How often did your husband shave his face?" Friedrich interrogated.

"Huh? What kind of question is that?"

"Just answer my question."

"...I don't think he ever shaved his face at all," she replied, thinking.

"Why is that?"

"I don't know. He never needed to."

"Because he couldn't grow facial hair?" Friedrich smirked. She was quiet. "Your husband has green eyes, doesn't he?" Her eyes widened.

"W—What makes you think that?" she asked. "You have never met my husband!"

"Oh, but I have," he replied. "I know exactly who your husband is."

"You do?" Heinrich asked Friedrich. He nodded.

"He was looking for you. Saying he had a duty to protect you. Lucky for you, he managed to escape from me. Don't worry. I guarantee that he's alive."

"He is?"

"Her husband's name is Gailimantas, son of Sarginus," Friedrich said. "He's a very dangerous man. Almost as dangerous as Herkus himself. You can continue your interrogation. My work here is done."

The woman just sat there frozen, in complete shock at Friedrich's deductive skills.

"Friedrich, how do you know—"

"It's the same man I told you about on the way here," Friedrich replied, heading towards the door, a smile plastered on his face. *Finally! This is my chance to get even with him! My chance to finally settle the score! To finally put this infidel in his place.* "Oh. And don't worry about your husband. I promise I won't have him executed," added Friedrich. "After what your husband has done, I'll make sure he suffers a fate worse than death."

Gailimantas awoke to a dimly lit forest again. He didn't know why, but he kept waking up at sunset and would get tired midday. Today, he was awake earlier than expected, since the sky was still mostly blue instead of pink, violet, and orange. Unless the sun was shining on his face, he would sleep through most of the day. Finding a shady place to sleep wasn't hard as of late. But when he came to a clearing, the sun was so bright and intense, he could hardly move unless he was covered by some sort of shade. Normally, he had no problems sleeping in uncomfortable places, but recently that was becoming impossible. However, traveling at night had not been an issue for him. He could see surprisingly well in the dark forest, and he encountered fewer problems at night. Wild animals were easier to find, and it was easier to keep warm since he always carried a torch with him. Best of all, he could avoid the Teutonic Knights by traveling during night time. He had two encounters with them so far, and they seemed to know his name for some reason. So every night he would hide himself before he slept. Gailimantas had been living in the forest for a few weeks now and so far, there was no sign of his comrades. Even though Pomeus had brought him to the forest, he had no luck finding him so far. He found a stream after a few weeks and kept following it, hoping to find some town near it.

On top of all of this, he had a terrible toothache that made his entire upper jaw throb in pain. It was mild at first, but as days progressed, it worsened to the point where he could hardly eat. He had to mash up whatever fruit he could find with a rock or fillet his meat into tiny thin strips. Gailimantas took a thick branch that would later become his torch and continued following the stream. Surely he would stumble across someone or some kind of civilization.

As he continued on, the pain in his jaw worsened. The soreness would come in waves. Every ten to fifteen minutes or so, a storm of pain would hit. Mild at first, but as the sun sank lower, he had to stop whenever the aches hit. By the time the sky was pink and orange, the agony was so unbearable, he had to stop and rest. This pain was worse than it ever was before and lasted much longer. He did everything he could not to scream in fear of attracting enemies or scaring away his later dinner. When the pain finally subsided, he began to think clearly again. *Water,* he thought. *Nice, cold water should ease this pain, right? Water is full of benevolent spirits. Surely they will calm this toothache.* Gailimantas turned to the stream next to him and noticed that the stream had become incredibly shallow, so shallow that water merely trickled along the rocks. *My mouth feels…fuller. But it could just be from the throbbing pain.* He examined his surroundings for another source of water. To his luck, he saw his saving grace out of the corner of his eye. A small, placid pool reflected the trees and sunset around it like a watery mirror. Gailimantas hurried over to the pool, scooped up the water in his hands and began to drink, the cool water slightly numbing his pain. Gailimantas stopped to catch his breath. His jaw was slightly throbbing as he watched the pool return to its placid state. *What is wrong with me? Am I still sick? No. This is something else. My teeth never ached like this before. I don't recall them ever like this. I thought the evil spirits had left my body.* When Gailimantas looked up, the pond had once more become a mirror.

Gailimantas looked at his reflection. His dirty, brown hair was down to his shoulders and needed to be washed. He had become thinner from the lack of available food. But something about him was somewhat alluring. Although he was dirty and had not eaten in a while, he did not look as terrible as expected. He gave a smile, as he often did when looking at his reflection. His smile quickly faded when he saw it. He stared closer at his reflection, thinking that what he was seeing was an illusion or a ripple in the water. In the water, it appeared as if he had long, pointed, white fangs. He stared at the pond for a while, trying to make sense of the image in front of him. He ran a finger along his teeth, feeling the elongated teeth on his finger tip before flinching after feeling a sharp prick. His finger held a slight imprint of the long canine, a slight dot of red marking the pointed end of the tooth. The reflection did not lie. He had fangs like a wolf. Like an evil spirit. Gailimantas wanted to scream, but his voice wouldn't come to him. It was as if he was being choked, but there was nothing around his neck. *What happened to me? What the hell is going on?* Gailimantas thought back to Friedrich before he attacked him. He thought about what he told him about being reborn as a revenant.

*I really did die…* Gailimantas trembled when he came to the realization. *I'm a corpse. I'm a reanimated corpse. I'm a revenant.* Gailimantas looked at his reflection again. He didn't look too different aside from the teeth. He didn't feel worse either. If anything, he felt better and more alive than before. He looked nothing like what was described in the stories he was told as a child. He wasn't bloated and his skin was a normal color instead of a dark red like the blood of the living. He looked very much alive, just like Friedrich did. But he knew deep down he wasn't human anymore. *Oh why did the gods let this happen? Why couldn't have I just died? I don't want to eat the blood and flesh of others! I don't want to be a monster! Why couldn't have I joined my family in the afterlife? Why am I stuck here? Maybe a cat or a wolf jumped over my corpse. Or maybe this is because I wasn't cremated properly. It's not my fault. Why do I have to suffer for this?* Friedrich's words then echoed in his head.

*Thanks to you leaving me there in the forest and running away like a coward, I was turned into this. And now you're going to pay.*

Gailimantas froze. Did Friedrich do this to him? Was this his way of getting back at him? Did he turn Gailimantas into a revenant like himself? Gailimantas's fear and panic turned into rage. One man had been the cause of all of his suffering. He took away his mother and his siblings, he took away his wife and family, and now he had taken his life and humanity. Gailimantas couldn't stand by anymore. *My priority is no longer to find Herkus. It is to find Friedrich von Rotenkreuz and take revenge for all he has done.* Gailimantas stood up and returned to the stream. *I realize now why the gods did this to me. I'm not here to take my revenge on the living. I'm here to take my revenge on the dead.*

# Chapter 13: Loss

The boar nibbled on the bush innocently, its tail flicking slightly. Its long tusks were intimidating, but the small berries it nibbled on made it seem docile. As sunset dawned on the forest, all was quiet and peaceful. Suddenly an arrow flew into the boar's side, shattering the peace. As the beast scrambled to its feet, another arrow hit it in the leg. It let out a squeal of pain. Gailimantas jumped out of his hiding place and tackled the boar, knife out and ready. But instead of finishing the boar off with a strike from his knife, instinct took over. With his long, sharp canines, he bit into the creature's neck, ravenously sucking the blood out of the pig. Soon, the boar fell to its side, the life drained out of it.

Gailimantas caught his breath before he grabbed the boar by the leg and dragged it back to his makeshift camp. It wasn't a big boar, but nevertheless he would cook the meat tonight for dinner. He had to change his direction after running into some Teutonic Knights a few days ago. He managed to slip away, but there was no way he was going to continue in that direction. He was following the river another way. He had been to Grewose before, but it was a long time ago. Not since his journey back from Kulm with his comrades. It was only slightly less than a day by horse. It shouldn't be too much longer on foot.

He continued until he found the fire pit he made. Gailimantas then started filleting the boar. The boar had been drained of every last drop of blood, so as usual, the meat was incredibly dry and brittle. But food was food.

Gailimantas heard a rustling from a distance behind him. It sounded like footsteps were coming towards him. The cooking would have to wait. He took out a large piece of cloth and spread it out on the ground. He gathered up whatever scraps of food that he had cut off and finished severing a leg of the boar, tying it up in the cloth before putting it in the hole in the tree behind him. He then climbed up the oak until he was high enough to see above, but still covered by leaves. He sat and listened to the footsteps approaching and the voices getting louder. As he identified the words, he realized that there were two people speaking Prussian. It was mostly one guy talking to another, the other person not responding to him.

"So Ardan shoots the deer in the butt. But not just in the butt. Up the butt. I have never heard a deer make a sound before, but now I know what a deer sounds like." The man then attempted to make a distressed deer noise. Gailimantas tried not to laugh from the story, knowing he had to stay quiet. He couldn't see the men, but just because they spoke his language didn't mean that they would automatically be his friends. They could be from an enemy tribe, though he could understand their dialect fine. Even if they were from his tribe, this could be their sacred forest. And if it was discovered that Gailimantas hunted there, there would be serious repercussions. Gailimantas knew that sacred forests held the spirits of their ancestors, thus it was forbidden to hunt there, and violators could suffer a bloody punishment. He hopped down to a lower branch to get a closer look, but the leaves still obscured his vision. He was only a couple meters from the ground, so if needed, he could jump out and run away quickly. His heart began to race when he heard the footsteps stop at his tree.

"Is that a freshly killed boar?"

"Something's weird about it though."

"Who would leave a perfectly good boar here like that?"

"Is that a fire? I think this is someone's camp."

Gailimantas recognized one of the voices. *Is that… Pomeus? Thank the gods! I've finally found him! But I don't want to startle him. What if he saw me die? What if he knows what I am? I hope he doesn't think I'm trying to kill him. What will I say? What will my excuse be?*

"Do you think the Teutonic Knights have been snooping around here?"

"I hope not."

"If they're searching this close to camp, this is bad news. Herkus isn't going to be happy. We're going to have to pack up and leave."

Gailimantas's heart began to beat faster at the mention of his leader's name. Uncontrollable joy began to take over Gailimantas's brain. *They found Herkus! Herkus is alive! By the gods, Herkus is alive!*

"They normally come in large armies. This looks like a camp for a couple of people."

"Who would be camping out here?"

"That would be me." Gailimantas slid down from the branches, startling Pomeus and another man he did not recognize.

Pomeus had a look of shock on his face, his jaw hanging open and his eyes as wide as the full moon. His beard and his hair had grown a lot since he last saw him, and he looked like he was frozen in place. His companion looked confused at Pomeus's behavior. Gailimantas just decided to put on a brave face and smile, pretending as if nothing ever happened.

"Gailimantas… Is that really you?"

"The one and only," he replied. "I'm so happy I found you. I've been out here for days." Pomeus grabbed Gailimantas by the arms as if to feel that he was actually there.

"By the gods… I thought you were dead…" he gasped. "I swore I saw you—"

"You must have been mistaken," Gailimantas cut him off. Pomeus had a relieved smile on his face.

"Well I'll be! You seem like a new man! Where has all this confidence and youthful vigor come from?" Pomeus seemed to return to his normal cheerful self.

"I woke up feeling as youthful as ever," Gailimantas explained. "My illness was gone, my wounds no longer bothered me… The gods have healed me from my ailments."

"Well that's great!" Pomeus said. "Because we need all the men we can get." He turned to his companion. "Skiris, this is Gailimantas, son of Sarginus. I know I've told you about him." Skiris waved a greeting, not saying a word. "Come. Let's bring you back to camp."

"Let's bring the boar," reminded Gailimantas. "We'll have food for the evening."

"I'll carry it," Skiris offered. Gailimantas gathered his leftovers from the tree and followed Pomeus. "Thanks for the boar."

"Our camp isn't too far away from here," Pomeus commented. "You got lucky."

"I heard you two talking about Herkus," Gailimantas began. "Is he really—"

"He's alive and with us," Pomeus finished. "He'll be happy to see you." Gailimantas felt young inside for a moment, excited to see his master again. Well, technically Herkus was merely a commander, but Gailimantas would serve under him as a slave if he could. "We built a makeshift camp in the woods and have been staying there for the past few weeks," Pomeus continued. "Have you just been living in the woods on your own?"

"Pretty much."

"We've been holding our own. So far, no sign of any knights, but we know they're looking for us."

"You haven't seen any Teutonic Knights?" Gailimantas asked, raising an eyebrow.

"You have?" Pomeus asked.

"I have encountered them more than three times over the past few days," Gailimantas said. "They even know my name. It seems they have a bounty out for me."

"Then we should be extra careful," said Pomeus.

The three arrived at a small camp in a thick part of the forest. Six makeshift tents made out of large cloths hung from the branches. A fire pit was in the center, a man currently working to start a fire for the night. The camp seemed barren, as there were only four men in sight. From the larger, thicker trees, ropes dangled down from the branches, showing that some men had to sleep in the trees.

"Things are not going so well right now," Pomeus said somberly. "Our numbers are very low at the moment." Gailimantas nodded, understanding. "There's barely even ten of us."

"I'm going to start cooking," said Skiris. Pomeus led Gailimantas to the makeshift tent by the biggest oak.

"Oy Herkus!" Pomeus called. "We have another man in our arsenal." Gailimantas froze when Herkus locked eyes with him. He had encountered this man numerous times and even had personal conversations with him, but he was still awestruck whenever this man graced him with his presence. Herkus not only looked older, but he looked tired. Gailimantas could understand why. Upon making eye contact with him, Herkus's eyes contained a light of hope and relief.

"I'm not sure if I can be much of help but—" started Gailimantas.

"One single soldier makes a magnanimous difference in this case," Herkus said, putting a hand on Gailimantas's shoulder. "Thank you for your contribution." Gailimantas hadn't seen Herkus in a while, so he forgot the energetic feeling he experienced every time he talked to him.

"What are your plans sir?" Gailimantas said diligently. "Your wish is my command!"

"My current plan is to regroup our numbers until we have enough to stand a chance," Herkus replied, a tone of discouragement lining his words. "We were so close. We almost had them. We crushed their will to succeed, we crushed their dreams, and we almost forced the Teutons out. But they still managed to turn the tides on us." Herkus's fists were clenched in anger. "But, we have been in worse positions before. And we will turn the tides once again. Although our numbers are few, we shall work together with other tribes and rise up once again!"

"But we don't have time to gather troops sir!" Gailimantas blurted. Herkus cocked his head. "I recently encountered Teutonic Knights not that far from here. They're going to find our camp eventually."

"How many were there?"

"They traveled in packs of three or four," Gailimantas informed him. "And they seem to be looking for you and me."

Herkus thought for a moment. "Pomeus, tell everyone that tomorrow morning we're packing up camp and leaving the area," he ordered.

"Yes sir," said Pomeus.

"Herkus!" Skiris said, entering the tent.

"By the gods, what is it?"

"Dinner is ready."

"Dinner?"

"Gailimantas brought a large boar for all of us," Skiris added. Herkus turned to Gailimantas with a smile, as if his stress was slowly ebbing away.

"We'll be right there," he said, exiting the tent. Herkus turned back to Gailimantas. "It is good to have you with us again, Gailimantas." As Gailimantas watched his commander exit, he felt energy build up inside him again. Herkus not only remembered him, but was appreciative to have him back. He felt like cheering in excitement, but held back as he didn't want to cause a scene.

*Perhaps this afterlife won't be so bad. Maybe this is why the gods brought me back. If I am to be an eternal servant to Herkus, then I will gladly accept that fate.*

"So, have you found their camp yet?"

"Unfortunately not, Komtur," Simon told Heinrich. "However, we seem to encounter them all in a specific area. I have marked it all on the map here." Simon handed Heinrich a map. Heinrich gently unrolled it to view a map of the coastal area dotted with small red marks. "They keep attacking around this area, so the camp shouldn't be too far away."

"It's a start at least," noted Heinrich. "You are doing well, Brother Simon. How are your men holding up?"

"We have lost a few to these barbarians, but so far, we have managed to fend off most of their attacks," Simon explained. "But there have been many times where my men have been outnumbered and forced to retreat."

"Would you like more men?"

"That would be greatly appreciated, Komtur," nodded Simon.

"I'll consider it," said Heinrich. "I just wish I knew where all these Prussians were coming from. If there's another settlement nearby, then why wouldn't we know?"

"Maybe it was recently built?" guessed Simon.

"But how would they build something like that so quickly?" wondered Heinrich. "I'll analyze this. You are dismissed, Brother Simon."

"Yes sir. God bless you." Simon bowed as he left.

"God bless you." Heinrich stared at the map in front of him. *That man always works so hard. He's such a genuine man, and an interesting one. Every time he goes into town, he talks to peasants about the Lord's word. I hope he doesn't overwork himself.*

Heinrich's thoughts were interrupted with another knock on his door. "Come in," he said. Friedrich entered the Komtur's office. "Ah, Brother Friedrich! Welcome."

"I just wanted to make sure my arrangements were set," Friedrich stated.

"Tomorrow you leave for Swintamīstan, right?"

"Yes," Friedrich said. "I am returning back to my troops there. Brother Bernard seems to be holding things together while I'm gone, but I must return to my duty. This is my mission."

"How is the search going?"

"When I went to check last time, they said that they saw a clean faced man in the forest, but he ran away from them," Friedrich reported. "They told me he's really fast. The last week I was there, there was no sight of him. I have a bad feeling he's fled the area."

"How about we go to the church and pray for your success?" said Heinrich. "We can ask Father Vincent to bless you before your journey."

"Evening mass is about to start in an hour. Let's hope he has time."

"And then I asked Skiris, if you didn't kill this, who did? And he said, my wife. I questioned him about that and… What exactly happened, Skiris?"

"Ugide told the kids that she saw a deer while going to the river to bathe. She then said that Perkūnas sent a lightning bolt from the sky and struck it dead for her. She probably just killed it herself, but she really loves to tell stories, doesn't she?"

"Your second wife is a strange one, Skiris."

"I know. Ugide is very young. Only about 14 summers. But she gets along with the other one well."

"Where did you buy her from, again?"

"Twangste."

Gailimantas and his friends were dragging back a deer for dinner. He felt a sense of pride with the deer he shot. He felt like a dog bringing back a rabbit to its master as a sign of love. Herkus would be so happy, and it would take his mind off the dire situation. After all, there were only about ten of them left in total and he was worried too. But this deer would be a distraction from their hardships. Tonight they would have a feast that would fill them with hope and motivation.

"A month or so ago I was out hunting and I saw this creature I've never seen before in my life," said another soldier.

"What did it look like?" Pomeus asked.

"It looked like a wolf, but it was twice as big as any wolf I've ever seen," he described. "When it stood on its hind legs, it was taller than me!"

"A wolf man?" guessed Skiris. "Like the ones that are born if a fox jumps over your corpse?"

"Maybe…" he replied. "Either way I don't want to run into that thing again."

"What was it doing?" Pomeus asked. "Was it docile?"

"Far from it," continued the soldier. "It was devouring a cattle farm. By far, it was the most terrifying creature I've ever seen."

"Annuse once told me she saw something similar in her dreams when she was little," added Gailimantas. "Maybe you were dreaming?"

"I know I wasn't," replied the man. "I know what I saw and what I ate for dinner that night."

"Perhaps your wife wasn't dreaming, Mantas," said Skiris. A pit of worry began to form in Gailimantas's stomach. *Am I going to become one of those things? Are these fangs just the beginning? Am I going to turn into some horrific wolf creature and kill everyone? Well, it's been almost a year since I was resurrected. So far I've just had to sneak out and drink boar and deer blood every now and then. Maybe an animal didn't jump over my corpse. Hopefully I don't ever turn into one of those monsters...* Gailimantas slowed down as he saw his friends stop.

"What's going on?"

"Shhh!"

"Wha—"

"Get down! I hear voices!" Skiris hissed.

Everyone quieted down. Gailimantas could hear voices. They seemed to be excited male voices, cheering in a foreign language. Gailimantas felt his blood run cold when he recognized the ugly, throaty language that the Teutons spoke. He carefully crept towards the camp and carefully peeked through the bushes. Several white invaders stood above the two dead comrades that were in the camp. The knights were gathered around a large oak tree near the center of the camp, cheering with glee as a knight drew his sword. The knight charged towards the tree and slashed at its branches a sword. Gailimantas moved so he could see better, wondering why the enemy knights were cheering over stabbing a tree with a sword. Then he saw that the sword was covered in crimson blood. He was confused until he looked at the large oak tree. The sight almost made him drop to his knees in despair.

Tied to the tree in the distance was a body, laying limp, swinging on a rope with the breeze. Life had already left the man who hung from the sturdy tree branch, blood steadily dripping down his side. Hanging from his neck from the gallows with a gaping wound in his side was none other than Herkus Monte himself. Gailimantas felt the air being choked from his lungs by an invisible force as he watched the life drain from his master's body. The mix of cheers and laughter from the Teutonic Knights faded as Gailimantas felt his entire world come to a grinding halt and his hope vanish from his heart. He just sat there, cursing himself for not being there to protect his master and enraged that these knights were laughing at his misery.

Gailimantas snapped out of his daze when an arrow went through one knight's head. He turned to see Pomeus with his bow, looking just as enraged as he was. Gailimantas's despair turned to rage as he impulsively drew his sword and charged towards the knights, screaming in fury. The knights outnumbered them all, but Gailimantas knew that he could take them. How dare they kill Herkus? The savior, his master, the man who would save his people from these invaders was now gone and they had cheered! Gailimantas was determined to cut their tongues out for celebrating Herkus's death. The first two knights quickly drew their swords and charged back at him. Two on one. Gailimantas knew that he was going to be disadvantaged during this fight, but he didn't care. It was about six of them against at least twelve knights. He had no armor to protect himself, but all he could think about was making them suffer. He swung at the first one, only to miss and have the second one hit him in the knee. The second one raised his sword to kill him but was suddenly hit in the shoulder with an arrow. Gailimantas took the opportunity to slice at his leg, causing the knight to fall to the ground. Gailimantas barely reacted in time, missing the second knight's sword. Out of desperation and instinct, he glared at the knight, drew his fangs, and let out an intimidating hiss. The knight's face turned ghost white as his body froze, giving Gailimantas the opportunity to fling the sword from the knight's hands and tackle him to the ground. Forgetting about his sword, he proceeded to beat up the man with his fists, delivering blow after blow to the man's head.

When the man was passed out in his own blood and his knuckles began to hurt, he stopped. He then turned to the other knight, who was trying to limp away, blood pouring out of his wound. Gailimantas pounced on him, wrapping his hands around the man's neck and began to squeeze as tight as he could. As he listened to the life choke out of the man beneath him, the chaos around him fading, he felt a sort of pride for getting retribution for Herkus. With every gasp for air and futile struggle, he felt no sympathy for this man and felt joy in watching him slowly suffocate. The man stopped fighting back after a few seconds. Gailimantas saw another sword out of the corner of his eye, but the knight quickly fell to the ground as Pomeus' sword went through his chest. Pomeus had a proud smile on his face, like he always did as he fought on the battlefield. That smile quickly disappeared as he was shot in the back with an arrow that pierced through his chest. After he fell to the ground, Gailimantas realized that he was the only man left standing. Five knights surrounded him, slowly closing him in, proud and sly smirks on their pale faces. Behind them were the bodies of his comrades and four other knights. His head clouded with despair, Gailimantas drew his fangs and let out a long, sinister hiss as a final, desperate act of intimidation. As the men stopped in their tracks, Gailimantas took his chance to flee into the woods.

Gailimantas ran as fast as he could away from the camp. He dashed through the forest, leaping over fallen logs, hopping over springs, and dodging trees as he sprinted for his life. *I let my emotions affect me on the battlefield. I should have just stabbed those guys! But...I wanted them to suffer. I suppose this is my punishment.* When he couldn't hear voices or movements anymore, he collapsed in exhaustion. Despair washed over him once more and hatred began to cloud his heart. He considered taking out his sword and driving it through his own chest. After all, Herkus, Pomeus, his family, and all hope he had to live was gone. It had all vanished with a glint of steel. Instead, he merely rose to his feet once more. *I'm already dead, remember? This will be futile. Besides, I still have a mission from the gods.* He stood up and began to walk further away from where he came. *For destroying my home, separating me from my wife and children, taking away my best friend, robbing me of my master, and turning me into a demon… I will not rest until his soul suffers in the fiery pits of the underworld and his body is eviscerated so he can never return. I will cut out his tongue so he cannot desecrate my beautiful mother tongue anymore. I will slice off his hands and fingers so that no one else will die by his mighty sword. I will cut out his black pit of a heart and sacrifice it to Peckols so that he can return to the underworld where he belongs. I will not have my peace until Friedrich von Rotenkreuz pays for what he has done to me.*

# Chapter 14: Fox

Herr Friedrich! Herr Friedrich!"

Friedrich looked behind him to see a young novice running towards him, his high-pitched, youthful voice repeating his name ecstatically.

"What ails you, Brother Andreas?" Friedrich asked. Andreas von Jungnau was about 14 and had just joined the Order, his first mission being Friedrich's quest to find Gailimantas while he was on probation. Friedrich found Brother Andreas's appearance unusual. His eyes were unusually dark to the point where his pupils couldn't be seen, similar to those from the far South or far East. He was apparently of noble German birth, but Friedrich wondered about his origins. Given that the boy could read and write before becoming a page, he had to have come from some money. Nevertheless he was a very generous boy, always offering to fetch water and other things that were needed. It was as if he didn't quite grow out of his page stage yet. Friedrich knew he shouldn't play favorites amongst his squires, but Andreas was definitely his favorite. He never gave him any sass or attitude and was always so happy to do anything, even if it was cleaning horse poop. He couldn't wait until his probation was over so he could bring him to the battlefield.

"We have just received glorious news!" Andreas replied, slightly out of breath. "I have been asked to bring you to the city square as soon as possible."

"What is the news?"

"Brother Bernard forbade me from telling you," Andreas replied, failing to hold back a smile. "You have to come to the center of town." Friedrich decided to go along with the boy's antics. After all, he had nothing better to do.

"Alright. Lead the way."

Andreas gave a small hop in excitement.

"You won't believe what happened! I saw these knights ride up to Swintamīstan with Brother Gottfried—"

"Wasn't he captured?" Friedrich asked.

"He was. But the knights from Christburg rescued him!" Andreas replied.

"Christburg? That's awfully far away. What are knights from Christburg doing all the way near Balga?" asked Friedrich.

"I'm not supposed to tell you that yet," admitted Andreas. "But you can find out now."

"There you are, brother," said Brother Bernard as he approached Friedrich. Brother Bernard was a half brother in charge of keeping the men in order while he was away. Everyone else in his troop was already gathered in the square, all in an upbeat mood and chattering with excitement. There were also three Ritterbrüdern and two novices amongst his own that he did not recognize.

"Who are these men?" Friedrich asked. "What are they doing here?"

"This is Brother Josef von Joachimsthal, Peter von Buchau, and Michael von Blumenberg," said Bernard. "They are members of the Komturei in Christburg."

"I learned from my Komtur that you were also searching for Herkus Monte and his comrades," Josef explained. "On my way to Balga, I ran into your men. Perhaps you can relay my message for me."

"They have delivered us some joyous news!" a younger knight cheered.

"So that's why you all seem excited," Friedrich smirked. He had a feeling that something wonderful had happened, since his troop had never been this excited before. They always were forlorn, resenting their failure to capture Gailimantas. The men turned to Brother Josef from Christburg.

"About a month ago, a few of us brothers of Christburg found Herkus Monte in the forest, alone in his camp," Josef announced. "So we surrounded Herkus Monte and killed him!" The crowd of brothers cheered loudly. Friedrich's heart skipped a beat. Could it really be true? Was Herkus Monte truly dead? Was the thorn in their side really gone? Without Herkus, victory in this crusade was secured. After a lifetime of fighting, watching his friends die at the hands of heathens, and almost losing hope in their cause, God had finally answered their prayers. He was a bit disappointed, as he wouldn't be able to take revenge on Gailimantas, but he knew that he couldn't let a selfish desire like that overtake this glorious news. The crusade was all but won now, and Friedrich couldn't believe it.

"Praise God… You all have done the Lord's work. On behalf of the Teutonic Order, your service is appreciated."

"It is our honor sir," Josef bowed.

"We ambushed him when he was alone, and then we hung him from the tree right away!" added Michael. "We were worried about him escaping again, so we executed him on the spot."

"What about his men?" Friedrich asked.

"We killed most of them," Michael said. "But one or two may have escaped."

"How many were dead?" Friedrich asked.

"About ten or so men, including Herkus," Michael answered.

"I wouldn't call those things men," Josef asked.

"What do you mean, Brother Peter?" Michael asked.

"One man was definitely not human," Peter answered. "He had fangs like a wild animal, and he *hissed* at me."

"…Fangs?" repeated Friedrich, feeling dread begin to bubble up in his stomach.

"He almost beat Brother Adalbert to death with his bare hands. I managed to hold him off, but he escaped," Peter continued.

"What did he look like?" Friedrich demanded.

"He was tall and slender in figure with unkempt brown hair," Peter said. "He had these merciless green eyes. But the strangest of all, he was the only clean-shaven man there."

"And you let him get away?" Friedrich snapped.
"That demon was trying to kill me—" started Peter.

"That was our target! Gailimantas, son of Sarginus!" Friedrich barked.

"*That* was your target?" Peter asked. "You were hunting a demon?"

"Brother Peter was not aware of our mission, brother," Bernard informed.

"Besides, Herkus Monte is dead!" said Peter. "What do we need Gailimantas for?"

"I would have given up the mission with Herkus's death, but now that we know that this man is a demon, it is too dangerous to let him run loose!" Friedrich lectured. "He could hurt or kill innocent Christians! We can't let one of Satan's spawn run freely! We need to hunt this creature down and make him pay for his crimes."

"We have encountered this man a couple of times after we killed Herkus, but every time he managed to escape us," Michael informed.

"The last time we spotted him, he was heading North, so he may be in this area soon."

"He's like a fox!" a younger knight added. "He's easy to spot and identify, but he's clever, cunning, and fast and he escapes every time!"

"I don't care what it takes!" barked Friedrich. "Find this man and capture him! Alive." He took a deep breath. "You three, keep a lookout. Congratulations on killing Herkus Monte. I shall inform Balga at once." Friedrich headed towards the door, but stopped short of the exit. He turned back to Josef. "You are from Joachimsthal?"

"Yes."

"You don't happen to know a young boy by the name of Weirich von Rotenkreuz, do you?" asked Friedrich.

"He is my step-brother's son," Josef replied. "My sister is taking care of him."

Friedrich smiled. "Next time you see him, tell him to take good care of my nephew," he said, waving as he exited the building.

The conversation replayed in Friedrich's head as he rode back to Balga. This was evidence that Gailimantas had been bitten more than once and now he was even more of a threat. *Great. The Komtur is going to have my head! How does this man slip away from us every time? He really is a fox, deceitful and elusive…* Friedrich thought about what his men had told him about Gailimantas and began to think about how fox-like he was. Cunning was definitely one word to describe Gailimantas. He had pulled tricks on him in the past, like when he tricked him into following him into the forest where he would be surrounded by pagans. Fast was another suitable word, as he ran like the wind, even when he was terribly ill. Clever and elusive was another way to describe him from what he had been told. But like a fox, Gailimantas was also cowardly. He ran away during the majority of their fights. He left Friedrich in the forest when he was attacked by a nachzehrer. He ran away from fighting Friedrich last time the two faced each other. Gailimantas even looked like a fox with his long, slender face, tall, lanky body, and long reddish-brown hair. He was a fox. And Friedrich was an angry farmer, tired of the fox's trickery. The fox that had bit at his heels, eaten his chickens, and tormented his livestock would do so no more, for he intended to trap him and finally slay him.

Friedrich saw the Balga fortress ahead. He was not looking forward to going back to the Komtur and reporting what just happened at first, but as he approached the stables, he realized that this was an excuse to keep the hunt for Gailimantas going since he was now a greater threat. *Perhaps God has arranged this so that I may get my comeuppance,* he thought. He led his horse to its stall and continued towards the hospital. He hadn't seen his brother in a few weeks, so he figured he would check up on him first. Besides, it was a way to avoid telling the Komtur there was another nachzehrer on the loose.

As Friedrich approached his brother's bed, he could hear audible hacking and gasping, as if someone was struggling to breathe and was suffering in pain. He stopped at the bed. His heart sank when he saw it was completely empty. He quickly hailed a nearby nurse.

"Hey! Where is Wilhelm?" asked Friedrich.

"Wilhelm?" said the nurse.

"Wilhelm von Rotenkreuz!"

"Oh. The traveler? He's in the bed across from this one," she replied. Friedrich sighed in relief, knowing that he was merely a forgetful dolt and his brother was still alive. When he turned around, however, the sight that he found wasn't much more pleasing. The loud sounds of coughing and agony were coming from Wilhelm, who looked like he was on the brink of death. All the color had drained from Wilhelm's face.

Sweat dotted his forehead, but he shook like he was freezing. His chest heaved dramatically, as if taking a single breath was like running up a hill. Wilhelm tried to put on a smile as he saw his brother, but it twisted into a grimace of pain.

"Brother, what has happened to you?" Friedrich exclaimed.

"Fritz…" Wilhelm sounded like he was going to run out of breath with every word he said. "You're back early…"

"Wilhelm, what happened? I thought you were okay. Why are you—"

"A lot has happened…since I last saw you..." Wilhelm rasped. "I can't even feel my arm anymore. All my insides hurt. I can't eat. I can hardly breathe or sleep… And my body…" Tears welled up in his brother's eyes. "I feel that I've already died and that I'm experiencing Hell on Earth. And my arm… My arm..."

"I'm sure your arm isn't that bad." Wilhelm removed the sheets that were covering his body. Friedrich almost threw up when he saw Wilhelm's arm. It was swollen and had changed to a variety of colors. The wound was black, purple, and green with disgusting yellow pus oozing out of it. Friedrich quickly turned away at the putrid smell of rotting flesh. The sight was so gruesome, worsened by the fact that this was happening to his own brother. Wilhelm covered his wound again.

"Horrifying isn't it?" Wilhelm rasped.

"What kind of evil spirit is this?"

"Apparently, not an uncommon one," Wilhelm answered. "But the healers have told me that no one has survived from it." Friedrich's heart stopped. He didn't want to accept it. He couldn't accept it. His brother— the only family he had left—was dying in front of his eyes. He could see how much his brother was suffering and felt so powerless in his situation. Of course, he could always bite him…

"Wilhelm, you'll be fine. I promise I'll find a way to heal you," Friedrich said, taking his brother's cold hand and holding it tightly. "I will pray however long you need me to. I will sacrifice my own health if I must. I love you more than the Lord loves His children. I'll find a way to help you. I promise!" Friedrich began to debate with himself. *Should I do it? Can I do it? Heinrich told me to let him live a life free from sin. To let him be a normal human. If I do this he will become what I am. But here he lies suffering. He's dying a slow, agonizing death. I have to bite him. It's the only way!*

"Wilhelm, can you close your eyes for a moment?" he started. Wilhelm obeyed.

"What's going on?"

"You'll see. Just keep your eyes closed."

Wilhelm squeezed his eyes shut. Friedrich came closer, trying to ignore the rancid stench. He drew his fangs.

*Let him be a man of God, free from darkness. Don't force this burden onto him just because you don't want him to die.* Heinrich's words echoed in Friedrich's head, causing him to hesitate. *Do I really want to force this onto my brother? Could I really bring myself to do that? Am I really thinking of his well being? Or am I thinking of my own selfishness? Would this be something that Wilhelm would want? To never be able to let the sun warm his skin again? To live off of the lives of others? To become a demonic being?* Friedrich withdrew his fangs, wiping away a tear. He couldn't do that to his brother. His brother was like a pure white holy light, untainted by this curse, and he was a mass of purple shadows. Friedrich felt that if he touched this light, his shadows would snuff it out, tainting it with sin.

"I…I just want this to be over…"

Friedrich looked at Wilhelm again, who was rasping and coughing again. His eyes were still closed, tears streaming down his face. "Part of me just wants to die and get this over with," said Wilhelm. "I just want to end my physical and emotional suffering and meet my holy Father in Heaven but…" Wilhelm choked. "I can't do that to my son… I'm all he has. The only one who can carry on the family name. He's the reason

I'm here in the first place. The reason I'm suffering and dying here right now." He stopped to gasp for air, catching his breath. "I want to live, Fritz. I want to see my son. I want to be a father. I don't want him to grow up without his family like I did. I want him to have a father. I'm not ready to die yet…" Wilhelm was struggling to breathe while crying. Friedrich felt a warmth inside him. He felt a sense of closure that he needed. His hesitation and uncertainty vanished. He didn't feel like a shadow tainting a white light anymore. Now he was an eternal flame trying to save a dying candle from being snuffed out. He wasn't a demon in this case. This wasn't a selfish act. He had a duty. A duty to use his powers for good. A duty as a healer. *I understand now, God. I understand why You made me like this. I understand what You want me to do. I am not a demon. I am a protector of life.*

"Wilhelm, can you answer me something?"

"What is it?"

"You would do anything for your son, right?"

"Absolutely."

"Even if you had to sacrifice your place in Heaven?"

"Sacrifice my place in Heaven?"

"Keep your eyes closed."

"Okay."

"Would you commit sin for him to live?"

"…I would."

Friedrich drew his fangs once more. Only this time, he didn't hesitate. He put a sheet over his and his brother's heads, bit into his brother's neck, and began to feed. He felt his brother flinch, but Friedrich kept going. He didn't realize how hungry he was. Wilhelm's blood felt so refreshing, but somehow not as delectable as his other meals. He wasn't getting full as fast as he normally did. His hunger began to take over, and he tried to slurp up as much as he could. *What am I doing? I can't stop! This is my brother! I'm supposed to heal him! Stop! Stop!* Friedrich forced himself away from Wilhelm's neck, blood dripping down his chin. He stared at Wilhelm, his ragged breathing now completely still and his wheezing and gasping silent. Friedrich looked over Wilhelm's body again. *Is he…dead?* Friedrich quickly withdrew his fangs as soon as he heard footsteps. He tried to quickly wipe off the blood before greeting Sister Zoe.

"I can't have you in here right now—" said Sister Zoe.

"S—Sister…" Friedrich muttered, trying not to choke. Zoe looked at Wilhelm, crestfallen. She quickly rushed to his side, checking for signs of life. The look on her face confirmed Friedrich's fears.

"I'm so sorry," she said.

Friedrich sat down, withdrawing deep into himself. It was as if the roof of the infirmary had collapsed and crushed him as the sister pulled the sheet over Wilhelm's head. *I failed. I failed to heal him. I couldn't protect my little brother and I let my selfish hunger kill my own kin. I really am a monster! A creature of Satan that can't be redeemed! A foul creature that taints everything he touches.* He put his hands to his face and began to sob. *I truly am nothing more than a demon.*

# Chapter 15: Capture

Friedrich watched the steadily blurring scene of the grave keepers digging a hole for the body wrapped in a white cloth embroidered with a black cross. It was a temporary grave until Wilhelm's family decided if they wanted to move him. He felt like he was going to burst into tears again, but he held back as much as he could. He couldn't let his novices, his subordinates, see him in such a vulnerable state. Bawling like a girl would make him look incredibly weak. He had to look strong, no matter how much the guilt ate at him. The cloudy sky seemed to match his somber mood. *Dear God, why did this have to happen? Was this a lesson for me? I only tried to do what was right and now, Wilhelm is dead. I don't know what I'm supposed to do now. I know you have kept me alive for a reason but I feel like I have lost my sense of purpose. Ever since meeting Wilhelm again, my goal hasn't been just to take revenge on all the heathens anymore, but to do so with my brother at my side. Dear God, am I really a demon? I was only trying to do Your will, but I ended up becoming a murderer.*

"Are you alright, Brother Friedrich?" Friedrich felt the Komtur's hand on his shoulder. Friedrich had come to him last night, bawling about what had happened. Friedrich expected to be yelled at, punished even, but to his shock, Heinrich seemed to be sympathetic towards him, lending him an ear and a shoulder to cry on. Friedrich knew he didn't deserve it. Heinrich went with him to confession and sat with him as he prayed until curfew was called. Friedrich now saw him as more than just a father figure, but a best friend. Right now, he couldn't look him in the eye. Not after showing him such weakness. Friedrich felt ashamed not only at his actions, but at his reaction. Since Wilhelm received Vespers before he died, he was allowed to be buried the next morning. As the men began to carry the body to the pit, Friedrich felt another wave of emotions hit him. He had disappointed the Komtur so many times as of late, he felt like he was a child instead of an elder. He was a failure at his powers, he let Gailimantas escape with the knowledge of what he was, he turned Gailimantas into a nachzehrer, and now he killed his own brother. He hadn't even told Heinrich about that yet. Failure wasn't permanent, but it sure felt like it for Friedrich. It felt like this failure would haunt him for the rest of his life.

"Why?" he choked. "Why are you so sympathetic towards me? I've caused nothing but trouble for you and the Order ever since I was reborn. You said that failure wasn't permanent, but then why do I keep making these disastrous mistakes?"

"But Brother Friedrich, you have succeeded so many times in your lifetime," Heinrich reminded him. "The number of victories outnumbers your defeats. Why do you believe you are a failure?"

"I've succeeded in military victories, but I seem to monumentally fail at the things that truly matter," Friedrich continued. "My family and the safety of others, doing God's will… I would rather have lost every battle I led if it meant that I could have kept this from happening." Friedrich swallowed. Did he really mean what he said? Would he really give up everything he had accomplished in life for his brother? As the priests chanted their haunting Paternosters, the shallow hole in the ground was about halfway filled.

"I believe I know why God did this, Brother Friedrich," added Heinrich.

"Why?"

"Brother Friedrich, when I first met you, you had one goal: revenge on the pagans," said Heinrich. "All you cared about was destroying the enemy. Now you're saying you would throw that all away for your younger brother to be at your side. The Lord is trying to tell you that life is meant for more than just war."

Friedrich was quiet as the hole was filled to the top. The rest of the crowd began to disperse. He went to his brother's grave, careful not to step on the fresh dirt. Teutonic Knights were not allowed to have grave markers or emblems on their graves. Too prideful. They were servants of God who were too humble to have such petty things. But Wilhelm was a volunteer and never a member, so his coat of arms would be on his grave. All of Wilhelm's estate would still go to his son. Now that the last surviving member of his family was gone, Friedrich felt alone once again. But never before had he felt such despair. It was as if he had a chill in his heart that had formed a thick layer of ice. *Maybe I should just quit the Order. I know I made a vow to commit for life, but I doubt that applies to demons. What if Heinrich is wrong? What if we can't be redeemed? What if we're doomed as minions of Satan and Heaven is forever out of our reach? A monster like me doesn't belong here with holy men.*

Before he turned to walk away, he saw the dirt beneath him move. It was as if the dirt was being pushed from underneath. He swore it was his imagination, when he saw it again, this time more noticeably. Friedrich yelped, causing the priest's prayers to die down.

"What in the devil is going on?" Friedrich yelled. "The dirt just moved!" Those still in the area began to murmur. Friedrich looked at Heinrich. The Komtur smiled at him.

"I don't think you killed him Friedrich," Heinrich whispered. Friedrich then realized why the grave was moving. Friedrich felt life return to him as his heart skipped a beat. Quickly, Friedrich began to claw at the fresh dirt with his bare hands. Those around him gasped.

"Brother Friedrich!" a priest scolded. "Why do you desecrate a man's grave like this?"

"He's alive!" Friedrich yelled. "He's still alive!" The clerics whispered amongst each other. Friedrich turned to the enslaved gravediggers.

"Well don't just stand there!" Friedrich snapped. "Dig him up! Hurry!" The two men shrugged and grabbed their shovels. Friedrich felt not only relief, but joy. He hadn't failed. He had succeeded at what God wanted him to do. He wasn't a monster. He was a healer. He was a servant of God here to heal knights. "Can't you dig any faster?" Friedrich barked. The grave diggers just grumbled something in Prussian and continued digging.

Eventually, a figure in a white sheet popped out of the dirt. Wilhelm ripped off his cloth and collapsed on the side of the grave, gasping for air. His eyes were wide with panic as he examined his surroundings.

"I…I can breathe…" he gasped. "Where…Where am I?"

"Wilhelm!" Friedrich cheered, tightly embracing his terrified brother. "I thought the Lord had taken you for sure!"

"I'm…alive?"

Wilhelm was slowly coming out of his state of shock.

"It looks like they buried you while you were still alive! Like they did with Brother Diederich," he said, laughing and patting his shaken brother on the back. Friedrich looked around at the concerned clergy. "It's okay! A false burial! He's okay!" The priests nodded and began to scatter.

"Why did they think I died?" Wilhelm asked.

"Well, you were sick for a while, remember?" said Friedrich. Wilhelm reached around to hug his brother back, realizing what had happened.

"My arm… I can feel it. I can move it…" he gasped. "I'm cured! The Lord has cured me from my suffering!"

"Praise the Lord!" said Father Johannes. "He must have blessed you. Be sure to give Him your praises tonight."

"Of course," Wilhelm said. "I feel like I was never sick to begin with. Like I'm a new person. Like the Lord has breathed fresh new life into me."

"I told you I would find a way to heal you," said Friedrich. "I prayed and prayed all night."

"Thank you," Wilhelm said, smiling. "Fritz, I could not ask for a better brother."

Friedrich put on a smile, but inside, he knew that what was ahead was far from being trouble free. He now had a heavy responsibility for Wilhelm. He had to explain to him how he was no longer human, watch him suffer through changes, and teach him how to deal with his new life. But for now, it was a time to be joyful. It was a time to be grateful and appreciate his family while he could.

# 1273

Gailimantas wiped the blood from his chin as the body beneath grew colder. He looked at the man who lay in the snow, more still than a placid lake, drained of every last drop of blood that he had. His pale, gaunt face matched his white uniform now speckled with drops of red blood. Next to him was his comrade that Gailimantas had eaten earlier. The full moon illuminated the scene with a bright pale beam, shining off of the snow and muting the red blood to purple. He continued forward, leaving the scene behind him. He knew that the rest of the knights would eventually find their two fallen comrades, so he had to leave before he would be attacked. He stepped out into the clearing. The full moon was large tonight, leaving very little covered by shadows.

Gailimantas had fallen into a routine. Wake up at sunset, continue searching for a pagan town that wasn't conquered, find some poor lost traveler on the road and suck the life out of him, and rest when the sun comes up. When he couldn't find any human, he ate the nearest deer or boar he could find, even though humans tasted much better and gave him more energy. He realized that he didn't need to eat normal food as much as he needed blood, but it was easier for him to find food. Lately, he had come across more Teutonic Knights, so finding a tasty meal wasn't a problem. Neither was finding warm clothes for the winter. The Teutonic Knights wore very nice fur coats.

Gailimantas stopped when he heard howling in the distance. *Of course. The full moon is out tonight. Naturally wolves and other creatures will want to hunt.* The wolf howled again, but it didn't sound like a normal wolf. Something sounded off. *Don't wolves normally have packs? Why do I only hear one wolf?* Another sound echoed in his ears. This time, it was the sound of people. No. Not people. Germans. Teutonic Knights.

*"The infidel has to be around here somewhere! I know it was him who did it!"*

*"Our infidel?"*

*"Does it matter? He's an infidel nonetheless! No good Christian man would do this!"*

*"Let's split up."*

That was Gailimantas's signal to start moving. He turned back into the forest to go around the clearing, avoiding it just in case anyone was nearby. He carefully tiptoed across the snow, trying to be as silent as possible, looking for a tree to hide in, but having no luck finding a good climbing tree. When he did see one, it was always covered in snow, which would only hurt his stealth. Suddenly, he heard a massive disturbance in the forest. Something was coming towards him, shaking trees and crunching snow as it made its way over. Something big and fast. The moment he heard distant snarling, he took off running. All thoughts of being silent and subtle had vanished as he ran for his life, fearing that it was a bear or a pack of wolves. He could hear the sounds getting closer and closer. Whatever was chasing him was faster than a hare. He didn't know what was behind him, but whatever it was, it was massive and Gailimantas could not afford an encounter. He sprung over logs and stumps as he sprinted as fast as he possibly could through the dimly lit forest.

Gailimantas glanced behind him for a second. The sight behind him made him shudder. He expected to see a pack of wolves or a large mother bear. Instead, he nearly gasped at the sight of the monster behind him. Chasing him was what looked like a wolf, but it was almost twice as large. Its limbs were long and lanky. Long, dark fur covered its body, and despite its long body, it was quite muscular. The beast emitted short snarls with every leap. The creature was catching up to him fast. *By the gods. This thing is going to eat me! Wait, what am I doing? I'm already dead! But I don't want to experience the pain of getting mauled by that thing. Please, Deywis, help me!* Gailimantas was fast, but this monster was faster. Gailimantas knew he couldn't outrun a four-legged creature. He could hear the creature's breathing and snorting as it was right on his heels.

Suddenly Gailimantas felt his foot sink through the ground. He gasped in shock as he began to fall down. As he fell, he reached his arms out to grasp onto the stone walls, slowing himself down slightly. When he landed, he landed hard on his posterior. It hurt, but there was a pile of snow on the bottom to break his fall. He looked up to see he was in a hole several meters deep. He watched as the creature that had been chasing him jumped over the pit, missing him. He then heard its movements stop and held his breath as it began to tread back towards his direction. He began to shiver as the monster's sinister, glowing white eyes glared at him, saliva dangling from the side of its enormous muzzle. After a few moments of terror, the beast snorted and left, deciding that being trapped wasn't worth such a small meal. Gailimantas sighed in relief, his heart still pounding in his chest.

*What a beast! That thing could have torn me limb from limb!* He stared up at the hole above him. The hole looked possibly narrow enough for him to climb out of, but right now he just wanted to stay here for safety. *Perhaps I can just sleep in this hole tonight. I'll crawl out in the morning.* He shifted in the snow, trying to find a comfortable position to rest in. The hole was surprisingly comfortable. The walls blocked out the howling winter wind, warming him slightly. The snow beneath him was soft and comfy. He was safe from most predators. Eventually, he covered his face with another fur and managed to relax enough to get some sleep.

⚜

The morning sun shone on Gailimantas's face, making his skin tingle unpleasantly. He tried to block out the light with his hands, but to no avail. He opened an eye to see dirt and stone walls surrounding him, the blue sky directly above him with the sun slightly peeking in. *Oh yeah. I fell into a pit. Alright. The walls look easy enough to climb. Hopefully it's not too icy. I think I can get out of here.* Using the stones that jutted out just enough, he hoisted himself up to the top of the square pit. He rolled over onto the snow, resting after using his strength to climb out. *That really drained my energy, but that pit saved me.*

Gailimantas examined the large animal prints in the snow. The back feet looked like large wolf tracks. But the front prints were nothing like he had seen before. They looked like very large human hand prints with claws at the tips. He shivered. *Thank the gods for this hole.* The moment he stood up to leave, Gailimantas heard a man cry out behind him.

"Halt!"

Gailimantas whipped around. At least ten Teutonic Knights were right behind him, each cloaked in thick fur coats, armed with sharpened silver weapons and ready to pounce on him at any moment. *Crap! I'm surrounded.* The knights looked surprised when he turned around. They all whispered to each other in their ugly language.

*"Is that him?"*

*"No facial hair…"*

*"That's him alright."*

*"We found him!"*

*"You are surrounded, infidel! Come with us, Gailimantas, and we won't have to kill you,"* one knight said. Gailimantas tilted his head. He recognized his name but had no idea what this man was saying. He took a few steps towards the men, close enough to hear them. Then, with the little German he knew, he spoke to them.

*"I don't speak German,"* he said. It was the one German phrase Gailimantas had perfected as it was the most useful. The knights lowered their guard and turned to each other whispering. Some seemed shocked that Gailimantas spoke to them, while others were asking around to see if anyone knew Prussian. Gailimantas noticed that there was a lack of knights to the left of him. *Wait, I see an opening! I can dash through and escape!*

*"I don't know his language, do you?"*

*"Why would I know that unholy language?"*

*"No. What language does he speak?"*

*"I didn't think he would actually talk to us."*

*"Brother Ulrich, don't you know some Prussian?"*

*"Some, but it's not very good."*

*"I told you we should have brought some peasants with us!"*

*"Where's Brother Friedrich when you need him?"*

*"This is Friedrich von Rotenkreuz's mission. He should have been here to talk to the heathen."*

"Friedrich von Rotenkreuz?" Gailimantas couldn't understand most of what was said, but he knew that he recognized his nemesis's name. Everyone else turned their attention back to Gailimantas. *He must be the same Friedrich von Rotenkreuz, right? If they know where he is, they can take me to him! I won't have to search for him anymore. This will make my job a lot easier. But how do I make sure that they take me to him?* With the little German his wife taught him, he attempted to commune with these knights. *"Friedrich von Rotenkreuz. You know?"* he asked. The knights seemed taken aback, surprised at not only their target's ability to speak their language, but at the mention of their commander.

*"Friedrich von Rotenkreuz? He is leading this mission,"* a knight said slowly. Gailimantas didn't understand a word the knight had said. He sighed, trying again.

*"You and Friedrich von Rotenkreuz? Yes?"* he spoke slowly, making gestures with his fingers and nodding his head to indicate he wanted a yes or no answer. The knights hesitantly nodded in response. Gailimantas thought for a moment. *Now what should I say?*

*"I want Friedrich von Rotenkreuz,"* he attempted. *"You take I…"* He sighed. *I should have learned more German!* Giving up, he returned to Prussian. "I will willingly surrender if you take me to Friedrich von Rotenkreuz." Gailimantas began speaking more slowly, making hand gestures towards the knights. "I will give myself to you—I go with you—to see Friedrich von Rotenkreutz."

*"Oh! I kind of understood that!"* said a fresh young knight no older than 14 who came forward. "Talk slowly please." Gailimantas sighed in relief. He tried to formulate his words more simply.

"You all can capture me if I can see Friedrich von Rotenkreuz," he said slowly. The knight looked confused. "Capture. Um…" He mimed out his sentence again. "You all," he pointed at the knights. "You all can capture me." He made a tying motion with his hands. "If I can meet with Friedrich von Rotenkreuz." The young knight's eyes lit up, finally understanding. He said something in German to the rest of the knights, who reacted with shock.

"No problem," the boy squeaked. "Hands behind you."

Gailimantas complied as his hands were tied behind his back. He hated to surrender, but if it would get him to Friedrich faster, it was a sacrifice that he had to take. His goal was inches away from him. Paradise was within arm's reach. All he had to do was comply with what these knights wanted and he could finally rest in peace.

As of late, it was Friedrich's duty to monitor Wilhelm's symptoms, so that meant the two spent almost every day together. When Wilhelm started experiencing insomnia and had a slight sunburn, Friedrich felt it was time to tell him. Wilhelm accepted the explanation pretty well and wasn't taken aback too much. He caught on pretty fast. Ever since his brother learned what was going on, their time spent together became more open and intimate. Every battle involved Wilhelm at his side, where he watched as Friedrich healed other soldiers by biting them. Friedrich was proud to have Wilhelm look up to him like this and be the big brother he never got to be when he was younger. But inside, Friedrich knew that he didn't know much more than Wilhelm and was still learning things himself. Maybe this was how Heinrich felt when this happened to Friedrich. This served as a distraction from his troop's failure to locate Gailimantas for almost three months now. The previous week, they had finally reported news of him around Balga. The campaign had spread to a few nearby Komtureis, bringing more soldiers into this cause. Friedrich figured that it would only be a matter of time before he was caught.

Almost a month after his "resurrection," Wilhelm's jaw began to hurt. As soon as Friedrich got word from a messenger sent by Heinrich, he rode back to Balga from Swintamīstan. Friedrich and Wilhelm found themselves in the Komtur's office, waiting for Wilhelm's fangs to grow in. The process seemed pretty slow for Wilhelm compared to when it happened to Friedrich. Friedrich would show up with water to try to ease his brother's pain. He had been suffering for about seven hours.

"Let me see…" said Friedrich. Wilhelm opened his mouth. "They are starting to move past your current teeth. But they aren't there yet."

"The pain is not as bad as my illness, but it still is very tedious," Wilhelm said, taking another sip of water. "By the way, how is the hunt for the infidel going?"

"My troops call him the fox, since he keeps sneaking away from them," Friedrich answered. "He was missing from this area for a while, since he was last spotted near Christburg, but he was spotted again a week ago. As of late, he's developed a new tactic of eating my men." Friedrich scowled. "A horrible demon. To make my men suffer a slow death of being drained of their body fluids… It's disgusting."

"Isn't that what you do?" Wilhelm asked.

"I stop before I kill the person," Friedrich replied. "I never eat to kill. I eat to heal." The two looked at the door as Heinrich entered.

"Ah. You two are still in here," Heinrich said. "When did you bring him here?"

"Seven hours ago. When the new teeth started growing in," Friedrich answered. "I took him in when it started to look suspicious."

"My, that's quite slow," noted Heinrich. "Slower than usual. You don't seem too troubled Brother Wilhelm."

"I've experienced far worse a month ago, Komtur," Wilhelm said, dismissively. "I nearly lost my life to that illness. This is nothing compared to that."

"You two really are brothers," commented Heinrich. He then began to take out a map and rolled it out on his desk. He sat down and began to study it.

"What's that?" Friedrich asked.

"A map of the coastal area," answered the Komtur, not looking up. Friedrich noticed a large red circle on the map not too far away from Balga. Dozens of small X marks dotted the area around the circle. He had seen many maps of the area, but none with these markings. It didn't even look like there was a town there.

"What are these markings for?" Friedrich asked.

"It's a new Prussian stronghold that sprung up while we were focused on Swintamīstan," Heinrich replied. "Or at least, that's where I believe it is. Each X marks an incident where they have attacked us. The barbarians from there have stolen so much of our equipment and our horses. Their settlement has become so big, they've established a village. Now women and children live inside there." Heinrich sighed. "The women try to provoke our Halbbrüdern, running around in the nude, using their charm and beauty to lure away our men and kill them. The children are like little devils, throwing rocks to distract the knights while their men ambush them."

"I've heard about a new stronghold, but I didn't know about all this," Friedrich said.

"It's because you were gone in Swintamīstan," Heinrich said. "While you were gone, I started my own mission to figure out where the camp is. And I think…" Heinrich pointed to the red circle. "It's somewhere around here."

"It's that close?" noted Friedrich. "How did they manage to build a settlement like that without us knowing?!"

"I think they've been hiding in what might be a large rocky hill," Heinrich speculated. "But that hill is probably acting like a wall."

"Once my mission is fulfilled, maybe my men can help."

"Brother Simon is actually leading this mission," said Heinrich. "Maybe you can ask him about it."

Friedrich smiled. "I haven't seen Simon in a while. It's about time we catch up anyways," he said.

"We're out of water," noticed Wilhelm.

"I'll go fetch some more," Friedrich said. "Thank you for loaning your office to us, Komtur."

"This affects me too, Brother Friedrich," Heinrich said. "It is important that we look out for one another." Friedrich smiled as he left. He normally would turn up his nose at fetching water. That was the servants' and novices' job. But he didn't mind today. Not for Wilhelm. It was the least he could do. After all, Wilhelm's suffering was his fault.

"Herr Friedrich!"

Friedrich watched as a familiar young novice sped down the hallway. Friedrich gave him a look. "Brother Andreas. What are you doing here?" Andreas was out of breath, exhausted from running all the way there. "Why aren't you in Swintamīstan with the rest of your troop?"

"I have… I have come to…" he huffed, trying to catch his breath.

"Catch your breath, my young brother."

"We set up a deer trap for dinner and left it overnight and all the sudden I hear this roar and there was the fox and—"

"Get to the point, brother."

Andreas calmed himself. "We've captured the fox," he revealed with a proud smile. "We have Gailimantas!" Friedrich felt excitement jolt his heart, making it skip a beat.

"Is he here? Alive?" Friedrich asked.

"We have him in custody. We were going to put him in the prison, but if you want him somewhere else…"

A warm tingling sensation spread through Friedrich's body. He couldn't believe it. "Tell the others to keep him in the lowest room in the prison tower. I will come for him soon." A gleeful, yet sinister smile was plastered on Friedrich's face, "I will handle his punishment myself." Andreas nodded and began to rush off. "Oh! Brother Andreas!" The boy skidded to a halt. "Could you find a slave to fetch some water and bring it to the Komtur's office?"

"I can do it myself! I'll be right back, sir!"

The young boy then vanished from sight. Friedrich turned around and dashed back to the Komtur's office. He could hardly contain his excitement. He burst through the door of the office, startling Heinrich and Wilhelm.

"By Satan's foot, Friedrich, do you not know how to knock?" Heinrich said.

"Water?" Wilhelm asked.

"Not yet. Brother Andreas should be coming with the water," Friedrich replied.

"Herrje, that's the biggest smile I've ever seen on your face, Brother Friedrich," noticed Heinrich. "What on Earth is the occasion?"

"My mission is completed," Friedrich proudly announced. "We have captured Gailimantas, son of Sarginus."

Heinrich raised his eyebrows and smiled. "Really? Well congratulations!"

"I can finally teach this infidel a lesson!" Friedrich smirked. "They're holding him in the prison tower."

"I am interested in meeting this man as well," said Heinrich. "After I'm done here, I will meet you there."

Friedrich nodded. "Wilhelm, will you be okay?" he asked.

"Don't worry about me, Fritz," Wilhelm lisped. "I can take care of myself."

Friedrich chuckled. "Are you sure?" He couldn't keep himself from smiling.

"What is with that smile on your face?" Wilhelm asked.

"You're lisping like you used to do when you were younger," Friedrich pointed out.

"O Jemine…" Wilhelm sighed in annoyance.

Friedrich laughed as he returned to the door. "God be with you," Friedrich said as he departed.

He hurried outside the building and headed to the prison tower. *I can't wait to see his execution! I wonder what fate that infidel will meet. Maybe we can boil him alive. But then I wouldn't get to watch as he was tortured. We could tear him from limb to limb. Or just suspend him in the air until he dies.* As Friedrich approached the tower, a strange sight came into view. The entrance to the tower was empty. Not a single guard was in sight. Friedrich had a bad feeling in his gut. This was too unusual. Not even a Halbbruder would be lazy enough to not take up a guard shift. It was one of the easiest jobs at the Komturei. He looked around the tower with caution. He had a feeling something dreadful had happened. Not only that, but he felt an uncomfortable presence in the tower with him.

"Hello? Is anyone here?" he called, backing up towards the entrance. He wanted to investigate further inside but something in his gut was telling him that something was terribly wrong and not to go inside. He retreated back outside, cautiously examining the rest of his surroundings. "Where are the guards? Anyone?"

"…Herr Friedrich…"

Friedrich heard a small voice from behind the tower and rushed to it. The sight he saw made his heart sink. Lying on the ground was Brother Andreas, a growing pool of blood staining the snow at his side next to a spilled pail of water. It looked like he had been stabbed in the stomach.

"Andreas!" Friedrich rushed to his side. "Who did this to you?"

"I went to get water and I saw…" said Andreas, his cheerful, youthful voice now submerged by pain and fear. "The fox… He broke free. I tried to stop him but…" Andreas sniffed, his eyes full of tears. "I'm sorry… I failed you."

"No, no. You did great. You fought back instead of running away," Friedrich coaxed. "I'm so proud of you."

"Herr Friedrich…" Andreas tried to put on a smile, but that smile soon broke. "I—I don't want to die… I—I'm not ready…"

"You're going to be okay," Friedrich growled. "I'll be sure of it. Damn it, I'm not going to let you die so young… Close your eyes."

"Why?"

"Just do it!"

"Yes sir!"

Andreas squeezed his eyes shut. Friedrich quickly drew his fangs and bit the boy. *That bastard. He's just a kid. How dare he? How dare he do this to a child! He's my best squire! I can't let him die! He has so much to live for!* Friedrich reluctantly tore himself away from the boy's neck and watched his dark eyes flutter shut again. His rage against his nemesis clouded his brain to the point where he could hardly enjoy his snack. His ecstatic smile had now become an enraged scowl. *That bastard…* He leapt to his feet and began to scan the area.

"Fox!" Friedrich yelled. "I know you're hiding here! Come out so I can make you suffer!" Friedrich noticed the camp was mostly empty. He then realized that it was about to be evening prayer time, which would explain why the camp was so deserted. He walked back around to the front of the prison tower. "Infidel! Don't be a coward! Come out from where you're hiding and fight me like a man!" The feeling in Friedrich's gut grew as he looked at the prison tower. Cautiously, he entered. As he stepped inside the tower, the delicious smell of blood flooded his nostrils, making him salivate slightly. The smell led him to the stone spiral staircase. Behind it were the bodies of two brothers that Friedrich assumed were guards of the tower. One was pale and thin, not a single drop of blood left in him. The other had a slit throat and was bleeding like a freshly slaughtered calf. *Why would he eat one but not the other?* Friedrich wondered.

Friedrich suddenly felt a force slam into him from above, driving him face first into the cold stone floor. His hands broke some of his fall, but his cheek made an audible smack on the ground.

"Looking for me?"

# Chapter 16: Flogging

His body against the stone floor, Friedrich tilted his head sideways to see Gailimantas on top of him, twisting his arms behind him and wrapping a rope around them. *I knew he was hiding in here! So he left one bleeding guard as a trap! That sly bastard! Deceptively hiding from me. Just like the cunning fox he is! Impressive, but now is not the time for games.* Gailimantas didn't look too different from the last time Friedrich saw him. His reddish-brown hair had grown slightly past his chin, but he looked rougher and dirtier. He didn't look so young and innocent like before. His eyes had a look of determination, burning with a desire to see Friedrich dead.

"You bastard!" growled Friedrich. "I knew you were in here! You really are a fox!"

He tried to get up, but Gailimantas slammed his head down when he did. *Damn it. He's a lot stronger...*

"I have been waiting for this moment." Gailimantas said. His tone was more serious too. It was always serious, but he sounded more confident and his voice didn't waver. He then began to tie Friedrich's feet tightly with another rope. "For so long…" Gailimantas said. "Running from knights, living in the woods for years, and finally surrendering myself just so I could find you."

"You turned yourself in?"

"It was the only way I could find you," Gailimantas replied. "I have been searching for you for so long, Friedrich von Rotenkreuz." He finished his knot and sharply kicked Friedrich in the side. "Friedrich von Rotenkreuz. A strange name. And a long one."

"Von Rotenkreuz is a family name. Oh right, peasants don't have those."

"I wandered through the forest, let myself get captured by the enemy... All so I could finish you and kill you for good." Gailimantas shoved him upright, his eyes glowing red for a second. Friedrich was taken off guard by the red glow, staring at it before it disappeared after Gailimantas moved his head.

"Whoa! How did you do that?" Friedrich asked. "I never knew we could do that."

"Shut up!" Gailimantas growled. "I am going to kill you again! And this time I'm going to make sure you stay dead. You are the only thing standing between me and the afterlife. And I will do what I must to have my peace."

"You and the afterlife?" Friedrich questioned. "You infidels have an afterlife?"

"The gods have given me new life so I could finish my destiny and kill you. And I cannot be put to rest until you are finally gone for good," Gailimantas clarified, taking out a dagger. As Gailimantas approached him, Friedrich struggled to try to free his hands, but the ropes around his wrists were so tight and painfully dug into his skin when he moved. Gailimantas squatted in front of Friedrich, running the knife along the skin of his neck, grazing his facial hair. "And I am going to make you suffer like you made me suffer," he hissed. "I am going to remove parts of your body, bit by bit, and sacrifice them to each of my gods." Gailimantas then took the knife and scraped it along Friedrich's face, shaving off his facial hair.

"You bastard infidel!" Friedrich snarled as Gailimantas cut off the rest of his beard. *My beard... I can't imagine how I'll look without it. None of my knights will take me seriously anymore! If his goal was to humiliate me before murdering me, he's succeeding.* "I don't want to be an ugly hairless heathen like you!"

"A man like you doesn't deserve self satisfaction," Gailimantas spat. "You lost that privilege the day you waged a war against my people." Friedrich felt the freezing floor against his face, his warm hair that used to cover it now gone.

"Well, if your people didn't kill my father and enslave my family, I wouldn't have had a problem with you," Friedrich retorted. He felt his hands touch the rope that bound his feet, coming in contact with a large knot. *Perfect!* He was suddenly taken off guard by Gailimantas grabbing him by the throat. He had to buy time so he could untie his feet.

"So, your wife is an interesting person," he quickly stated. Gailimantas released his grip.

"You met my wife?"

"Yes," he replied. "She's stubborn and annoying like you. A real headstrong peasant. She tried to protect you. So I had to pry the information out of her." Gailimantas paused for a moment as Friedrich felt the knot loosen. Gailimantas's grip suddenly tightened again.

"What did you do to her?"

"Nothing! She's safe!"

"Where is she now?" Gailimantas asked.

"Don't worry," Friedrich said. "She has been relocated to Elbing with the kids. The others in your village were enslaved, but since she was a loyal Christian, she had the opportunity to relocate. She'll live out the rest of her days in peace. How you got a Christian woman to marry you,

I have no idea." Friedrich could feel the knot coming undone. He was so close. Just a bit more time. "If you're nice to me, I can let you see her one last time before you—"

"Shut up! Stop wasting my time!" Gailimantas wrapped both of his hands around Friedrich's neck. "You're going to come with me back to the forest. Where I will make sure your body is eviscerated. And you will go with me willingly."

"Or else?" challenged Friedrich.

Gailimantas put his thumbs on Friedrich's trachea, pressing firmly as the fingers around his neck squeezed tighter and tighter. Friedrich gasped and struggled for air as he felt his throat being crushed. He finally kicked off the ropes and flailed his legs, kicking at Gailimantas. He felt the pressure leave his neck, his head spinning as colorful splotches clouded his vision. He gasped for the dry winter air, coughing and sputtering. He couldn't use his hands, but his legs were free at least. Before he knew it, Gailimantas was on top of him again, sitting on top of his legs. Gailimantas raised his dagger, ready to plunge it into Friedrich's forehead, but Friedrich quickly jerked his head to the side. He suddenly felt a sharp sting in the right side of his forehead. He yelped as he felt the pain begin to spread as Gailimantas dragged the dagger downwards, cutting through more of Friedrich's skin.

"You son of a whore!" Friedrich cursed, his voice hoarse from the choking. Blood from his wound splashed into his eye, tainting his vision red.

"From what you said about your mother, it sounded like she was the one who was used as a whore," remarked Gailimantas. Friedrich was now overflowing with rage. He felt his body begin to shake and his eye began to twitch. Friedrich screamed furiously, his mouth dry as a bone. Out of instinct, he drew his fangs and bit Gailimantas in the arm. Gailimantas flinched and loosened his grip. Friedrich didn't care if he couldn't use his hands. He wanted this man dead for degrading the one woman in the world he cared about.

"You satanic son of a bitch!" Friedrich screamed as he charged at Gailimantas. "I'll maim you for saying that!" Gailimantas had just stood up on his feet when Friedrich barreled into him. He slammed back down on the floor. But without his arms, Friedrich couldn't do much. Gailimantas punched him in the head, giving him the opportunity to pin Friedrich down again. Friedrich was in a daze, colorful shapes blotting his vision again as a high pitched tone rang in his ears.

"I suppose I'll just have to kill you here," said Gailimantas. "I'll burn your remains for the gods later." Gailimantas pulled out his dagger again. He then began to cut the clothes around Friedrich's stomach, ripping a hole in his tunic until he got to the soft flesh of his stomach.

"Wh—What are you doing?" Friedrich gasped. Across his stomach was a line that was a mere dent in his skin now, but was once a fatal blow dealt by Gailimantas. It had been years since that scar was a wound, and when it was, it almost cost Friedrich his life in a very painful way.

"So it is still there," said Gailimantas. "I really did kill you. You really are undead like I am."

Friedrich knew what Gailimantas was about to do. Friedrich had heard about a horrific practice by the pagans where they would cut open men's stomachs and remove all their insides while the men were still alive. He heard from Brother Florentin that Brother Kitan had died that way. It sounded like a very painful way to go.

"Finally, my suffering will end. But yours will begin," said Gailimantas with a relieved smile on his face. "Farewell, Friedrich von Rotenkreuz."

Friedrich braced for the final blow, preparing himself for death. He was ready to be stabbed in the heart or have his bowels ripped out. But instead, he felt the weight on top of him vanish, accompanied by a few sounds of struggle. Freidrich looked above him. To his surprise, a knight had come out of nowhere and tackled Gailimantas. Friedrich sat up and saw that Heinrich had pinned Gailimantas down. Gailimantas's dagger was far out of his reach and Heinrich was tying his hands.

"Komtur! Just in time! Praise God!"

"Thank the Lord that you told me to meet you here," Heinrich said as he struggled to keep Gailimantas bound. "Well, don't just stand there, Brother Friedrich!"

"Um, my hands are…" Friedrich turned around.

"Just sit on his legs," said Heinrich. Friedrich obeyed. "No wonder why you wanted this man captured. Clearly he is a dangerous individual. We need to execute him as soon as possible." Gailimantas tried to struggle, but Heinrich gave him a sharp blow to the head, knocking him out. Heinrich then went to untie Friedrich, sitting on Gailimantas just in case. The Komtur flinched when he looked at Friedrich. "O Jemine! What in the world happened to you, Brother Friedrich?"

"The fox put up quite a fight," Friedrich remarked. "It's not too bad is it?"

"There's blood in your eye!"

"I know. I'm hideous now aren't I?" Friedrich rubbed his smooth face. "This heathen attempted to humiliate me by cutting off my beard."

"Don't let him be successful," said the Komtur. "Don't let something so trivial like your appearance take away from your victory. I expected you to be happier after you finally captured the man you sought after for years." Friedrich paused. Adrenaline scrambled his brain, so it was taking him a while to catch up to the current moment. Friedrich finally caught him. His greatest rival was now lying unconscious on the floor, limbs bound by rope. As he breathed, it was as if joy and pride replaced the air in his lungs. Sure, he had Heinrich help him, but now Gailimantas had no escape and Friedrich could do whatever he wanted.

"I did it… It's finally over," he breathed, his breath clouding in the air. "I finally captured the infidel…" Friedrich then felt the pain and exhaustion that he had shoved to the back of his mind resurface. His face began to throb, his throat felt raw, and his limbs became heavy, blood rushing back into his hands. He leaned against the wall.

"Just go to the infirmary and get patched up. I'll deal with him," assured Heinrich. Friedrich forced himself to stand. "Are you okay getting there yourself?"

Friedrich nodded. "I'm not helpless," he dismissed. "I'm just exhausted. The fox put up quite a fight." He gave a smile. "Don't start without me. I'll be back." As Friedrich left the tower, he looked up at the gorgeous sunset that was hiding behind the castle, surrounding the building in pink, purple, and dark blue. *God, thank You for giving me the strength and patience to do this. Thank You for giving me the perseverance to fight and defeat the infidel. Everything in my life has come to this moment. The Lord in Heaven has finally answered my prayers.*

Friedrich frowned at the reflection in the window in front of him. He hadn't seen himself without a beard in years. He looked so young and it changed the shape of his face in a way that was alien to him. Though he had to admit, he had a pretty nice jawline. *Maybe I should keep a shorter beard.* There was a bandage wrapped around half of his face from when Gailimantas almost stabbed him in the eye. The cut stretched from his forehead to just below his cheek, so it was hard to bandage it. Right now, only one of his eyes was visible, so the bandaging made his injuries look a lot scarier than they actually were. It looked like he had lost an eye or that half of his face had fallen off. But this would definitely leave a disfiguring scar on his face. Another small bandage was on his opposite cheek from when his face had smacked the floor. His treatment had taken longer than expected since there was a spot on his head that had to be sewn shut. Friedrich stood up and began to walk out of the infirmary. *Maybe the scar won't be so bad,* thought Friedrich. *Maybe it will make me look like a war hero. It will mark the sign of my struggles with the fox. Proof that I took down one of the most dangerous infidels on the Prussian coast.* He noticed a slave out of the corner of his eye, setting down a pail of water. Friedrich then remembered that since Brother Andreas was injured, Wilhelm never received his water.

"You there! Servant!" Friedrich called. "Fetch some water and bring it to the Komtur's office." The servant nodded, rushing back outside. *Poor Wilhelm. I would go check on him, but the Komtur's office is away from where I want to go. I have made him wait long enough. I'm worried that they'll start the execution without me.*

As Friedrich approached the prison tower, he saw Heinrich standing outside, studying the map from earlier. He rushed to the Komtur.

"Komtur, are you waiting for me?" Friedrich asked. Heinrich nodded. "Why so?" He could hear muffled screams of pain coming from beneath them. The screams were definitely coming from Gailimantas, as Friedrich recognized his voice. "Is that—"

"Indeed," said Heinrich. "Right now he is being flogged. He tried to escape again, so we have to punish him for that." Friedrich continued inside the tower and descended down the stone stairs to the lowest, coldest cell they had. As he moved closer, the screaming became louder, but eventually fell silent. "I have finally figured out where the potential camp of those infidels is," said Heinrich. "It's so close to us. Not even thirty minutes from Balga. I can't believe we didn't see it earlier."

Friedrich nodded. "That's great news," he said. "Looks like both of our missions are going smoothly." Heinrich knocked on the cell door. An older friar answered.

"Ah. Brother Heinrich. Who is this you have brought with you?" he asked.

"Brother Franz, do you not recognize Brother Friedrich?"

The friar blinked. "Ah. Forgive me," he excused himself. "I didn't recognize you with that bandage on your face." Friedrich's mood dissipated, but immediately returned to its original state when he saw his archrival in a vulnerable position. Gailimantas was stripped of his clothes and his wrists were tied to the top of a tall post, his feet barely missing the ground. Laced across his back were fresh whip marks, his back dripping with blood as he caught his breath. Friedrich noticed that Gailimantas was a lot more muscular than he thought. He had been hanging up on that pole for at least an hour and had been flogged severely, so he looked exhausted. Friedrich approached him.

"How does it feel?" sneered Friedrich. "How does it feel to finally get what you deserve, infidel?" Gailimantas glanced down at Friedrich, scowling.

"Just get it over with," Gailimantas said. "Just kill me already."

"A quick and painless death is out of the question for you," Friedrich replied. "If we had one, I would break you at the wheel."

"Just do it already instead of wasting time," Gailimantas growled.

"Oh no. I plan to savor every moment of this," Friedrich said with a smirk, fidgeting with the whip in his hands. "Ah. Justice feels so good."

"You son of a whore…"

"Shut up!" Friedrich struck Gailimantas hard across the back, causing Gailimantas to cry out again. Friedrich gave a few more lashes before taking a deep breath and turning back to Heinrich. "What are we going to do with him?"

"I'm still thinking about that," Heinrich replied.

"Should we parade him around the convent and humiliate him first?" Friedrich asked.

"I would prefer not to do that," Heinrich replied. "He is notorious for escaping, isn't he?"

"True. But simply being hung is not enough pain for him. Should we put him in a box full of rats?"

"No," declined Heinrich. "There aren't enough rats around here. Plus, then we would have a bunch of rats around us. None of us want that."

Friedrich thought for a moment. "Oh! I have an idea," he smirked. "We should take a page from his book and have him disemboweled alive. Just like he was about to do to me. I heard that's what happened to Brother Kitan after he was captured. May his soul rest in Heaven. It seems like a perfect barbaric punishment for a barbaric infidel."

"We shouldn't stoop to their level," lectured Heinrich. "Don't be selfish, Brother Friedrich. Think about what you have to put the executioner through. We have to bring him all the way from Christburg."

"He deserves a fate worse than death itself!" Friedrich snapped. "Do you know how many of our men he has murdered? If I had not come in time, Brother Andreas would have died. He's only a boy! And this man had no doubts about killing him!"

"He…almost killed Brother Andreas?" Heinrich said, surprised.

"Brother Nathaniel and Brother Diedrich are also dead because of him. As well as Brother Tomas, and I'm sure many others. Not to mention, he's also a nachzehrer." Friedrich became serious. "In fact, I have a better idea." Friedrich's smile grew wider. "I'm going to do to him what his people did to my father. We should burn the heretic alive!"

"I need to think if that will harm him or not. Since he is in the second stage, he should be able to…" Heinrich trailed off. It appeared as if inspiration had struck him like a lightning bolt.

"Komtur?" Friedrich called. "Komtur, what is wrong?"

"…Brother Friedrich, God has given me a perfect solution," Heinrich replied. "A solution to solve all of our problems. And it all relies on this man."

"What is it?"

"Bring me a carriage and constraints for this man," commanded Heinrich to the friar at the door. "Please hurry." The friar left, leaving Friedrich, Heinrich, and Gailimantas alone. "Friedrich, lock the door." Friedrich was confused, but was in no position to question the Komtur's orders.

"Please…kill me," Gailimantas begged in broken German. Tired, he switched back to Prussian. "Just kill me! Please! I just want to rest in peace. My family is gone, my commander is gone, my home is gone… I have nothing left to live for. Please just execute me and get it over with!" He fought back tears. "Please… I just want to rest in peace and go to the afterlife…" Heinrich approached Gailimantas, a glare in his eyes. He stepped on the stool next to him, so that he could look down on him. Friedrich was about to translate what he said, but Heinrich cut him off.

"No. Hell is not enough suffering for you," said Heinrich. Friedrich was surprised to hear Heinrich speak in Prussian. "For your sins I shall give you a punishment worse than death. Although you will be going to Hell eventually, you will first live Hell on Earth. You will live your life here as a night dwelling, blood sucking monster. Your skin will burn in the sunlight. You will have to feast upon human beings each day to live. And you will watch everyone you know and love slowly die while you live on for eternity." Gailimantas stared in terror at the vampire above him, who had drawn his fangs. He began to scream, but he was quickly cut off with a bite to the throat. Friedrich watched with his mouth open as Heinrich began to feast on Gailimantas's blood. The Komtur seemed to be hungry, but he soon broke away. Gailimantas soon fell unconscious, his limp body still dangling from the post. Friedrich was aghast at what just happened.

"What was that? Why are we keeping him alive?" Friedrich exclaimed. "Why in God's name did you make him a full nachzehrer? He'll just come back as an even stronger soldier and slaughter us!"

"Because Friedrich, I have a plan that will tactically benefit us," Heinrich said. He knocked on the door and asked the friar on the other side of it, "Is the carriage ready yet?"

"Yes Komtur," said a voice on the other side of the door.

"Get this man's body in the carriage quickly," Heinrich commanded as he opened the door. "Hurry. Make sure you keep the binds on him and blindfold him." The men took Gailimantas down from the pole.

"Why do we need a carriage?" Friedrich asked. "Where are we going?"

"To that pagan settlement near us," Heinrich stated. "We need to hurry. Before he wakes up."

"But why?"

"Brother Friedrich, it's time you learned what happens after you are first reborn as a full nachzehrer," Heinrich said, beckoning Friedrich into the wagon. Friedrich uneasily followed Heinrich inside, his mind in a blur of conflict and confusion. He sat next to Heinrich, flinching as Gailimantas was loaded behind him, blindfolded and tied. The wagon was small, so Gailimantas was fairly close to Friedrich's feet. Heinrich snapped the reins, causing the horses to take off. Friedrich was surprised that dusk was still setting in. He expected it to be darker outside. Friedrich had a strange feeling that he was forgetting something as the castle disappeared behind the trees. He shook his head. *It can't be too important if I forgot about it.* Friedrich began to reach for the lamp in the corner of the carriage so they wouldn't be left in the dark.

"That won't be necessary, Brother Friedrich," said Heinrich.

"The lamp?"

"Pagans will see us and attack us and we are clearly outnumbered."

"But it is dark. How will we see? How will you drive?"

"You may not be able to do so yet, but I do not need light to see in the dark."

"I can do that when I become a full nachzehrer?" Friedrich started to get excited again.

"It's another benefit of being a monster."

"What else can I do when I'm a full nachzehrer?" asked Friedrich. "There's so much I've learned, but yet, still so much I have yet to learn."

"There isn't that much we can do," Heinrich replied, not taking his eyes off of the path in front of him. "Whatever power we have is mostly unstable."

Friedrich was quiet for a moment. He stewed in his disappointment. For years he had waited to settle the score with this man. He finally had him in his grasp. He was ready to give him the punishment he deserved. And then the Komtur did the exact opposite and took away his prize. Then again, the Komtur did help catch him, so he deserved to have at least some say in the punishment. Friedrich was nevertheless disappointed. He looked back at the lucky bastard who got to live, whose back was still dripping in blood. Friedrich pressed a finger against his back, gathered a bit of blood and licked his finger. He wanted to lick his back like he would lick the inside of a soup bowl, but he knew that Heinrich would yell at him for it. *But all that blood is going to waste. Perhaps one lick wouldn't be so bad...*

"Brother Friedrich, what are you doing?"

*Damn it! How does he manage to catch me every time?* "Sorry, I'm hungry! I ate a bit of Andreas's blood, but it wasn't much," Friedrich complained.

"That does not mean you are to lick every bloody man you see. Have some self control! It really feels like you're still a child sometimes..."

"Sorry Komtur…" Friedrich said, ashamed. Friedrich respected the Komtur, but he always made him feel 20 years younger than he actually was. When the Komtur turned back to him, Friedrich was startled by the sight. The Komtur's eyes were glowing red. With a tilt of his head, the glow disappeared.

"Are you alright, Brother Friedrich?"

"Sorry," replied Friedrich. "I thought I saw your eyes glow. It must have been my imagination."

"That's how nachzehrer eyes are," said Heinrich. "They glow like a cat's when you look at them from certain angles."

"Oh. So I wasn't seeing things," said Friedrich. "So, are you going to tell me why we are taking this infidel out to the middle of the woods?"

"Newborn nachzehrers have an insatiable bloodlust that cannot be stopped," explained Heinrich. "When a man becomes a full nachzehrer, he loses control of his body and soul. He becomes a demonic beast, eating everything in sight. You are no longer a person until you feast on everyone in sight until the sun rises."

"And so we're bringing him to the woods because…"

"We're going to eliminate that pagan settlement once and for all without wasting a single soldier," answered Heinrich.

"But all those men against just one nachzehrer?" said Friedrich. "Surely they'll defeat him. What is the difference between us killing him and the pagans killing him?"

"Don't worry about it," replied Heinrich. "The camp will be gone by morning."

"Did the same thing happen when you became a nachzehrer?" Friedrich asked. Heinrich didn't answer. Friedrich figured that maybe now wasn't the time. Perhaps a story for another day.

"When we return to Balga, you'll understand."

"What do you mean?"

"Brother Friedrich, I can't have you nearly die on me again. So I've decided that now would be a good time to make you a full nachzehrer."

Friedrich's eyes lit up. "Really?" he said.

"I'm going to have to keep you in the dungeon for a few days, but just…" Heinrich sighed. "After these close calls, I realize that you tend to put yourself in dangerous situations. So I have to do this in order to keep you alive." Friedrich felt a mix of nervousness and excitement. He then remembered what he forgot.

"Ach! Herrje! I forgot about Wilhelm! I hope the servant didn't forget his water."

"I'm sure he will be fine," said Heinrich. "He seems to have a high tolerance for pain."

"Yeah. Better than me," said Friedrich, hating to admit that his younger brother was better at something than he was. "But I'm worried that he may come and look for us."

"I told him where I was going before I left and ordered him not to leave my office. I'm sure he will be fine," assured Heinrich. There was another long pause. Going through the forest at night was eerie, and darkness blanketed everything outside of the wagon. Friedrich was confused at how Heinrich could even see through this darkness since all he saw was pitch black. Wolves, bears, demons, infidels… Anything could be hiding out in the woods. Chills went down his spine as he felt himself becoming more and more anxious. *Maybe talking with Heinrich will break the tension.*

"Komtur, can women be nachzehrers?" asked Friedrich.

"I have never met one," answered Heinrich. "So I don't think so."

"But I swear I saw one. A woman bit me once…"

"Perhaps it was a young man," explained Heinrich. "Women would be too soft to handle this curse."

"Women seem to suck the life out of things just fine," commented Friedrich. "I think they would adapt to this curse fairly well."

Heinrich chuckled. "You don't like women very much, do you Brother Friedrich?"

"What reason do I have to like women? They're useless beings. They don't fight and risk their lives for God. All they do is stay at home, cry, and scream all the time. And they tempt men into sinful acts. The only good thing they do is have children and become nuns. Nuns are the only useful women as they help our cause."

"Well perhaps you'll meet a woman who will change your mind someday."

"I would never break my vow of celibacy for something stupid like that," Friedrich scoffed. "My duty to God is greater than the power of any temptress. Never in my life have I been tempted by any women, something I am very proud of."

"As you should be," Heinrich said. "I'm shocked you haven't even had the slightest temptation to be with a woman."

"I don't see how any man can," said Friedrich. "But alas, I know the Lord wishes for us to start families that will carry on his will, so I know it is a necessity. But my devotion is to God and God alone."

Friedrich suddenly remembered how many of his comrades had echoed the same thoughts as the Komtur. Not once had he come across someone who agreed with him about women. Every time he had to go into town, his fellow brothers would slobber all over women, something that he could never understand. Not that he ever attempted to relate to his lusting comrades. He just assumed that he had a stronger will to avoid sin. The Komtur's answer made him think about how everyone looked at him whenever he talked about women.

"Komtur, are you tempted by women?" Friedrich asked.

"Of course. God made men and women for each other," Heinrich replied. "And I was a regular knight before I was bitten. I had a wife and children."

"What was it like?"

"Pardon?"

"What was it like to have a wife?"

"My wife…" Heinrich thought for a moment. "Last time I was married was over a century ago. Her name was Katarina. She was a lovely woman. My parents picked a really beautiful girl for me. I only saw my children once or twice before I died. They've probably perished now." Friedrich thought he heard Heinrich's voice waver, but it could have been due to the bumpy terrain. "I used to dream of teaching my son how to become a knight, eating a nice warm dinner with my family, and ending the night passionately with my wife. I had to give that up to keep my family safe. But part of me still wishes for that dream."

"I can't relate to that at all," Friedrich said. "I know becoming a knight brother was my destiny, but everyone around me wants exactly what you described, even the other knight brothers. My younger brother has already married and had children. I can't help but wonder if I'm supposed to want that too."

"Brother Friedrich, what you speak of is not a curse, it's a blessing," Heinrich explained. "I have seen many knights slip and fall into the hands of lust. Claiming that God is rewarding them for their quests." There was a hint of disgust in Heinrich's voice. "I've never seen a man with as much devotion to the church and the battlefield as you. That is because you have a strong will and are not distracted by things such as women. The Lord gave you this resilience because you were created to be a knight brother." Friedrich remained quiet. "I greatly admire your resilience, Brother Friedrich," Heinrich continued. "You have a resistance to temptation that most men lack. You should be proud of that."

Friedrich did feel proud to hear those words. His insecurities and doubts had vanished with affirmation from Heinrich. For many years Friedrich had looked up to Heinrich, seeing him as the father he never had. But hearing Heinrich express admiration for him made him feel accomplished as a holy knight, as if he was on the same level as the Komtur. He felt more like an adult and a real Ritterbruder, the childish feeling from earlier disappearing. Though the age gap still made him feel like a child, Heinrich's words made him a strong, confident man. *I am perfectly happy on the battlefield with my fellow men. This life brings me joy and pleasure. My ideal life involves slaughtering heathens on the battlefield, coming back to my Komturei, bathing with my comrades, whittling while discussing my day, and sleeping with my men under the candlelight. It's all part of God's plan for me, and it's something I will happily accept.*

To Friedrich, it seemed to be an eternity spent in the wagon, even though the journey took not even a half an hour. Riding through the snow created a bumpy, unpleasant ride, but thankfully, the snow wasn't too thick. He talked with Heinrich whenever he could to distract himself from the darkness surrounding him. Eventually, the horses came to a halt in a spot in the middle of the forest. Friedrich could hear distant sounds of people, but they seemed to be far enough to be away from their attention. As Heinrich took Gailimantas's upper body, Friedrich took the lower half and the two unloaded him onto the forest floor, right beside a large rock. Heinrich then returned to the wagon.

"We're not staying?" Friedrich asked.

"Of course not!" Heinrich answered. "I may be fine, but he will drain the life out of you. We should get out of here now." Friedrich returned to the wagon as Heinrich cued the horses to start moving again.

Friedrich stared out at the darkness around him. The sounds of the crickets and the other animals of the forest made the journey a lot more peaceful on the way back. The moon had risen higher now and he could see some of the birch forest in the moonlight, the light dripping down the leaves like white rain. Friedrich looked back at the fading figure of his rival's unconscious body. *This is farewell for now, fox. But as sure as the stars in Heaven, I refuse to die until I know that your unholy presence has left this Earth. By God's holy fate, I am positive that we will meet again.*

# Chapter 17: Bloodbath

Gailimantas awoke feeling terrible. His body was cold and sore all over, the orange sun was in his eyes, and he felt incredibly nauseous. It was as if he ate a whole boar by himself and was so full that he felt like throwing up. He had only experienced this feeling once in his life when he was a child and was fed a full meal after eating hardly anything for a month. He tried to roll over on his back, but was met with a burning pain as his back touched the ground. He yelped and sat up, his back throbbing from the pain. He touched his back, wincing when his wounds responded with a sting. Gailimantas then remembered what had happened the previous night. How he almost killed Friedrich, but was stopped by a man, who he assumed was Friedrich's superior. He remembered the whipping and the torture and then… Everything was black after that. He couldn't remember what happened.

*Where am I now?* Gailimantas looked next to him and was met with the shocked, pale face of a dead woman. She looked like she had all her blood drained out of her. He yelped in shock and skirted away from the body, only to bump into a wall. His eyes dashed through his surroundings, trying to see where he was. It appeared to be a messy hut quite similar to his own. It even had a statue of Perkūnas on the table. *How the hell did I get here? Why am I in a house? Whose house is this?* An awful smell wafted into his nose. He quickly covered it, though he knew that stench all too well. The smell of death and decay. He thought it was from the dead woman in the house, but the smell was much stronger than normal. It smelled like there were dead bodies everywhere.

The nausea doubled as he rose to his feet. Gailimantas felt as if his stomach was going to burst. *What did I eat last night? By the gods, I've never felt so full in my life.* He groaned as he leaned against the wall of the house. *What is going on?* He trudged to the door of the hut and opened it, the cold, outside air hitting him in the face. What he saw made him shake in fear. It looked like a Prussian settlement, but it was completely void of life. All the life that should have inhabited the village was lying on the ground, unmoving, painting the snow with red dots. At least three people were motionless in the center of the village. He felt his legs tremble as he hesitantly stepped outside, the trees providing shade from the sun. *So many people… And they're all dead.* Finally, Gailimantas couldn't take it anymore and threw up. The contents of his stomach stained the snow with a milky red color and the taste of stomach acid and blood filled his mouth. He felt a bit better, but was still nauseous and overly full. He continued walking through the village, examining every house. Every home was full of corpses. Most of the bodies were in their beds, all with puncture wounds on their necks. *Who would do such a thing? Who would kill all of these people? And why do they look like they were sucked dry by an undead? I would think that's what happened, but how could an undead kill so many people? Maybe there was more than one…* He stopped when he heard soft crying. Someone was still alive in this town. Maybe they could help him out and tell him what happened. He followed the sound of the crying to one of the houses with a door cracked open. He quietly peeked inside. The house was completely torn apart and spattered with bloodstains. Inside was a young woman weeping over an older man dressed in warm clothing. She looked like a recently bought young bride. The older man was dead like the rest of the village, but the woman only had a smear of blood on her neck. Gailimantas accidentally pushed the door open further, causing the woman to instantly notice him. Before Gailimantas could ask her anything, she let out an ear shattering scream. She had a desperately terrified look on her face, as if she was staring death in the face.

"Excuse—"

"GET AWAY!" she shrieked, beginning to sob harder.

"Wh—What is—"

"NO! PLEASE!" she continued to wail. "HELP! DEMON! DEMON!"

"Demon…" Gailimantas stepped backwards until his foot stepped on something. When he bent over to pick it up, he realized his hands were stained with blood. He looked down at himself and noticed his chest was dotted with red droplets. He backed away from the house, his heart beating faster and faster as he began to piece together everything around him. "No… This… It can't be… I couldn't have…" He looked at the object in his hand. It was a small hand mirror. He hesitantly flipped it around and peeked at his reflection. Blood was smeared all over his chin and around his mouth. His teeth were stained pink. Most shocking of all, his irises had changed from forest green to ruby red. The mirror dropped from his hands as he began to scream. Gailimantas felt a wave of nausea and panic wash over him.

*I did this… I killed all these people…* He dropped to the ground and screamed louder, unable to contain the reality of what had just happened. He didn't want to accept that he could have done such a horrible thing, and to his own people no less. *I ate them. I ate all these people. I ate my own people!* The nausea became overwhelming, and Gailimantas threw up once again, gasping for air as he panicked. He just sat there for a while in a daze, staring at what was once his meal, formerly part of another person. Just that thought almost made him want to throw up again. He put his hands in his face. *What have I done? Why would I do something like this? Why don't I remember anything? Why did this happen? Why!*

*For your sins I shall give you a punishment worse than death. Although you will be going to Hell eventually, you will first live Hell on Earth. You will live your life here as a night dwelling, blood sucking monster.*

The knight's words echoed in his head as he withdrew within himself. He sobbed into his hands. *Why… Why would the gods allow me to turn into something so horrendous? Something so evil that I slaughter my own people? Why?!* Gailimantas sobbed for a bit longer until the smell of decay became stronger. He couldn't take it anymore. He would lose it if he had to stay in this village longer, staring his crimes in the face. He trembled as he stood up and swiftly walked towards the forest, staring at the ground to avoid looking at the death and destruction he had caused. Gailimantas made the mistake of looking back one last time and felt his heart be smashed with guilt and horror as he saw the haunting scene again. He returned his gaze to the ground and walked faster, continuing until the shade of the trees disappeared, exposing his body to the sun.

Gailimantas suddenly felt his body become unbelievably hot, despite the winter chill. It was as if he was surrounded by fire coming dangerously close to his skin. He felt like his body was becoming heavier and heavier as the sun beat down on his skin. Everything around him was so bright, it hurt his eyes. It was almost like he was staring directly into the sun. He dashed back into the shady safety of the forest and felt his skin begin to cool. He fell to his knees, slumped over in despair.

*Why didn't the gods just let me die?*

Gailimantas continued to trudge through the snowy forest, withdrawn from the outside world as he walked past thick, unchanging pine trees. He didn't know where he was nor where he was going. He had nowhere to go. No goal, no family, no friends, no people to protect. He had nothing. He was nothing. Nothing but an evil being that caused pain and suffering wherever he went. He felt like a dead snail, but the snail had died and rotted away, making the shell still gorgeous on the outside, with a disgusting decaying snail corpse on the inside. *My life has been a series of loss and suffering, hasn't it? Whenever I have something good in my life, it seems like the gods snatch it away.* He continued to mindlessly walk through the forest, making subconscious turns every now and then. It seemed like walking in the woods was all he could do. Walking in the woods was what he had done for most of his life.

In the middle of his journey, he found a dead Prussian man slumped against the tree, slowly rotting away. Gailimantas envied him. *All those times I prayed to stay alive, now it's coming back to mock me. How can the gods be so cruel?* He then realized that the man had a nice cloak, whereas he was shivering in the bitter wind with nothing but his pants. Gailimantas snatched the cloak and the dagger that the man carried and journeyed on. He wandered through the shady forest as the sun rose, peaked, and set. *I want to disappear. Someone like me should just vanish from the Earth. I just want to die. Why couldn't the gods have just let me die when I was sick? Why do they force me to suffer in this miserable existence? Do I still have to kill Friedrich in order to pass on? Why can't the gods just let me die!*

A sound snapped him out of his daze and brought him back to reality. It was the sound of rushing water. After hours of continuously walking in the woods with nothing but the uniform trees by his side, he finally encountered something new. He followed the sound to a clearing in the trees. There he saw a large roaring waterfall that emptied into a wide rushing river. The cliff he stood on was tall enough to the point where the trees at the bottom blended together to make one spikey green and white patch. The large drop made his spine shiver and his stomach feel uneasy, the fear of falling clutching his mind in a powerful grip. He stared at the cliff. Something about the foamy water at the bottom seemed welcoming and comforting. The wide, blue river was calming, and surprisingly not frozen. The whole scene was accented by sparkling snow and shimmering icicles, clumped together to form natural crystals. The beautiful natural sight changed his fear into awe at the gods' creation. The fear of falling was turning into the temptation to jump. He sighed, wishing to be submerged in those crystal clear waters, drinking from its riches like it was a bath from Heaven. Gailimantas realized that this was the place. The beautiful sight that he wanted to die with.

*I know what I must do. The gods can't make me stay alive.* Gailimantas felt a smile come to his face as he stared down at the roaring river and the merciless rocks at the bottom. *Finally, for once in my life, I will finally know peace. I will meet my mother and father for the first time in so long. My siblings, Pomeus, Herkus… I can't wait to see them all.* He looked back at the forest, inching himself closer to the drop until his heels were touching the edge of the cliff. He took out the dagger that he had found earlier and unsheathed it. The silvery blade glinted in the golden sunset, nice and sharp enough to do its job.

"I shall now have my peace," he whispered. He then placed the knife against his throat and slit it open. Gailimantas felt himself fall backwards off the cliff. The falling sensation that would normally terrify him was somewhat calming. Gailimantas closed his eyes and smiled.

*Peace at last.*

# Epilogue

Heinrich cautiously entered the cell, locking the door behind him. The moment he stepped inside, his nose wrinkled at the smell of decay. Heinrich observed the creature that was chained to the wall of the prison. It looked like his energy had run out, and he was too hungry to continue on, so he lay there, slumped against the floor, groaning. The vampire gave an unenthusiastic grunt as he heard the door shut. Heinrich approached with caution, nervous that he would be attacked again, trying to conceal the basket he had behind his back. But the young vampire could smell the delicious substance in the basket. He dragged his body across the floor, so hungry and desperate for anything. Heinrich had noticed that after four hours with no food, the poor thing began to look like he was dying. But as soon as he had a taste of human blood, the energy would instantly return to his body. The newborn drooled as he stared at Heinrich, having gone another three hours without food. Last time, the poor thing only had a few drops of blood and bit Heinrich's hand while he was being fed. He looked up at Heinrich, red eyes full of tears, begging for food. Heinrich recoiled at the sight. The vampire looked like an animated corpse. His skin was tinged a reddish color and some parts of his body had started to bloat. There appeared to be a festering sore on his neck. The smell of decay was starting to emanate from the starving creature. Heinrich felt his hands begin to shake. *Is this what happens when newborns don't eat? Will the same thing happen to me if I don't eat?* The vampire let out a pained groan. Heinrich opened the glass jar and carefully pushed it over to him.

"I'm sorry I kept you without food for so long, Brother Friedrich," he apologized. "I was…curious. I'm sorry. I didn't know this would happen." Before biting him for the final time, Heinrich had locked Friedrich up in the prison tower so that he couldn't eat anyone. It was hard to believe that the moving corpse in front of him was a man just a few hours ago. This was the same man who had sat in a cart with him to drop off another new vampire in the forest. Friedrich shakily dragged his body towards the jar and began to take a small sip from it. He then quickly sat up and finished the jar off in a matter of seconds, his energy returning to him. The bloating seemed to dwindle and his open wound had mostly scabbed over. He slammed the jar down, cracking it a bit, before springing up and bounding towards Heinrich, only to be snapped back by the chains. Heinrich gave a sigh, shaking his head. Friedrich desperately tried to pull on the chains to get to him, struggling snarls escaping from his fanged mouth. The man was acting like a wild dog, salivating at the sight of the jar of blood that Heinrich pulled out from the basket. Heinrich had always frequented the infirmary, being sure to attend every bloodletting he could. He had accumulated numerous jars of blood over time, but he knew that this newborn would want at least half of his collection. Friedrich put less energy into his efforts, showing Heinrich that he was already getting tired. Of course, he had only given him a small jar. He opened the bigger jars, setting them on the ground and pushing them towards Friedrich. Before Heinrich could pull his hand away, Friedrich launched himself at him and sank his fangs into his arm, trying to suck the blood out. Heinrich let out a yelp of pain, trying his best to contain his curses as this was one of the most painful bites he had experienced. He was surprised how powerful Friedrich's bite was. He had been bitten by angry vampires in the past, but none had a bite this strong and painful. Heinrich's eyes became cloudy as it felt like his arm was being crushed. He took a deep breath.

"That's quite the jaw you have," he commented. "But I'm afraid I won't be very tasty." Friedrich's eyes soon widened as he released his grip, gagging and spitting at the foul taste. He hissed and scuttled off into the opposite side of the room, crouching in the corner. His red eyes glared at Heinrich, hissing at him. Heinrich understood this as a way of saying get out. Heinrich finished opening the jars and pushed them closer to Friedrich. As he was moving the last jar, Friedrich suddenly bolted from his place and charged at him, barely missing Heinrich's sleeve. Friedrich began swinging, chains preventing his fists from Heinrich's face, and let out an angry wet hiss. Heinrich quickly retreated out of the cell and slammed the door behind him, locking it. He took a deep breath. *I should get the rest of my blood. I don't want him returning to that state.* Heinrich hurried up the stone stairs, leaving the snarling, hissing creature behind him.

# 1285

*"Well what do you know, it is a man! For once, you were right, Mainotas."*

*"I told you! I know a dead man when I see one!"*

*"Well this is quite the catch. We should cremate the poor man so he can have a proper send off to the gods."*

*"More like so he doesn't come back and kill us. Let's row the boat in."*

*"Yes sir!"*

*"Um, I think that it's too late for that."*

*"What do you mean?"*

*"Look at him."*

*"Wait… What the hell?"*

*"This man is still alive! He's moving!"*

*"There's a lot of water coming out of him. Especially if you kick him."*

*"Sir! Sir! Can you hear me?"*

Gailimantas instinctively began to cough. All the water that had entered his lungs was now being painfully forced out through coughs and vomiting. *Where am I? I don't remember anything! Why don't I know anything!* As he purged the water from his body, the four men rowed the boat back to land. He groaned. His head hurt as much as his lungs and his memory felt like a blur, but it was slowly returning to him. *I know who I am. My name is Gailimantas, son of Sarginus. I come from… Where am I from? Think! What's the last thing you remember? Okay. I jumped off of a cliff… I think. But why? Why did I do that?* By the time he was finished retching he felt his body being lifted out of the small fishing boat. He gasped for air as he gazed up at the setting sky, his eyes half open, as the four bearded fishermen's conversation faded to the background. *I can hardly remember anything about my childhood. I fought in a few wars. I am 24 summers old. I'm sure of that. I have a wife and kids that I had to flee… I know I have a wife. Annuse. Yes! I know her name. I have a little daughter and do I have one more? I don't know. But why did I have to leave them? Why didn't I stay with my lovely family? And why can't I remember most of their names? Oh! I'm a vampire. I know that. And I remember my nemesis, Friedrich von…something. I remember mostly everything up until Swintamīstan was attacked… Swintamīstan! That's where I'm from! Wait, Swintamīstan was attacked? No. I must be confusing that with my childhood home…*

*"What do we do with him?"*

*"I don't know."*

*"Maybe we should ask our leader."*

*"What is he?"*

*"He looks really young."*

*"Let's just sacrifice him!"*

*"No you idiot! Let's make some money off of him! I say we sell him as a slave."*

*"He's probably an escaped slave or a prisoner."*

*"Then perhaps he can be our servant."*

*"But no slave would have hair that long! He must be of some status."*

*"I still think we should sell him."*

*"Do you think he's a German?"*

*"No. All the Teutons have white or black uniforms. He looks like a nobleman."*

*"Why don't we just ask him?"* said a man, pulling the small boat to shore. He knelt beside Gailimantas, making eye contact with him. *"Where did you come from?"*

Gailimantas could somewhat understand what the man was saying. The language he spoke was so similar to his own, but just different enough to the point where he was unsure whether his interpretation was correct or not.

"Where did I come from?" he rephrased the words in the language he understood. The men looked at each other, continuing to talk in the semi comprehensible language.

*"He's a Prussian!"* exclaimed a younger fisherman.

*"A Prussian? Don't Prussians live by the sea? What is he doing all the way over here?"*

*"Many Prussians have been fleeing to us since the Teutonic Knights attacked. Remember?"* replied a man with red hair. *"Kirkis, do you think you can communicate with him?"*

*"I can try. But if he's a Pomegesian, I'm out of luck,"* said a young man who crouched down to Gailimantas. "So, you speak Prussian?" He had a Sambian accent, but Gailimantas could understand him fine. He sighed in relief.

"Where am I?" Gailimantas asked.

"We'll answer your questions later," the young man halted. "Where are you from?" The way the young man asked him questions made him feel as if he was being interrogated, but by a man who was half-assing his job.

"Swintam… Natangia," Gailimantas replied.

"That's pretty far away from here. What are you doing in Lithuania?" Gailimantas blinked. *Lithuania? How did I get all the way to Lithuania? The sea is incredibly far from here!* Gailimantas had heard many things about the Lithuanians. They were formerly at peace with the Teutons and the Livonians after their king converted to Christianity, but the war reignited after he became pagan again. They were known to be incredibly strong to the point where they could fend off almost any Christian order that attacked them. The Lithuanians were known to terrorize their neighbors back in the day and inspired many heroic stories. Many Prussians fled there when the Teutonic Knights began to take over, so Gailimantas assumed that he could let his guard down a little. Besides, these were only fishermen. But Gailimantas was still piecing his memories together. He wasn't sure how to respond to the man.

"I—I don't know," Gailimantas answered. "My memory… I can't remember. I don't know how I got here. I know I'm at least 24 summers old. I have a wife and children. I fought in numerous wars and I…"

"What is the last thing you remember?"

Gailimantas thought hard. "I remember my town being attacked by the Teutonic Knights, I think. Everything is spotty after that. But I think the last thing I remember is probably being captured by the Teutonic Knights." Kirkis said something back to the other men.

"*I knew he was a prisoner,*" said the red haired one. "*Okay. It's settled. Let's sell him as a slave. We could make some good money off of him.*" Gailimantas could understand every other word that these men spoke if he concentrated enough, but it was hard to focus since he was so confused and exhausted. Suddenly, the men picked him up and began leading him somewhere.

"What is your name?" asked the Sambian.

"Gaili…" Gailimantas coughed again. "Mantas. Just Mantas."

"*Well Mantas*," said the red haired man. "*Let's hope you make us some money.*"

"Wh—What?" Gailimantas wasn't sure if he misheard the man when suddenly, his hands were bound by rope. Two men held him down as he struggled. "What are you doing? Let me go!" Gailimantas received a sharp kick in the side.

"Don't struggle," the Sambian said. "It will only make things worse for you." After his legs were bound, Gailimantas was thrown into a wagon.

"*You're quite strong*," commented a fisherman. "*You're bound to fetch good money at the market.*" With that, the reins snapped, and Gailimantas felt the cart move, taking him towards an unknown land to be sold as a slave.

# 1286

The tavern was mostly empty. It was around closing time, so it was to be expected. Reiginas listened as a couple of regulars chatted away. This tavern had become quite popular with the Prussians of Elbing, but Germans were still a daily occurrence. Reiginas had made a nice cozy life for himself. Working at a tavern was the perfect job for a vampire. This way he could avoid the sun, make a nice living, and have easy access to booze. What more could a man want from life? Of course, being a former sailor, he always missed the sea. Every night after the bar closed, he would grab a pint, sit by the sea, and watch the ocean, reminiscing about his life before he had met his partner. *Ah yes… Today marks a year, doesn't it?* Reiginas thought. His everyday grin suddenly disappeared. *I never thought I would miss the lad so much. I guess he was the closest thing I had to a friend in this life.* Reiginas then remembered how lonely his year had been. He was used to being alone, after all, it was hard to meet other vampires like himself, especially vampires that were friendly to their own kind.

"Hey, why so glum, Reiginas?" said one of the regulars who seemed to notice his shift in mood.

"It's been a year…" Reiginas sighed. "It's been a year since he went missing." The regulars at the bar frowned.

"Mantas?" one Prussian guessed. "I almost forgot about him."

"I didn't. What happened to him spooked me," said the other. "The man completely disappeared without a trace. He had a life and family here and suddenly he's just gone."

"He wouldn't just leave without telling me. Maybe he was taken hostage by the Teutonic Knights," Reiginas wondered. "He was in a lot of trouble with them, but when I went to them they said that they had no one in custody with that name."

"I miss the old fox. All my jokes flew over his head, but it was always fun to make him smile," said the first Prussian, taking a sip of mead.

"Meh, I don't notice much of a difference. Reiginas is the life of the party," said the other drinker.

Reiginas looked at the sky. It was about closing time. He would let these two finish their drinks then close down the bar and return to the cemetery. He sighed. His friend had always handled the finances and technical stuff. He rarely came out to interact with the customers unless Reiginas wasn't there. The two had come to this town together, starting off as graveyard watchmen before starting this tavern together. The last day Reiginas saw his partner, he gave Mantas a beautiful, mesmerizing red ring he had found to use for his daughter's dowry. He didn't see him again after that night. *Where did you go? How does a man just suddenly disappear?* Reiginas noticed that the two regulars had finished their drinks and were currently chatting away. The sun was going to rise soon, so he had to hurry these two out of here, lest he be stuck in the tavern for another night.

"Alright you two, it's getting late. You don't have to go home, but you can't stay here," Reiginas said.

"Oh come on, Reiginas. Can't we at least finish up our conversation?" one customer complained.

"You can do that outside. I'm really tired tonight, boys," Reiginas said.

"Why I—"

"Hey," the customer interrupted his friend. "Not today. Let the man grieve." The other man quietly got up from his stool and left the tavern. "See ya tomorrow!"

"See ya then!" Reiginas called out. He then locked the doors behind the men. *Am I really grieving for him? Well, he is most likely dead, but I just have a gut feeling he isn't. My gut has always been right in the past, so I'm sure it's right now.* Reiginas went to the back of the tavern and grabbed the bucket and a rag to wash the sticky floor. *I have good reason to grieve for him, I guess. No one in my life had ever shown me such kindness before. To be starving and on the verge of becoming feral and give food to another feral vampire who has done nothing for you… Not even my mother had shown me such kindness.* He looked around the tavern. Not that much of a mess tonight. Ever since that new tavern around the corner opened, it had been taking his business. Nights were getting quieter and quieter. Reiginas wasn't used to the quiet. His life had always been bold and full of adventure. In every century he lived, he always had something to risk his life for or somewhere interesting to go to. He wasn't used to being stable and placid like this. He missed the journey. Reiginas had always hoped to take his partner on an adventure, but now that was out of the question. Reiginas paused for a moment.

*I suppose I am in desperate need of an adventure. This place has become boring to me. And I know just what my next quest will be.* The former Curonian viking looked out the window at the barren streets of Elbing, a smirk on his face. *I'm going to come find you. Even if it takes years, it's nothing to me. I know you're out there somewhere, Gailimantas. I will find you. It's been a while since I went on an adventure, after all.*

# Endnotes

1. Wyatt, Walter James (1876). The History of Prussia, Volume 1. London: Longmans, Green and Co. p. 33–200.

2. Ibid.

3. Urban, William (2003). The Teutonic Knights: A Military History. London: Greenhill Books. p. 290.

4. Wyatt, p. 33.

5. Urban, p. 23.

6. Ibid.

7. Wyatt, p. 50.

8. Urban, p. 100.

9. Ibid.

10. "The Composition of the Teutonic Order: The Universal Leadership." The Teutonic Order of the Hospital of the Virgin Mary in Jerusalem. Accessed September 26, 2022. http://www.imperialteutonicorder.com/id26.html.

11. Ibid.

12. Wyatt, p. 214–216.

13. Urban, p. 23.

# About the Author

J. Kruza has traveled to over 40 nations but fell in love with Eastern Europe. J. has studied this region of the world for six years and wishes to bring light to an often glossed-over region of the world.

After obtaining a Master's in Global Policy, J. sought to accomplish a childhood goal and publish a book. It is uncertain where J. will be living by the time this book is published, but J. would like to thank you for your interest in this book series